"I'd be a fool not to listen to gossip," Ro said.

"Quark, by any chance?" Odo said the name as if it had a slightly unpleasant flavor.

But Ro laughed, memories of many tales told out of turn by her Ferengi friend coming to mind. "Quark is *always* gossiping. As I'm sure you know."

Again, the snort. "And Quark would, it pains me to say, be quite right. I've been . . . let us say that I have been taking advantage of quiet to reflect upon my past and consider my future."

"I understand the monastery at Trishella is very beautiful," Ro said. "A balm to the soul."

Odo's face remained expressionless, but a low rumble sounded at the back of his throat. (*Does he have a throat?*) "Quark *has* been keeping tabs on me. I must return the favor."

"Feel free," Ro said. "But tell me what's brought you out of . . ." She hunted for the right word.

"Out of my hermitage?" Odo suggested with a sigh. "A favor for an old friend."

"An old Cardassian friend?"

Odo studied her dispassionately. "Will that be a problem, Captain?"

STAR TREK
DEEP SPACE NINE®

THE MISSING

UNA McCORMACK

Based on *Star Trek®* and
Star Trek: The Next Generation®
created by Gene Roddenberry
and
Star Trek: Deep Space Nine®
created by Rick Berman & Michael Piller

POCKET BOOKS
New York London Toronto Sydney New Delhi Ab Tzenketh

Pocket Books
A Division of Simon & Schuster, Inc.
1230 Avenue of the Americas
New York, NY 10020

This book is a work of fiction. Any references to historical events, real people, or real places are used fictitiously. Other names, characters, places, and events are products of the author's imagination, and any resemblance to actual events or places or persons, living or dead, is entirely coincidental.

This book is published by Pocket Books, a division of Simon & Schuster, Inc., under exclusive license from CBS Studios Inc.

First Pocket Books paperback edition January 2015

POCKET and colophon are registered trademarks of Simon & Schuster, Inc.

For information about special discounts for bulk purchases, please contact Simon & Schuster Special Sales at 1-866-506-1949 or business@simonandschuster.com.

The Simon & Schuster Speakers Bureau can bring authors to your live event. For more information or to book an event, contact the Simon & Schuster Speakers Bureau at 1-866-248-3049 or visit our website at www.simonspeakers.com.

Cover design by Alan Dingman
Cover art by Doug Drexler

Manufactured in the United States of America

10 9 8 7 6 5 4 3 2 1

ISBN 978-1-4767-5023-1
ISBN 978-1-4767-5025-5 (ebook)

For Verity, my little runabout,
And for Matthew, deep space Dad,
With love from the mother ship

HISTORIAN'S NOTE

The events in this story take place in late November 2385, after Kellessar zh'Tarash of Andor takes the oath of office for president of the Federation (*Star Trek: The Fall—Peaceable Kingdoms*).

One

Captain's Log, Personal.

It has long been my intention to set down some general thoughts on the nature and purpose of exploration, with some particular observations on first-contact missions. This is as good a time as any to attempt to organize my thinking: not only because Beverly remains away but also because war is, at last, over, and it is my hope that Starfleet can, as a result, return to its primary mission of peaceful exploration. My small hope is that these reflections might prove of some use to a reader embarking upon voyages such as those that have been the boon and the challenge of my life.

What is the purpose of exploration? Why do we search? What draws us on the quest and makes us leave behind the considerable comforts that our homeworlds might offer? What makes us absent ourselves and choose to make a transient home among the stars?

The pursuit of scientific discovery, of course, has driven many of my colleagues: to be the first to document a new species, or hear a new language, or see the ancient ruins of a civilization that was gone before life had emerged from Earth's oceans. There is, too, a fascination with the unknown:

to chart not only the farther reaches of space but the farther reaches of knowledge as well. And then there is the challenge of it all—not simply the logistics of crewing and commanding a vessel such as the Enterprise, *but the challenge that one sets oneself: to be pitted against the unknown and to find within oneself the capacity to respond not with fear but with curiosity, empathy, and humility.*

War has, for too long, distracted us from these purposes: from the pursuit of knowledge for the benefit of others; from the pursuit of self-knowledge for the benefit of ourselves. Let us hope that peace will usher in a new era of discovery . . .

Doctor Katherine Pulaski knew that people didn't like her, and she didn't care. She led a good life—a life she loved, full of travel, adventure, and a handful of excellent friends who did not trouble her beyond her interest or inclination to socialize with them. Above all, she had her work, to which she was devoted passionately and with a degree of absorption that made it the primary love of her life. Friends, lovers, husbands—they came and went, but work was always there, a companion, a challenge, and a source of great satisfaction and pride. She was an expert in several fields and had made breakthroughs in genomic therapy that had markedly improved the lives of many people. She was successful and busy, and had never compromised her ideals or opinions to get where she was. So why the hell should she care that others thought she was cantankerous and awk-

Part One

Old Women Ought to Be Explorers

ward? That was exactly what she was—and she knew herself well, loved what was there, and didn't worry about the rest.

And now Katherine Pulaski had a spaceship to play with, the fruit of many hours browbeating the decision makers at the Rosalind Franklin Institute for Biomedical Research until they gave her exactly what she wanted in the hope that she would go away for a long time (it was a technique that worked, so why would Pulaski pass it up?). The ship was called the *Athene Donald* (after a scientist Pulaski had long admired), and it was, she was pleased to tell anyone who asked (and a few who didn't), a *civilian* science and exploration vessel. There had not been enough of these in recent years, in Pulaski's opinion. In grand old-fashioned style (Pulaski was both grand and old-fashioned), this ship—with its crew of scientists and researchers—was going to travel into uncharted space to explore what was out there, doing science all the while.

Pulaski had wasted no time in assembling a team, and right now the *Athene Donald* was on its way to Deep Space 9 for some final pickups before setting off on its maiden voyage. She had exactly the crew she wanted. First, as the ship's director of research (and de facto commanding officer), was Pulaski's old friend Maurita Tanj. Pulaski and Tanj—a joined Trill—went back to postgraduate days, when Pulaski (kicking and screaming, naturally) had been forced by her advisers to do an interdisciplinary study with another student from the xenosociology department. Pulaski thought that the social sciences were pretty much a waste of time (not even decades of friendship with Tanj had entirely altered that opinion), but Tanj—a specialist in interspecies group dynamics—had known from the get-go how to handle her difficult study partner, and their project (looking into different care strategies for patients across five separate species groups) had won several academic prizes that year. Pulaski, who set store by results, had thus been convinced that Tanj's specialty had at least some worth, and Tanj, who found the other woman's spikiness and frankness hilarious, had warmly accepted Pulaski on her own terms. They had been friends ever since, and Pulaski knew that the person to make the *Athene Donald* the success that she wanted (and who was interested in failure? Not Kitty Pulaski) was her old friend Maurita Tanj. The Trill knew how to handle people: not only Katherine Pulaski (that was always a bonus) but also the very special crew that they had assembled.

Because the *Athene Donald*'s big sell—what had made the folks at the institute balk initially at giving her the ship but had eventually persuaded them of the worth of the mission (with a little oil on the joints from Tanj; Pulaski was no fool)—was that the crew was multispecies.

So far so good. But the Federation by definition comprised many species, so plenty of its vessels had multispecies crews. The *Athene Donald* had gone farther. Pulaski had invited colleagues from Ferenginar and the Klingon Empire; there were several Cardassian females crunching numbers in data analysis. And that wasn't all. What Pulaski had wanted—and what she got (with more help from Tanj than perhaps she realized)—was a truly multispecies crew. Several Romulans had signed up to participate in some of the more obscure branches of temporal warp physics. But the cherry on the top of the cake that was the *Athene Donald* was the person running the genetic-screening program. Her name was Metiger Ter Yai-A, and she was the first Tzenkethi ever to be permitted (by both governments concerned) to travel on board a Federation vessel. Pulaski had read her papers and wanted her: not only for Metiger's expertise but also for the message that her presence would send.

"Science," Katherine Pulaski informed the board of Rosalind Franklin Institute in her presentation (quite aggressively and with no apparent sense of irony), "will do what diplomacy can't."

"This project will be the first of its kind," explained Tanj (more calmly, and with an eye on how the board members were reacting). "The first to be truly serious about peace among all species across the Khitomer Accords and the Typhon Pact. There's been too much tension and strife in recent years—unnecessarily so. It's time to set this aside and put scientific research and the exploration of space back at the heart of what the Federation does. And that means reaching out in friendship to those whom previously we would have treated with suspicion. Peace with the Klingons was a massive achievement. We can replicate this with the Romulans, and we can replicate it with the Tzenkethi—if we put our minds to it. Think of the *Athene Donald*"—and here Tanj's eyes had lit up, because this was the heart of the project for her, the reason she was on board—"as a laboratory not only for the scientific research it will carry out but also for discovering strategies that will enable all the species concerned to live in peace and mutual respect."

The board loved that, and Pulaski thanked her lucky stars that Maurita Tanj seemed to know exactly how to phrase what Pulaski could say only with gruff impatience. Not only did they have their ship, they also got their Tzenkethi.

"What do we think of Metiger?" Pulaski said to Tanj as the *Athene Donald* made its approach to Deep Space 9.

Doctor Maurita Tanj looked up from the notes she had been studying. "She's an outstanding scientist. Closed, of course, but she's opened up to me once or twice in the past few days."

"Oh, yes?" Pulaski's eyes sparkled in fascination. Everyone wanted to know something about the aloof Tzenkethi and their mysterious homeworld. "What's she told you?"

"Not much," Tanj admitted. "A few hints here and there about how their research projects are organized. She was surprised, but not disappointed, at how freely we all shared our information. Nothing

I couldn't have guessed given what we know about them already, but I'm taking heart that she's opening up to us."

"Are you happy with how it's going so far?" Pulaski asked anxiously.

Tanj held out her arms to encompass their beautiful new ship and the promise it contained. "Look around you. How could I not be happy? We're doing again what we're *supposed* to do, and we're being bolder than ever. Everyone should be happy."

Pulaski smiled. "Let's hope so."

"Katherine Pulaski? Coming *here*?"

Ro Laren, unused to seeing her chief medical officer as anything but calm in the face of trouble, almost took a step back. "Is that going to be a problem?"

They were in the medical unit, a well-lit and spacious area where no effort (or expense—Ro couldn't help thinking in pre-Federation terms sometimes) had been spared on either equipment or staff. The current chief medical officer was a case in point: Doctor Beverly Crusher was one of the most eminent and well-respected CMOs in Starfleet. She'd been assigned to DS9 after the previous CMO, Julian Bashir, had been court-martialed and convicted for his part in using classified data from the Shedai metagenome to work on a cure to the Andorian infertility crisis. Ro didn't know how long Crusher intended to stay: the doctor had a husband and child back on the *Enterprise*. But in the meantime, Ro was glad to have the best at her disposal. She certainly didn't want her CMO unhappy.

"Problem? Well, no," Crusher admitted. "At least I hope not."

"Do you want to fill me in on this? Is this something to do with the part she played in Julian's escapade? If there's going to be trouble, I should know—"

"Trouble . . ." Crusher frowned. "It's not that she's *trouble*. More that she's difficult."

"Difficult?" Ro laughed. "Is that all? Difficult I can handle. People think that I'm difficult, and I can handle me."

"There's difficult and there's difficult. Pulaski is brilliant, of course. An inspired researcher."

"What's her specialty?"

"Well, it was her expertise in genomic therapy that made her interesting to Bashir," Crusher said. "But that's not all she's worked on. She's a whiz at statistical modeling, for one thing, and that always made my head hurt at the academy. But she's cowritten papers in several disciplines."

"Multiple specialisms?" Ro was impressed. "She must have a first-class mind."

"She does," Crusher said unequivocally. It seemed the doctor's professional respect was not undermined by whatever personal matter lay between the two women. This would be important to getting the next few days to go smoothly, Ro suspected. Keep them off the personal and on the professional. "She's an excellent doctor too," Crusher said.

"So what's the problem?"

Crusher paused to consider her words. "She's an excellent doctor if you're not too bothered about bedside manner."

Ro gave a crooked smile. "Ah. I think I'm starting to see."

"Then let me not put too fine a point on it. Katherine Pulaski is self-centered, bad-tempered, and blunt to the point of offensive. In sum, she's a pain in the damn neck."

"I'm liking this woman more and more by the second," Ro said.

"That's your prerogative," Crusher said. "And you can have the pleasure of her company when she gets here."

"There's more to this, isn't there? Come on, Beverly, give me the full story."

"Very well, since you asked, although I hate bringing personal animosities into professional life, and I'll thank you not to breathe a word of this beyond these four walls. Simply put, I don't like her. She held my post on the *Enterprise* for a while, during which time she was extremely thoughtless toward Data. I've never quite forgiven her for that."

Ro whistled under her breath. "You *really* don't like her."

"I don't like her at all. Jean-Luc can't stand her either. She knows exactly how to raise his blood pressure."

Here Ro had to suppress a smile. The thought

of the usually supernaturally serene captain of the *Enterprise* driven to distraction by his chief medical officer—and a woman, to boot—was far too enjoyable. But Beverly's anger was so clearly deeply felt that she resisted the urge to tease. "What happened with Data and Pulaski?"

"She saw Data as a curiosity to be examined and explored. But Data is a person in his own right. There was a terrible fight at the time to prove that, and I'm not sure Pulaski ever understood what it was all about. I got the impression that given half a chance she'd have opened up Data like a tin can, as if he were nothing more than a specimen suitable for investigation." Crusher paused for breath. "All of which is hard to forgive, but I do admire her mind. I'd give anything for a quarter of the dedication and brilliance that she's shown in her research over the years. Why exactly is she here?"

"She's on the crew of a civilian science and research vessel that's heading off into uncharted space. The *Athene Donald*."

Crusher nodded. "Yes, I've heard about its mission. The kind of thing I might have signed up for myself once upon a time." Her lips twitched in sudden amusement. "So Katherine Pulaski is heading off into uncharted space? I hope uncharted space is ready."

"I'm sorry about Data," Ro said, "but you do realize you're selling this woman to me? Bad-tempered, brilliant, gets the room jumping when she walks in. She sounds like who I want to be when I grow up."

"Hmm. Well, wait till you meet her."

"I'm already looking forward to it. Anyway, she's not the only face from the past putting in an appearance over the next few days," Ro said. "We're also expecting a visit from Odo, the former chief of security here."

"The Changeling?"

Ro lifted a finger. "I think these days we're meant to say 'Founder.' "

"Yes, yes, of course . . ." Crusher looked embarrassed. "That's me told. So why is *he* here?"

"I don't know much yet," Ro said. "Except for one thing: it involves Cardassians."

"Cardassians?" murmured Crusher. "Oh, dear."

"I know," said Ro. "Cardassians. There are always Cardassians. They're something of a constant in this universe."

A little peace and quiet, thought Ro as she made her way to her office to meet Odo. The new station, barely a year old, had already been the site of too many crises and dramas. What Ro wanted now was to be in command of a station that was functioning normally. She didn't want to be bored—may the universe preserve her from boredom (and the associated paperwork)—but she did want a little time to enjoy her new station. Just a day or two to see how smoothly station and crew could operate when untroubled by galactic politics, assassination attempts . . .

Ro shook herself hard. They were still recovering from the shock of the death of President Bacco, here on DS9. It had hit them all hard that it had happened here, and it had hit her security chief, Jefferson Blackmer, particularly hard, since the death had happened on his watch. That was another good reason to want some quiet time. So that the crew could see exactly how well they were able to work together and, perhaps, get a little confidence back. It had hardly been the most auspicious start for the new place and its people. But that would change.

The door to Ro's office opened smoothly. Odo was already waiting for her there, and Ro crossed the room to greet him. Whatever had brought the former security chief of DS9 from Bajor, Ro could only hope that his mission would not cause her too many complications.

Odo rose from his chair and gave her a brusque but by no means unfriendly nod. He gestured around. "Most impressive." His voice was a kind of growl, the voice of a man who liked to stamp his authority on any given situation. "Nothing like the old place."

Ro, smiling, took her seat, and Odo followed suit. "I can't help missing the old place, though," she said. "It had . . . let's call them idiosyncratic charms."

Odo snorted. "Too idiosyncratic, if you ask me," he said, and—was that a sniff? Could a Founder even sniff? Whatever it was, Ro warmed to this gruff no-nonsense man with the strange half-formed face.

"You're very welcome here, Constable," she said.

Odo lifted his hand, as if to stop her. "Just Odo. I am no longer a constable. I am simply Odo," he repeated, much more softly.

"Nevertheless, I'm glad to welcome you here, although I have to admit I'm curious. Of all the former crew, I'd heard that you were the one least likely to drop by."

"My reputation precedes me," Odo said, and Ro swore that was a twinkle in his eye. Could Founders twinkle?

"I'd be a fool not to listen to gossip," Ro said.

"Quark, by any chance?" Odo said the name as if it had a slightly unpleasant flavor.

But Ro laughed, memories of many tales told out of turn by her Ferengi friend coming to mind. "Quark is *always* gossiping. As I'm sure you know."

Again, the snort. "And Quark would, it pains me to say, be quite right. I've been . . . let us say that I have been taking advantage of quiet to reflect upon my past and consider my future."

"I understand the monastery at Trishella is very beautiful," Ro said. "A balm to the soul."

Odo's face remained expressionless, but a low rumble sounded at the back of his throat. (*Does he have a throat?*) "Quark *has* been keeping tabs on me. I must return the favor."

"Feel free," Ro said. "But tell me what's brought you out of . . ." She hunted for the right word.

"Out of my hermitage?" Odo suggested with a sigh. "A favor, for an old friend."

"An old Cardassian friend?"

Odo studied her dispassionately. "Will that be a problem, Captain?"

"I don't know," Ro said. "You haven't told me about the friend yet."

Again, the low rumble. "This old friend," he said, "and make no mistake, this is a friend, came to me on behalf of her son. He was a glinn in the Second Order at the end of the Dominion War."

"Second Order . . ." Ro thought for a moment. "They were on the Romulan front, weren't they?"

"Indeed they were. When the war ended, the Cardassians serving there were taken prisoner by the Romulans. Since then, most have been repatriated. But some have not. My friend's son is one of these."

"He's *still* being held captive by the Romulans?" Ro was astonished. "It's been ten years!"

"And so you see why I want to help. There is an injustice here, Captain. I don't like injustice—not even," he added slyly, "toward Cardassians."

Ro, who didn't in general mind seeing a little retribution in action when it came to Cardassians, had to agree. Ten years was a long time to be a prisoner of war.

"According to my friend—her name is Mhevita Pa'Dan, by the way—I have acquired something of a reputation as a peacemaker," Odo said. "She believes that my intercession might spur the Romulans toward some kind of resolution. Ideally, that would be the release of her son and the others still being held. But some communication would be a good place to start."

"And I guess you want to use DS9 as a neutral friendly space to hold these negotiations?" Ro said. "Shall I be expecting a Romulan representative any hour now?"

"Not quite. We don't have anyone with whom we can negotiate. I gather from Mhevita that the Romulans are silent on the matter. Impenetrably silent."

"Then I'm not sure what I can do," Ro said. "This seems to be something that the Cardassians and the Romulans need to sort out between them. Your friend should be speaking to her own government—"

"Also proving unhelpful. This is partly why we have come to you. Not only are you a high-ranking Starfleet officer, you also are Bajoran. If a Bajoran is willing to intercede on behalf of Cardassian prisoners of war, then perhaps this will send a signal to the Romulans that it's time to put this enmity behind them and let these people come home."

"That's an interesting idea," Ro said, "and I respect the principle behind it. But I'm not sure I like the idea of meddling in the affairs of others, and I'm not sure my superiors would like the idea either—"

"In fact," Odo interrupted, and he did, Ro noticed, have the decency to sound slightly embarrassed as he did so, "I've taken the liberty of speaking to your superiors at Starfleet Command. They are of the opinion that assisting me can do no harm, and, even better, it will show support for the Cardassian-Federation alliance and possibly even foster the opening of channels of communications with the Romulans. I gather," Odo continued, "that your superiors are keen to see relations with the Romulans shift from hostile to merely mildly chilly. Any chance to negotiate with them is a chance to gather some goodwill."

Or irritate them beyond measure. And they wouldn't be the only one. "You spoke to my superiors?" Ro said, a chill creeping into her voice.

There was a slight pause.

"You might like to check your recent communications," Odo said politely.

Ro did so. And there it was: a friendly message from the powers that be asking her to give Odo all reasonable assistance.

"I'm sorry to have gone behind your back—"

It was Ro's turn to growl.

"—but I couldn't risk your turning me down, and I do want to help Mhevita. It is a very good cause, Captain. At the least, will you meet her? She's here on the station right now. Will you listen to what she has to say?"

Ro sighed. What choice did she have in the matter? There were her orders. "Of course I will."

Odo gave a rumble of satisfaction. "Thank you, Captain."

"Hmm." Ro's eye fell on the next message down. It was from a Commander Peter Alden, of Starfleet Intelligence, advising her of his imminent arrival and requesting a meeting with her as soon as possible. Another sigh. If Cardassians were a universal constant, then so was Starfleet Intelligence. And neither of them was likely to contribute to the longed-for peace and quiet.

Two

Captain's Log, Personal.

One hears a great deal of cant about natural leaders—those who are born to rule—mostly from the mouths of those who fancy themselves in such a role. But a wise captain knows that he or she is nothing without the crew and considers carefully how an effective and harmonious team can be assembled and maintained. A good team is more than the sum of its specialisms and expertise—that surely is plain enough. But are there means by which one can guarantee an effective and harmonious team? Is there, in short, a "science" of sorts to assembling a crew?

I confess that I am doubtful of such a project. Can one have a "science" of people? I have found myself that intuition and experience come more to the fore when judging which people will suit me best. This, however, is not helpful for a reader of these notes, who is surely looking for generalized lessons to take away from reading!

Such a reader, immersing himself or herself in the softer sciences, might quickly become lost in a long history of studies, all using mutually incompatible jargon. There are some gems out there, however, and I would refer the reader here to Doctor Maurita Tanj's work, particularly her book The Diversity Paradox. *While this might be seen as a "popular science" book, it does provide a good grounding in some of the theoretical difficulties of research in this field and offers many solutions from which practical guidance might be drawn.*

A ship such as the Enterprise *is a provider of case studies—it is, in a way, a laboratory of sorts—but only of species from Federation worlds. As we inch toward peace, I would like to see how a crew drawn from various powers might be formed: how might a Federation ship accommodate Romulan crew members? Cardassian crew members? Perhaps even, one day, Tzenkethi crew members? Tanj hints in the conclusion to her most recent paper ("Identifying Key Drivers of Success in Diverse Teams") that this is the direction in which she is moving, and I will certainly read any further work with interest . . .*

Corazame—now she had no other name. Once upon a time she had been Corazame Ret Ata-E, part of a six-person unit tasked to maintain the coral surfaces that comprised a series of government offices around the central lagoon of Ab-Tzenketh, the Tzenkethi homeworld. She had been among the lowest of the low. To anyone who asked (not that anyone would bother), Corazame would have said that her function was to serve the Autarch joyfully and unquestioningly in the tasks that he had allotted her when determining her station in life. She would have denied knowing what purposes the offices she passed through each day served—they were not *her* purpose.

But even then—when Corazame had no thought of ever leaving her ravishing, complex, beguiling world—she had known that a wider universe existed. Each day she bent to clean the walls and floors of the Department of the Outside, where Corazame's superiors discussed and made policy toward those worlds that lay beyond the Autarch's grace, and she could not help herself. Because even if you closed your ears completely, or sang songs to cover the conversation coming from above; even if your superiors sometimes lapsed into a dialect that you were not supposed to know (but you did), you could not help but hear, and however hard you tried to suppress your understanding, you could not help but grasp at least some of what you heard. All of which made Corazame Ret Ata-E an interesting prospect for the new friends she had made after leaving her homeworld. Those friends were from Starfleet Intelligence, and they had turned out to have great interest in Corazame's people and planet.

Corazame—but let us call her Cory, the name she has been using since coming to the Federation, and as we are prying into her private thoughts, we should at least show her the courtesy of using the name she is using—Cory had not ever intended to leave Ab-Tzenketh, and most assuredly she had not intended to find herself living among the enemies of her people. A year ago, Cory had been quietly and unobtrusively spending each day traveling from her billet to her work, where, between her tasks, she quietly and unobtrusively observed her workmate Mayazan Ret Ata-E, who was proving of great interest to Cory's quietly curious mind. During her break times, in quiet and unobtrusive conversation with the other members of her unit, she would discuss Mayazan—Maymi—about whom they all worried, because Maymi seemed to get so much *wrong* . . . Odd questions, strange gestures. It was all a puzzle.

As it turned out, the solution to that puzzle was not what Cory would have guessed. Mayazan Ret Ata-E was not an EE server who had been recalibrated upward and was now struggling to understand her new function. She was Neta Efheny, an undercover Cardassian spy, sent to record what was happening in the Department of the Outside for her superiors back on Prime. But Efheny had been so beguiled by the compelling beauties of Ab-Tzenketh and the comfort of the unthinking life she led there that when the time came for her to leave Cory's world, she decided instead to stay, sending Cory in her place. In doing so, Maymi—Efheny—had certainly saved Cory from the enforcers, but she had also thrust the girl into a strange and frightening new world. Yes, Cory had *guessed* that there were alien worlds out there (that knowledge was specialized on Ab-Tzenketh and certainly not appropriate for one of Cory's status to know). Yes, she knew these worlds must be populated by alien beings—but the intellectual knowledge of something is quite different from the physical reality, and what Cory had seen since leaving Ab-Tzenketh surpassed her wildest imaginings. There were more alien worlds than she would ever have guessed, and not all of them were friendly to hers, and not all were friendly to each other, and there had been wars and struggles and events of which she had no knowledge and thought she would never quite sort out in her head. Were the Dominion the same as the Borg, or were they different? Why were the Vulcans good and the Romulans bad? Was it true that an individual Trill could be two people within one body? Were there even more species that she knew nothing about? How many? Where were they? Would she have to understand them all, learn how to serve them and placate them? For Cory had not yet quite shaken the belief that, in some way, she was destined to serve others. Not quite. And this despite (or perhaps because of) Peter Alden.

Commander Peter Alden had been among the first to speak to Cory when she found herself thrust suddenly into exile. She had been terrified: the gestures and signals she used habitually had been suddenly useless and she had known no way to placate these strangers and assure them that she was no threat. But Alden—*Peteh*—had been kind. He had taken her hand until she was calm and, despite his steely gray eyes that made him look like an enforcer, Cory believed him when he said that he could trust her.

Cory had been with Commander Peter Alden ever since. She had followed him to his home (Earth, she had understood that), where she had met his colleagues (from Starfleet Intelligence, she had certainly understood that) and had been asked questions (politely, there had been no pressure, no sense that she might face a punishment such as reconstruction) about her home and her way of life. At first, Cory had answered fully—joyfully, even, and unquestioningly—until one evening, Alden put a seed of doubt in her mind.

He had taken her to a big city that he called London. He was clearly very proud of it, but Cory thought that it was dull and rather dirty. There were no sparkling coral buildings, no sweet shared songs to soothe the soul, and certainly no great lagoon as broad and deep as her capacity for love. Instead there was discord, bustle, variety, and laughter. Alden took her to the theater, which baffled her, and then for dinner, which she liked: it was hot and spicy and—best of all—salty. Having established, indirectly, that Cory had not thought much of *The Duchess of Malfi*, Alden leaned back in his chair and said, "You don't have to be so free with everything, you know. You can hold something back."

At first Cory did not understand. She thought that he meant she had said too much about the play—which had looked pretty and sounded beautiful, but the story had been silly—and then she realized he was talking about her conversations with his colleagues. She began a placatory gesture but suppressed it quickly. Peteh hated it when she did that.

"This one . . ." she said. He frowned, and she tried again. "I . . . thought that was what you wanted me to do."

Impatiently, he began to pull apart a piece of naan. "I want you to do what *you* want to do, Cory. Have some sense of your worth! You're handing them everything on a plate. Telling them everything without any thought for what that might mean for you. What they might do for you."

She was confused. These were his friends, were they not? Why would she not tell them everything? They had asked about her homeworld, and she loved Ab-Tzenketh: its rich colors and the gentle unchanging steadiness of the way of life she had led there. Sadly, she looked around the gray city to which her friend had brought her.

"I know you were safe there," Alden said softly, "and I know you didn't choose to leave. But you're free now. Completely free. You can do whatever you like."

She did not know what to say. She wanted to please him, to thank him for the kindness he had shown her during this past wrenching year. His job, she knew, was to find out as much as he could about Ab-Tzenketh, and she had been amazed to discover how little he and his friends really knew. She pressed her hand against her breast and began to tap slowly.

Unconsciously, she dimmed the tone of her skin to a more respectful level.

"You don't have to let people use you," Alden said. Then he reached out for her hand, taking it within his and gently, but forcefully, stopped the tapping motion. "And, please, don't do that. You don't have to do that either. There's no one here you have to serve." He held her hand tightly. "I want to see you shine, Cory."

This conversation had preyed on her mind. At first, she did not know what to make of it. It was clear that he and his friends wanted—needed—her to tell them about her life and her world. But now he was saying that she didn't have to. That she mustn't? Was this in line with what his superiors wanted? Or was Peteh, who always seemed so strong and safe and certain, experiencing doubt himself? Cory would not have dared to ask, but she pondered these questions as she continued under Alden's care, and she listened even more closely.

After a few months, Alden took her on some short travels around the Federation: to Earth, of course, his home, but to other worlds too. Some of these trips she understood were for her education; on others the purpose was less clear, and she might find herself once again answering questions about her world and her people. But after the conversation in London, Cory had gone back to the strategy that had served her throughout her life as a Ret Ata-E: to show that she knew only what was appropriate for someone of her station.

"I am afraid that this one . . . that I do not know," she would sometimes say gravely to her questioner. "This one served as . . . I was only the cleaner." This turned out to be a good strategy. They found it amusing that Alden's great catch knew nothing more than how to scrub floors, and they never pressed her further.

Cory enjoyed the travels for a while, but after a few months she knew that the dull heavy ache she carried with her everywhere could not be ignored for much longer. She missed her home, and all these new worlds only served to make that absence more painful. Alden said she was free. Was this what freedom felt like? Would she always be so lost, so sorrowing?

It was another day, and another journey. Alden had told her that they were traveling to a place called Deep Space 9. She had listened to his briefing and had dutifully read the files he gave her, but these strange places were now blurring into one. Nevertheless, she tried hard to commit to memory as much as possible of the ship upon which they were traveling. She suspected that she would need this information as currency—if ever she found herself on Ab-Tzenketh . . .

Home. Would she ever see it again? Would she dare to return? She had never heard of someone of her station so dramatically, so disgracefully, breaking rank. Had it ever happened before? What would they do to her if she returned? Would the knowledge of all she had seen of the Federation be enough to protect her from reconstruction? Would they want to preserve something of her in order to learn what she knew? Or would punishment for her outrageous transgression take precedence?

"Cory?" Alden was sitting beside her. "Are you okay?"

She turned to face him. He was tall and lean, with dark hair, and those grave gray eyes could have a steely look that she still on some level feared.

"I am . . . okay."

He smiled. "Well, you sound it at least. But your skin tone . . . Well, that one usually means that you're sad in some way."

"I am thinking about home," she said simply.

"Ah," he said, and looked out the porthole by which she was sitting, contemplating the emptiness of space.

She lifted her hand to her breast—but his hand was there, stopping any motion she might make. (And not for the first time, Cory wondered whether it was *right* for him to constrain her in this way—to take her hand and stop her showing how she felt because he didn't like to see it.)

"Don't," Alden said gently. "You're free now. You don't have to placate anyone."

Except you, Cory thought.

"Not even me," he said.

Carefully, she retrieved her hand. "Peteh," she said, and stopped.

"Please tell me what's worrying you." He looked at her earnestly, honestly. Could she open up to him?

"You know that this one . . . that *I* am grateful for all the opportunities you have given me." She watched him repress his irritation at this and she pressed on. "But I miss my home." That brought a gleam of pity to his eyes, so she risked continuing. "I know how much you despise my civilization—"

"Cory, it's more complicated than that—"

"Please, Peteh, let me finish. I know that it is contrary to all that you hold dear."

He was listening carefully, sympathetically. He was not a bad man. He wanted her to be happy. But how could she?

"But it is what made me," she said. "It is all that I knew for my whole life—until the past year. For which I *am* grateful."

He thought for a moment. Then, bluntly: "Do you want to go home?"

Her skin tone dulled sadly. "They will destroy me if I go home. I have told you almost everything I know."

"But if there was no danger . . . if somehow I could send you back . . . a different person . . . not Cory . . ."

She thought about this for a while. She knew enough now about Peter Alden's world to know that this was possible. Yes, it was tempting, but what she missed at least as much as the sight of home were the familiarities of her old life: the quiet camaraderie of her workmates; the comforting small space of her billet; the gentle, lulling rhythms of her old way of life. She could not return to those. But to get a glimpse of home again? Would he be able to persuade his superiors that this was a worthwhile use of her?

"Could you do that? Send me back?"

"Probably." He rubbed a hand against his eye. Something was troubling him. The thought of her going? The thought of sending her back? When he spoke again, his words came quickly, tumbling from him. "But you don't have to. You can do what you want. You can stay here with me. You can go wherever you like. There's a whole universe out there! You've barely even started. You can seize the opportunity—see it all!"

"Is that what you have done with your life, Peteh?"

He looked at her, startled. Then he smiled ruefully. "I'm not sure . . . I did explore—I explored your home."

"Only long enough to find that you did not like it. That you liked your home better."

"You're right." He smiled. "You know, you often are."

She folded her hands on her lap and looked out again at the stars. "Perhaps that is what I am discovering. That I like home better." But how could this one go back? Peter Alden had returned home, yes, but if this conversation had made one thing clear, there was no going back for Corazame Ret Ata-E. If this one returned to Ab-Tzenketh, it would be as a different person—and one serving new masters. Was that freedom? Cory did not think so. But perhaps it was a price worth paying.

* * *

Whatever she privately thought of Katherine Pulaski, there were their public personae to consider, and Beverly Crusher couldn't think of a good reason not to agree to see the other woman when her message came asking if they could meet. She wondered whether Pulaski would have extended her the same courtesy. Katherine Pulaski, Crusher suspected, wouldn't bother seeing anyone she didn't like, unless she felt in the mood to insult her.

Pulaski made herself at home in the new medical unit. She examined workstations, quizzed nurses, and generally poked around until, with a satisfied grunt, she pronounced the facility "excellent."

Crusher bore the intrusion with surface cheer. With stern quelling glances at her staff, who were all silently signaling, *Who the hell is this?* she shepherded Pulaski into her private office. "Take a seat," she said. "Let's shoot the breeze for a while." *But not for too long.*

"Glad to." Pulaski settled herself comfortably into the nearest chair—not Crusher's, at least. "This really is a first-rate facility. But are you getting any work done?"

"Bits and pieces," Crusher said, not eager to give anything away.

"I guess Starfleet Medical has you slaving away over that blasted Shedai meta-genome data, making sure no more of it gets loose."

"It's taking up a fair amount of my time," Crusher

said evasively. "But what are you up to? I've read about the *Athene Donald*. It's an exciting project."

Pulaski beamed. "Isn't it? Exploration and research. Follow our curiosity and see where it leads us. Taking us back to what Starfleet is really about."

"Yes," Crusher said softly, "I think we're all tired of war. It's long past time to see what adventures peace can offer us. So what are you working on while you travel?"

Pulaski smiled. "The secret of eternal life."

Despite herself, Crusher burst out laughing. "Setting your sights low, as ever?"

"I like a challenge."

"So you've switched from medicine to alchemy?"

"I *think* that was about making gold. Perhaps I'll try that after I've cracked this. But I'm serious, Beverly. Our species grows older than it ever has in human history. Why can't we grow older still? And what do we need to do, on a genetic level, to make that extended period of life as healthy and fulfilling as possible?"

At the back of her mind, Crusher remembered Jean-Luc telling her about events that had happened during Pulaski's tour on the *Enterprise*, when the ship had visited the Darwin Genetic Research Station, and Pulaski had contracted a virus that aged her rapidly. It had been a near miss for her, apparently; they had only by chance been able to reverse the effects. Crusher wondered whether this preyed on the other woman's mind and was directing her current path of research.

"Hold back aging but keep the quality of life high throughout?" Crusher thought about this. "A noble endeavor. There'll be some pretty significant ethical and social consequences, of course—"

"We're already seeing those with our current levels of longevity. Look at you, starting a second family this late in the day. For most of human history that wouldn't have been possible."

"For most of human history I would have run the distinct risk of dying during childbirth," Crusher said tartly, irritated at the personal turn the conversation was taking.

"Hooray for medicine," Pulaski deadpanned.

Again, despite herself, Crusher laughed. "Yes indeed. Hooray for us."

Pulaski smiled. "But you're right. There'll be consequences. But then, there are always consequences."

"What will it mean for our civilization," Crusher mused, "if the old don't die, or their deaths are delayed even longer than they are now?" She glanced at the other woman. "How long are you thinking?"

"Three hundred years? Four?"

Crusher whistled quietly. "You know, I visited a place like that recently. The Venette Convention."

"Never heard of it."

"No, they keep themselves quiet. But the old were very old. Lifetimes in our terms."

Pulaski was interested. "And were there problems?"

"Not that I observed," Crusher said. "In fact, it all

seemed to work rather well." She reflected again on her brief time among the Venetans, whose homeworld she had visited as part of an attempt to stop this ancient civilization, which was making its first steps into the politics of the quadrant, from getting too close to the Tzenkethi.

"So what worked?" Pulaski said. "What did they get right?"

"I think the danger would be that the old would crush the young," Crusher said. "Not intentionally, but because they'd seen it all before. You'd always be surrounded by people who knew best. The worst case would be if the needs of the older people were put ahead of the young—or vice versa, for that matter, although I think the former has the potential to be more injurious."

"Sending the young to fight old men's wars?"

Crusher nodded. "That kind of thing. But it didn't work that way among the Venetans. The older people guided the young, but they didn't serve them or prevent them from learning. And the younger people respected the old but weren't in thrall to them or awed by their knowledge. They added, well, *freshness* to what could easily have been a stagnated society. Yes, it all seemed to work very well."

"Can I take a look at your files?" Pulaski said.

One good thing about Pulaski was that she wouldn't ask if she wasn't genuinely interested. She wouldn't bother to be polite. "They're on their way."

"I'll enjoy them. I'll come back to you with questions, if I may."

"Of course. They made a real impression on me. There was some delicate diplomatic business going on . . ."

Crusher stopped speaking. Pulaski had taken out a padd and was already skim-reading the files. Crusher sighed quietly. No, Pulaski didn't bother to be polite.

"And some spy business, I see," Pulaski said after a few moments scanning the files.

"Oh, inevitably. That was interesting in itself as far as the Venetans were concerned. The older people were simultaneously deeply naïve about all the scheming and yet were able to wrong-foot us in ways we didn't expect, because their assumptions about what counted in life and what constituted sensible behavior were so different. They couldn't see the point of our rules and regulations—"

Pulaski guffawed. "Good for them!"

"And they certainly couldn't see the point of spy games."

"I may have to retire there when the time comes," said Pulaski. "But, you know, it strikes me that it could easily have gone the other way: live too long, and you get into habits, don't you? You acquire funny little ways."

"Speak for yourself, Katherine."

"I wouldn't dare speak for anyone else," Pulaski said. "But imagine a whole society like that. Rule-bound, baroque, serving only those who've been alive long enough to master the intricacies."

"Like a Mervyn Peake novel."

"Huh?"

"*Gormenghast.* Never mind," said Crusher, seeing Pulaski's blank look. "I wonder which way the Federation would go, if we became as long-lived as the Venetans."

Pulaski was still flicking through the files. "Jury's out on that one," she said offhandedly.

"You'd have liked it there," said Crusher. "They were straight talkers. No nonsense and no pussyfooting about."

Pulaski laughed. Tucking her padd under her arm, she stood up easily from her chair. "When are you coming over to the ship?"

Crusher smiled. Of course Pulaski would assume that Crusher would have nothing better to do than to interest herself in Pulaski's work. And, in fact, she was interested. "I'll schedule something for tomorrow, if you're available."

"I'll make myself available. Thanks for the tour, Beverly." Pulaski headed for the door. "Superb facility. You deserve it."

If Pulaski knew that Crusher didn't like her, she certainly didn't care. But Crusher had the distinct impression she hadn't even noticed. Perhaps this way was better, skipping the animosities and getting on with learning from each other. It was refreshing. Crusher opened her appointment schedule and cleared the whole of the following morning.

* * *

Sadness lay heavily upon Mhevita Pa'Dan, like fog on a winter morning without any hope of spring. It was there in the slight stoop, in the wiry gray streaks in her thick dark hair, in the slow way she stood when Ro and Odo entered the room. She raised her palm gravely in greeting to them.

"Thank you for your time, Captain Ro," she said. "I know that you have a busy schedule and more on your mind than my troubles. Even if there is nothing that you can do, I'm grateful simply to have this meeting with you. It makes me believe that people are still listening."

Ro gestured to the other woman to sit down. "If I can help, I will," she said. She sat down opposite Pa'Dan across a low table set with tea and cups. She poured from the pot, handing a cup of hot tea to Pa'Dan in a near-universal ritual of comfort and courtesy. Odo, she noted, had quietly created his own cup. "But it would help if you explained more about your situation and what you think I can do. Odo has given me the basics, but there's more I'd like to know. For example, how do you two come to know each other?"

Pa'Dan gave Odo a slight smile that leavened her weary sadness a little. "We met during the Occupation," she said. "I was a nestor in Ashalla." She stared down into her tea. "Forgive me for mentioning the Occupation. I know that a Bajoran has no reason to help a Cardassian in need."

Ro's hand clenched instinctively around the

handle of her cup. *A Cardassian lawyer in the Bajoran capital? What atrocities had this woman allowed?*

"Mhevita is doing herself an injustice," Odo said softly. "I came to know her as the nestor who could always be relied upon to take on cases defending Bajorans."

"Bajorans had fewer rights in Cardassian courts than even their own citizens," Ro pointed out bitterly.

"Nevertheless," said Odo, "if there was a case that I thought surpassed even the Occupation's standards of inequity, it was Mhevita I would approach. And she always came. Even to DS9; even to offer a defense for Bajorans to Dukat himself, on two or three memorable occasions."

"Attracting Dukat's attention was my big mistake," Mhevita said sadly. "When he came to power, after the Dominion occupied Cardassia, he settled a lot of old scores. Who would have thought he would remember the nestor who came his way once upon a time?"

"You nearly got Eris Juze freed on a technicality," Odo growled. "He wouldn't have forgotten that.

Pa'Dan had been one of the good guys—insofar as anyone had been able to be good during that time. "What exactly did Dukat do?" Ro said.

"After he took power," Pa'Dan said, "there was a period of intense national pride. A lot of young people joined up to serve the Union in the war against the rest of the quadrant. Once the losses began piling up, however, that fervor quickly died away. But there was still a war to be fought. And what came next . . ."

"They call it Dukat's Draft," Odo said grimly. "Conscription. But too often of a targeted kind—forcing the relatives of his enemies into the army and sending them to the most dangerous places."

"My son was drafted. Sent to the Romulan front." Pa'Dan closed her eyes. "My son, Terek, was—*is*—an artist. The least warlike young man you could hope to find. Dukat sent him to fight Romulans."

Ro breathed out slowly. The Cardassian-Romulan front had been the epitome of brutality during the Dominion War. It would have been a cruel awakening for a sensitive young man. Dukat's malice was always finely honed. "I'm sorry," Ro said. "But if I understand correctly, your son survived?"

"That's right," said Pa'Dan. "When so many others didn't, on either side. But he didn't come home."

"They took him prisoner," said Ro.

"On Sekula, shortly before our government switched sides. And they've kept him prisoner ever since. It's been ten years since the war ended, and Terek has been in Romulan hands all that time."

"Have you heard *nothing*?" Ro said.

"A few messages, early on. Telling us he was alive."

"Treated well?"

"Treated fairly, he said."

"You said 'early on,'" Ro noted. "Have the messages stopped?"

"They stopped four and a half years ago," Pa'Dan said. "Suddenly there was nothing."

Ro paused to think. "Nestor," she said after a moment, "I have to ask—"

"Do I think it's possible that Terek may be dead?" Pa'Dan smiled back at her sadly. "Of course I've thought of that. But if that is the case I would like his body or his ashes. And if there is nothing left of him, then I would like to know the circumstances of his death. I gave up on the dream of bringing him home years ago. But I would like this uncertainty to end. To know for sure one way or another, and to know how it happened."

Ro nodded. "Thank you. I know that can't have been easy to say. May I ask, has your government been unable to help?"

Pa'Dan snorted.

"That'll be a no, then," said Ro.

"Why would they help?" Pa'Dan said bitterly. "After the war, people had other worries on their minds. Nobody wanted to remember the war or our part in it. They wanted to make peace with the Federation and the allies as quickly as possible."

Ro sighed. "And these days nobody wants to rock the boat with the Romulans if there's the slightest chance of peace between them and the Khitomer powers."

"A handful of soldiers left behind on the Romulan front ten years ago are not worth a diplomatic incident," Pa'Dan said.

"They've been forgotten," Odo said softly. "Either unintentionally or on purpose, nobody wants to help."

Ro put down her cup. "I'm sympathetic," she said after a while. "I genuinely am." And she was, Ro found. The war was a long time ago—the Occupation even longer—and Pa'Dan had not deserved this treatment in exchange for her courage during the Occupation.

Pa'Dan looked at her ruefully. "You're sympathetic—*but*. I imagine you're about to tell me why you can't help."

"Not quite that," Ro said. "I'll help if I can. But I can't see how. I don't have any contacts within the Romulan government—"

"I have a name," Pa'Dan said quickly. "A contact in their War Office. There's a repatriation committee before which prisoners of war have to appear."

"But you've had no luck?"

"Communications from them dried up about the same time they did from Terek. I think the Romulans may have forgotten our people too."

"Meanwhile," said Odo, "I shall be speaking to the new castellan to try to get some movement from the Cardassian government. He owes me a favor or two."

"I'm impressed," Ro said. "But again, I have to ask—what do you want from me?"

Odo and Pa'Dan smiled at each other. "We know that you have to keep your involvement semi-official," Odo said. "But a little Starfleet muscle never did any harm."

Ro smiled back. "Starfleet muscle. Yes, I can do

muscle." She lifted her palm to Pa'Dan. "Give me the name of that contact on the repatriation committee. I'll be happy to help."

Crusher had to admit that the *Athene Donald* was exceptional. A tweak of envy passed through her when Pulaski showed her the labs, and for a second she thought about signing up, getting back on the exploration trail . . . She reminded herself sternly that joining the crew would involve spending long hours with Pulaski. If Beverly Crusher really was going exploring again, she could surely do it in more congenial company. But Crusher was not a vindictive woman, and she gave credit where credit was due.

"The ship's beautiful, Katherine," she said as they entered the turbolift to make their way toward Tanj's office. Pulaski was very keen for Crusher to meet her friend, and Crusher in turn was intrigued to meet the kind of person willing to sign up for those long hours with Pulaski. "Everything about it—the design, the facilities—"

"The bar's well stocked too."

Crusher smiled. "You'll need that after a couple of years in each other's company."

"I hope not," said Pulaski as the lift came to a halt. "The idea—well, I'll let Maurita explain. She understands that part of the mission much better than I do."

Crusher liked Tanj at once, a quick-moving Trill

with long dark hair tied back in a brisk ponytail and sharp eyes that didn't miss a trick. "Another friend, Katherine?" she said as she shook Crusher's hand. "I thought I'd met all your friends by now. There can't be that many."

"Shut up," said Pulaski, easing herself into the nearest chair. "This a good time?"

"Would it make any difference if it wasn't?" Tanj smiled and gestured to Crusher to sit. "I have a meeting with Metiger shortly. She wants to discuss some of the supplies coming on board at DS9."

"Metiger?" Pulaski turned to Crusher. "If you can hang around, Beverly, you'll get to meet our Tzenkethi."

Crusher was slightly embarrassed to have been so transparent, but as soon as Pulaski had mentioned that a Tzenkethi doctor was on board, her interest had been piqued. Tanj looked at her with amusement. "Don't worry, Doctor," she said. "Everyone wants to gawp at our Tzenkethi."

They talked for a while about the project, and Tanj opened up when Crusher asked about her purpose for the ship. "Scientific research works only when there's an open culture," Tanj explained. "The whole purpose of the *Athene Donald* is to provide a space away from political or social pressures to allow the people traveling together to put them out of their mind and get on with working with each other."

Crusher was interested. "So a fixed space—a base

or a space station—you don't think they work as well?"

Tanj shook her head. "Too easily embedded in everyday squabbles—or, perhaps I should say, in wider institutional agendas. The *Athene Donald* is a bubble away from all that. Traveling and solving problems together naturally fosters community."

"That's the idea behind ships like the *Enterprise*," Crusher said.

Tanj nodded. "Yes, Starfleet knows this instinctively with its research and exploration ships, but this will be the first time that someone specifically observes and documents the processes with a crew that is not only multispecies but also comes from several different powers. Of course"—she smiled—"we could all get cabin fever and end up throttling each other." Beverly could have sworn that Tanj licked her lips at that prospect.

"Maurita's a sociologist, Beverly," Pulaski put in. "And yet we're still friends."

"And Kitty is bad mannered and difficult. And yet we're still friends."

Pulaski laughed. Give the woman her due, Crusher thought, she didn't pretend to be anything other than she was.

The door chimed. "Enter," Tanj called.

In walked the most beautiful creature Crusher had ever beheld. She had seen Tzenkethi before, but even Alizome Vik Tov-A had not been as lovely as this. Metiger *glowed*—there was no other word for it.

A silvery sheen came from her skin, as if she carried some kind of light within her. She was taller than all three of the other women, perhaps easing toward seven feet, and supple. Her skin rippled like quicksilver as she moved. Crusher thought faintly that this would be how an angel might look.

"Doctor Crusher," said Tanj, "allow me to introduce Metiger Ter Yai-A, our specialist in genetic screening. Metiger, this is Doctor Beverly Crusher, lately of the *U.S.S. Enterprise*, and now chief medical officer on Deep Space 9."

Then there was the voice: low and melodious, as if someone was strumming gently upon a harp. "I am glad to meet you, Doctor Crusher."

Such simple words, and yet the effect . . . *You could be lulled by a voice like that*, Crusher thought. *You would obey that voice without question.* She ran through what she knew about Tzenkethi status markers. *Ter*: a leadership role of some kind. Yes, you would want someone with this status to be obeyed without thought . . .

Crusher collected herself. "I'm very glad to meet you too." She thought her own voice sounded squeaky in comparison, like a child's.

Metiger nodded, as if she agreed that Crusher should be glad, and then turned to Tanj. "I do not wish to intrude, but we had a meeting arranged."

"We were just leaving," said Pulaski, standing up. "Beverly, let me introduce you to the bar."

The two doctors scurried into the turbolift like schoolgirls caught in the staff room. "Where did you find *her*?" Crusher said as the lift doors closed. "How on *earth* did you get her to come along?"

"Nothing to do with my charms," Pulaski said. "Maurita was contacted by her after she gave a paper on the *Athene Donald* at a research conference. She asked to come along."

"She *asked*?" Crusher was amazed. "Since when have the Tzenkethi started to become so open? I can't believe they're letting her travel. And she's genuinely a scientist? She's not a spy?"

"The two aren't mutually exclusive, you know, but, yes, I'd read a couple of her papers in the past and I've quizzed her since she came on board. She's the real deal. What do you think?"

"What do I *think*?" Beverly shook her head. "I don't know what to say!"

Pulaski gave a wry smile. "Astonishing, isn't it? She has . . . Well, the only word I have for it is 'glamour.' In the original sense. It's as if people are enchanted. Maurita is slightly besotted with her. Fascinating to watch."

They entered the bar. "Get me a gin and tonic," said Beverly to the barkeep. When the drinks arrived she knocked back half of hers. "I've met Tzenkethi before—but nothing like this. That one—Alizome Vik Tov-A—was definitely a spy."

"Vik Tov-A . . ." Pulaski pondered this. "Did you work out what the markers meant? I can't quite get my head around them."

"I think I got the hang of some of it," Crusher

said. "Alizome and Metiger are personal names. The Tov in Alizome's name is a status marker, signaling she's one of the governing class. Metiger has Ter—that signals leadership in some way. My hunch is that it means somebody whose orders should be obeyed by members of any follower class, regardless of their functional specialism. Because"—Crusher smiled—"and here's where I start winging it, names also indicate function. For Alizome, Vik marked that she was empowered to negotiate on behalf of the Autarch. And for Metiger, well, I'm guessing, but I imagine that the Yai is something to do with scientific expertise. She has expert knowledge of some kind. That would be my guess. What do you think?"

"Works for me," said Pulaski with a nod. "All conjecture on my part. Metiger isn't exactly effusive. Where on earth did you meet a Tzenkethi before?"

"Same mission as the Venetans. Alizome was there advising them. We thought the Tzenkethi were trying to militarize the Venetan frontier. Alizome came close to triggering war with the Federation before she backed down."

Pulaski whistled. "That was kept quiet. But do they seem different? Alizome and Metiger?"

Crusher pondered this. "Yes, I think they do. I felt Alizome was always watching us. With Metiger—well, I only have a couple minutes' exposure to go on, but I felt that I didn't quite signify. I'm not important enough to observe."

"She can be a little dismissive."

"Hell, Katherine, I've met a lot of research directors like that and they don't have the excuse of being Tzenkethi."

Pulaski laughed. "I guess I'll just have to observe her in turn and see what she gives up. I'll send you my notes if you like."

"I would like," Crusher said. "Are they deliberately secretive, do you think? The Tzenkethi?"

"Hard to say, isn't it? I don't go out of my way to explain how Federation society works when I first meet someone. It's the water you swim in, isn't it?"

"But Tzenkethi society is so complicated . . . Their genetic science must be well ahead of anything we know."

Pulaski grunted. "Between you and me, and having had a peek at what Metiger is working on—"

"A peek?"

Pulaski waved her hand. "Technical term. But I don't think their genetic programs are as impressive as we think they are. In fact, I think it's all baloney, propaganda to keep the serfs in place. You know, tell them they've been bred for a specific purpose to stop them thinking they can do anything else. Like in that hymn."

Crusher thought she might be starting to feel the effect of the gin. "Like in the what?"

"The one about the rich man in his castle and the poor man at his gate." Pulaski tuned it, or perhaps cawed it was closer. " 'The rich man in his castle, the poor man at his gate. God made them, high or lowly, and ordered their estate.' "

"You're full of surprises, Katherine Pulaski."

"You better believe it, Beverly Crusher. But you see what I mean? I think the Tzenkethi serfs believe they exist to serve because they're told that the Autarch has ordained it that way, and they believe that because it's biological rather than cultural it can't be changed. Which is stupid on several counts. Because biology is as easy to change as culture, isn't it, and increasingly so. Isn't that what we're all trying to do here? Muck about with biology." She eyed Crusher. "Like you and your second family. At your age!"

Crusher sighed. "And I was starting to like you."

"Oho!" Pulaski laughed. "Don't ever make the mistake of liking me!"

"I certainly won't again."

"So, how is it going in the Crusher-Picard household?" Pulaski said. "I was surprised that the kid wasn't with you. René, isn't it?"

"René, yes, and you should respect how we choose to bring up our child. Wesley didn't suffer from being in a single-parent family."

"But everything is okay, isn't it? I know that some marriages work better when the people concerned are nowhere near each other, but yours didn't strike me as one of those."

Crusher looked into her half-empty glass. "There have been some complications."

"Complications?"

"You know there was a prior attempt on Bacco's life?"

"I heard," Pulaski said grimly.

"Jean-Luc dived to protect me rather than the president."

Pulaski tutted. "I bet that pissed you off."

Crusher looked at Pulaski in surprise. "Yes, it did. How did you guess? I've had a hard time getting people to understand."

"Easy," Pulaski said. "Because his job is to protect the president, not his wife or the mother of his child. You can do that yourself."

"That's right."

"Bet he made you feel guilty for feeling that way."

"He didn't *make* me, but I did feel guilty. I wanted a little time away to think. Deep Space 9 came up for other reasons, but it offered that opportunity."

"I see."

Crusher shook herself. "Anyway, if we're getting personal—didn't you ever think of having children?"

"Are you kidding me? I tell you what, though, I did think of asking Jean-Luc to marry me."

Crusher nearly spat what remained of her gin over the table. Pulaski was eyeing her with what could only be described as mischief.

"Imagine it," said Pulaski. "It would have been like a screwball comedy."

"It would have been a bloodbath!"

"That too. But fun while it lasted. And hilarious to watch." Pulaski leaned back comfortably in her chair. "What I'm saying is that marriage, in my experience—and I've got three times of experience—

requires more than readiness to work at it. It requires the presence of each other. That's what blew up my marriages—and why I didn't want kids. I was more interested in my work. And while it made me feel sad not to be near whichever husband happened to be around at the time, it didn't make me sad enough to give up the chance to do my best work. So I guess I'm asking—is time and space for reflection really what you and Jean-Luc need?"

Crusher sighed.

"You'll know your own marriage best," Pulaski said, "but I know full well what made mine fail. I didn't put in the hours. And you've got to put in the hours. I put them elsewhere. And I'll keep on putting in the hours there until I drop."

The hours, thought Beverly, finishing her gin and tonic. *You've got to put in the hours* . . . Good advice, whatever the source.

Their ships were small and various, like beads strung together by a child. They were tiny and ragtag against the sleek new station. The travelers upon them were ragtag and various too. They called themselves the People of the Open Sky.

Three

Captain's Log, Personal.

Let me reflect a little upon first contacts, since these are the missions that seem particularly to intrigue the layperson, if numbers of requests for anecdotes are to be considered significant data! Charting untraversed regions of space, documenting nebulae, measuring photon densities—these are the day-to-day scientific activities that take up most of our time on an exploratory vessel such as the Enterprise, *and with which the crew is most generally busy. But the layperson has little understanding of such matters and even less interest. Instead, the romance of first contact has captured the imagination, and that is what civilians wish to know about.*

And indeed who can blame them? Even the most seasoned starship captain, with many thousands of hours of voyaging, cannot help but feel a quiet thrill to realize that he or she has embarked yet again upon that most delicate but rewarding of missions: learning to communicate in a meaningful fashion with a hitherto unknown species.

Perhaps laypeople might be less enthusiastic if, like the rest of us, they had been obliged to read through the extensive protocols for first contact devised by what must be some of the most fiendish minds ever to pass through Starfleet. Finding themselves in such a situation, they would quickly come to appreciate this documentation, assembled as it has been over years from extensive experience and with considerable thought. While we embark upon space exploration wishing to be discoverers of the new, there can be considerable consolation, when embroiled in a difficult or confusing new situation, to find that someone has been this way before . . .

"Thank you, Captain Ro, for showing us such interest. We are simply travelers. We do not mean to stay long."

Starfleet protócol stated there should be more pomp and ceremony to first contact, but you could hardly force that on people if they didn't want it. And these people clearly didn't want it. They had introduced themselves as the People of the Open Sky, asked for permission to dock—and that had been it. No formal greetings, no "We come in peace," nothing other than the fact that the station seemed suddenly to be full of children. Lots and lots of children. Shouting, laughing, generally making noise and having a good time. Blackmer wasn't pleased. He suggested they be asked to keep to specific areas. "They might," he said, when pressed as to why, "cause trouble."

"They're hardly delinquents," Crusher said dryly. "Some of them barely come up to my knees. Personally, I think they're delightful. They brighten up the place."

Ro agreed entirely. "If the day ever comes that it isn't safe for kids to run around this station, we all need to pack up and go home."

Nevertheless, she took herself over to the quarters where the People had been assigned, in order to make a more formal introduction, as per the book. But formality was firmly off the table. The rooms, with the doors wide open, were busy with chattering adults keeping their eyes on the very smallest children while the older ones rushed in and out. A few elderly folks were snoozing in chairs here and there, cracking open an eye every so often to see the little ones and smile. Ro couldn't see who was in charge—was anyone in charge? It looked like chaos. Eventually, from numerous short chats and conversations, she worked out that the person she needed to be speaking to was called Oioli. Oioli would be back soon, it seemed, but had popped out to take some of the toddlers for a stroll along the Plaza.

Ro waited for half an hour, then an hour, and was about to give up and go back to the Hub when the door opened and a tall thin alien with olive green markings across the temples came in. This, Ro guessed, was probably Oioli. Accompanied by at least a thousand toddlers, Oioli looked tired (not surprising) but happy (some people were like that with kids, or so Ro had heard).

Five more minutes passed. Ro began to think she had been forgotten, and then suddenly Oioli flopped into the seat beside her, giving her a friendly, lazy smile. "Well now, Captain Ro. What brings you here to see us?"

Ro, with no small amount of self-parody, said, "Allow me to introduce myself. My name is Captain Ro Laren, commanding officer of the Starfleet station Deep Space 9. First-contact protocol says that I must formally welcome you. So"—she lifted her hand—"hi."

Oioli burst out laughing. "A very pretty greeting, yes! I think you understand us!"

Ro spent two hours among the People, a most relaxing time. The smaller children were firmly but kindly sent off for naps, whereupon the rooms became merely pleasantly full of quiet chatter. Cups of a very nice green tea appeared at regular intervals. At some point she loosened her uniform jacket. And she learned something about the People of the Open Sky. Not that there was a great deal to learn, as Oioli kept on insisting. They were travelers. They traveled. That was it.

"But you're not all one species, are you?" Ro said. She was well able to observe, even with her feet up.

Oioli smiled. "Well done, very good! It seems you have been watching. There are one or two of us who share a common background. Others come and others go. But everyone is welcome."

That was all Ro got, and she was willing to believe that was all there was. There were three adults of the same species—Oioli, Ioile, and Ailoi—with the same olive green markings and the same casual way of introducing themselves, and the same wide and unblinking eyes that kept you fascinated. Oioli and Ioile had been traveling together for many years, Oioli explained, with Ailoi a later addition from their home. Often, when they came to a world, someone would choose to join them, and sometimes people decided to leave their ships, settling on worlds where they felt at home. There was no pressure to remain.

"But for most of us, our home is always moving," Oioli said. "We've found our place among the stars. We do not need to settle."

"There are a lot of children traveling with you," Ro said.

Oioli smiled. "Yes, there are. Lots of them. They keep us very busy!"

And that was that. Oioli had no more to say, and it all seemed pretty self-explanatory to Ro. Ailoi then began to press Ro about the station, and Bajor, and the Federation. She gave her audience a quick sketch of Bajoran history—they were profoundly interested in the Prophets, the wormhole, and the Orbs. Ioile's pale eyes flashed in anger when she explained the Occupation, but Oiloi's face saddened, the green markings at the throat deepening almost to jet-black.

"So much loss and so much grief," Oiloi said quietly, before Ioile could speak. "Too many times I've seen this. There must be many people here who lost their homes and families. Some of us have suffered this. I hope your people thrive now."

Ro was touched. The Occupation seemed to be

passing into history—a matter of dates to be learned and events to be memorized. There was a new generation growing up on Bajor for whom the Occupation was part of the past. Yet Oioli had immediately thought of the millions of people whose small quiet lives had been destroyed: the children who had grown up in camps, the homes that had been destroyed, the families that had been ruined or had never happened. "I think we're thriving," she said softly. "We have an ancient culture dating back thousands upon thousands of years. We won't let the Occupation become the defining moment of that history. We are so much more."

Oioli smiled. "There, now, that's the start. The way to proper healing."

They talked a little more about what the People hoped to do while they were on board the station. This amounted to nothing more than seeing the sights and collecting some essential supplies. Oioli asked if they could make use of the medical facilities, and Ro readily agreed. They parted in friendship, but when Ro got back to her office, Blackmer was waiting for her, hovering around like a small storm cloud ready to burst.

"Well?" he said.

"Well what?"

"How did the meeting go?"

Ro eased herself into her chair. "I had a very pleasant afternoon," she said as Blackmer was saying, "I'm monitoring their movements around the station."

There was a pause.

"I'm not sure that's strictly necessary," said Ro.

"A precautionary measure. We don't want any . . ."

They stared at each other. *Dead presidents,* thought Ro. "No," she said. "Thank you, Lieutenant. Keep on monitoring whatever you think needs monitoring. It's very sensible."

"What do you want to do while we're here, Cory?"

She jumped at Alden's voice. She had been miles away, back home, as ever, where the Spring Festival would be under way. Her workmates would be taking a half day from their tasks to walk beneath the coral canopies by the lagoon. That evening there would be songs in the square and food, gifts from their Ap-Rejs, their superiors, acting on behalf of the Autarch. They would raise their hands to the Royal Moon and thank the Autarch for the blessings that he bestowed upon them and the comfort that he gave them, and they would all sing together how much they longed to serve throughout the coming year and every year of their lives . . .

"You could take a look around," Alden said. "The old place was certainly worth a look." He glanced around their quarters. "Anything's better than sitting in here all day."

"I am happy enough to do that."

Alden sighed. "Only if you want to."

She thought carefully about what to say next. "When did you visit the old station, Peteh? I thought that it was a very unhappy place."

"It was, for a long time. It was bleak under Cardassian rule, a facility operated by Bajoran slaves. Then it was a war zone for several years when the Federation ran it."

"The Dominion War, yes?"

He looked at her steadily. "You've learned a lot. More than you give yourself credit for."

"The teacher has been good. What brought you here, Peteh? To such a sad place?"

"I passed by during the Occupation. I looked Bajoran then . . ." Alden shook himself. "Let's not dwell upon the past. This new place is a real sight. Go and look around. Take a walk along the Plaza. You can hire a bike, go all the way around. It'll be nice. You deserve some fun, Cory."

She uncurled herself from her sitting position. "Will you join me?"

"What?" He was already busy with his comm. "No, I have some work to do. I have to meet Captain Ro later today and I need to do some reading beforehand."

"I could assist with your preparations?"

"No, no, it's okay. Go and have a nice time."

He was lost in his files. Cory waited a moment longer, in case he remembered her, and then slipped out the door.

For several reasons, she would, in fact, have preferred to remain quietly in their quarters. For one thing, she was tired of Federation architecture, which she increasingly compared negatively to the beauties of the coral structures in which she had grown up. Even the modest billets in which E followers, such as she, spent their rest hours were more to her taste, being small and cozy, and with the sounds of your workmates through the walls to keep you company. The Federation made too much use of open space, which was anathema to the Tzenkethi. Go for a walk? A bike ride? Cory shuddered. She would find a covered corner and do what she liked best: sit, and watch, and think.

She wandered unhappily along a wide, bright corridor filled with greenery. There was another reason she disliked being out in the open: people stared. They had never seen a Tzenkethi before, and even Cory, with her unobtrusive ways and her dull copper skin tones (she carefully maintained the workmanlike hue of her daily life back home, like someone who prefers modest dress), attracted attention. Look now—someone wearing Starfleet uniform was watching her (a security officer, Cory noted, because whatever she believed about her capacity to learn, she in fact was very receptive to everything she saw). And there—the tiny person with the great ears . . . Watching, watching, everyone was watching.

Ordinary Tzenkethi do not like open spaces, not even on their homeworld, which has plenty of outstanding natural features that, as a result of the claustrophobia of the lower echelons, can remain the playgrounds of the elite. Ordinary Tzenkethi—whether by custom or design—prefer to congregate in covered areas, with plenty of their own kind around them. After only half an hour or so wandering along the Plaza, Cory felt shaky. She needed to be alone—no, not alone; she needed to be with her own kind, but that was not an option, so alone would have to do, away from all this space and all these watchers. She saw a little door ahead and caught a strange appealing scent coming out. Pausing for a moment's silent decision, she slipped through the door and into the Bajoran temple.

"I hope this isn't a bad time, Your Eminence."

On the view screen, the castellan of the Cardassian Union gave the other man a very sharp look. "*That is not my official title, Constable, as well you know.*"

"I meant it in the sense of éminence grise."

"Also inaccurate. An éminence grise is a power behind the throne. I, for my sins, am very firmly stuck on this throne."

Odo folded his arms. "Public life not suiting you, Garak?"

"Public life suits me very well. No, I tell a lie—"

"Surely not."

"Public life would suit me very well were it not for the constant demands that I justify my decisions. This time next week I shall be addressing the assembly in order to tell them my agenda for the next session." Garak pursed his lips. *"What a ridiculous pantomime! As if I'm going to say anything remotely truthful: 'My*

aim is to outmaneuver those idiots on the benches over there so that their political capital is reduced to the equivalent of a few leks, because they are reactionary fools whose continued election never fails to baffle me.' No, I have to recite a long list of legislation that all political sides would enact because they are palpably the best thing to do— Am I boring you, Odo?"

"On the contrary, I am considerably amused."

Ro watched this conversation with no small amount of amusement of her own. She had on occasion had call to speak to the castellan, but she was impressed at how direct Odo's channel had turned out to be. Garak had even apologized at how long it had taken him to respond, explaining that the castellan's annual Shape of the Union address was scheduled for the following week, and he was naturally busy preparing for that. Ro was amazed, too, at how much liberty Odo felt able to take with this powerful, notorious man. He spoke to the castellan as if he were speaking to a criminal—which, Ro thought, Elim Garak pretty much had been, once upon a time. A war criminal, and therefore eminently suited for the highest office in the Cardassian Union.

"I'm glad I'm offering so much entertainment."

"No doubt I'll derive as much pleasure from seeing your speech. I'm sure you'll enjoy having all those holo-cameras pointed at you. The Cardassian people are showing good sense keeping you under near-constant surveillance."

The castellan shuddered. "*Don't.*"

"It's good for you."

"*I know,*" said the castellan mournfully. "*But much as I would love to spend the morning sitting here being baited, I do have work to do. How may I help?*"

Quickly, Odo explained the plight of Mhevita Pa'Dan and the others whose family members were still in Romulan hands. Garak, Ro noticed, looked increasingly impatient.

"*This really is a very minor matter, Odo. Can't you take it up with the relevant people at the respective offices? The Romulans have some sort of repatriation committee, if I remember correctly.*"

"They do indeed, but they've long since stopped responding. Mhevita has not had news of her son for over four years."

"*That is a long time,*" Garak conceded. "*Any idea why?*"

"When I say no news, I mean exactly that. The Romulans have gone completely silent on the subject."

The castellan's eye ridges went up. His blue eyes were now very sharp. Ro had the impression that the matter now had his undivided attention. "*That's alarming. I wonder why I hadn't heard about this . . .*" Turning away from the screen for a moment, he spoke softly into a nearby comm. "*Akret, I'm sending across details of some prisoners of war being held by the Romulans. Could you send me everything we have? Immediately, please.*"

"Not quite on top of everything, Garak?" Odo said.

Palpably irritated, Garak said, "*Give me a little time, Constable.*"

"You used to be on top of everything."

"I used to be sitting in a shop with nothing to do. Now I'm running an empire."

"From where I'm sitting, it looks like the empire is running you. Are you still calling it that, by the way? I thought Cardassia had forsworn imperial ambitions."

"If my previous trade taught me anything, it would be the importance of window dressing. Did you want my help, Odo?"

Odo gestured with his hand.

Garak's comm chimed. "*Thank you, Akret,*" he said, and then he turned his attention away from Ro and Odo in order to read.

Ro tapped Odo on the arm. "Will he help?" she whispered.

Odo nodded. "Of course he will."

"*Well,*" said the castellan after a few minutes. "*This is all something of a surprise. I simply had no idea how many of our citizens were being held by the Romulans. This is not good. In fact, I would go so far as to say that this is unacceptable.*"

"You may thank me for bringing this to your attention."

"*Yes, I'm always grateful for having my life made more complicated.*"

"Consider it payback for all the times you made my life more complicated."

Garak beamed. Suddenly, he turned to Ro. "*The constable is far too familiar with me, don't you think, Captain?*"

Odo growled. "I'm not a constable, Garak."

"*No, I'm the one with the title now—which should surely earn me a little respect.*"

"And yet instead my heartfelt pity goes out to the Cardassian people. If it makes you feel any better, you'll always be plain, simple Garak to me."

"*Another insult,*" Garak said gravely. "*All this could be the basis for a serious diplomatic incident. How do you think I should respond, Captain Ro?*"

Ro shrugged. "I'm keeping out of this one. But thank you both. I'm enjoying the show."

"*We do go back a long way,*" said Garak.

Odo growled again.

"*I even had reason to interrogate Odo once,*" Garak said with breezy nonchalance.

"I had reason to interrogate you on many occasions."

"*Showing great wisdom as ever, Constable.*"

"I'm not—"

"*I know. That's why I keep on saying it.*" Garak smiled, which caused Ro some unease. "*Well,*" he said, "*this really can't go on. Rest assured this has the full attention of my office, Odo. I'll get back to you as quickly as possible—*"

"You mean someone in your office will?"

"*No, I mean* I *will—personally. But now I must go and consider further how to justify my policies to the representatives of the Cardassian people. What a strange and frankly inefficient system of government democracy is.*"

"It's the worst system," Odo said, "apart from all the others."

Garak smiled again and cut the comm.

"He seemed . . . slippery," said Ro.

"Yes," Odo agreed. "He found his calling in life when he turned to politics."

"But will he help?"

Odo gave a grim smile. "Oh, yes. He'll help. In his own inimitable way."

Pulaski could smell a spy a mile off, and Commander Peter Alden—in her less than humble opinion—reeked.

"So with your permission, Doctor Tanj," Alden said, "my associate and I will travel on board the *Athene Donald* for the first leg of your journey. We'll leave at Outpost 293 and return from there to Federation space."

"Your associate?" Tanj said.

"They always come in pairs, Maurita," Pulaski muttered. "One to ask the questions, one to turn the thumbscrews."

"This is a very straightforward request," Alden said mildly. "We want to come along only for a short while and observe how things are getting on. Starfleet Intelligence naturally has a great deal of interest in your mission and wants it to be a great success."

Pulaski snorted. In her opinion, there was nothing straightforward about Starfleet Intelligence. They were, in fact, what was wrong with Starfleet these days. Too many spooks and not enough scientists.

"You didn't mention anyone else before now," Tanj said. "Is this a colleague?"

"No, not exactly—"

"What exactly?" Pulaski shot back.

Alden studied her calmly. "Cory is a refugee," he said. "She is under my protection. She is my friend."

"A refugee?" Tanj said. "Where from?"

Pulaski didn't miss the brief hesitation before Alden replied. "Cory," he said, "is Tzenkethi."

Pulaski leaned back in her chair and laughed. "Oh, *now* I get it! That's why you're interested in us."

"I have many interests—"

"Don't talk to me like I'm senile." Pulaski leaned across Tanj to use the interface on her desk. "There we are—Commander Peter Alden, Tzenkethi Affairs. It isn't hard to guess why you've come out of the woodwork. This is about Metiger, isn't it? You're here to spy on her."

Alden smoothed an invisible crease from the sleeve of his uniform. "It's not as simple as that."

"I bet it is as simple as that. So what's the idea?" Pulaski went on. "You think she's up to no good, don't you? Something on behalf of her government, some covert op or whatever it is you people call your playground games."

"We won't be on board long," Alden said, addressing Tanj.

"You won't be on board at all," said Pulaski. "You can get off this ship now and crawl back under whatever stone Starfleet Intelligence keeps on top of you when you're not on the loose causing trouble."

She turned to her friend. "Maurita, this goes against everything we're trying to achieve—that you in particular are trying to achieve. How do we create a cooperative ethos on the *Athene Donald* when we start the journey with a blatant display of mistrust? Worse than mistrust. Contempt. What will Metiger think if we let this man come on board?"

There was a pause. Alden turned away from her and looked pointedly at Tanj.

There was an uncomfortable silence.

"Maurita?"

Tanj turned to Alden. "Thank you for coming to see me, Commander. I'll consider your request and let you know in due course."

Alden smiled and stood up. "A pleasure to speak to you both."

When the door closed behind him, Pulaski exploded. "Maurita, no way are you going to allow him and his associate—whatever the hell that means—to come on board this ship—"

"The problem is, Kitty, that I don't have the authority to prevent him coming on board—"

"This is a *civilian* ship! We're sponsored by a private research body!"

"But the ship, the physical hardware"—she rapped her knuckles against her desk—"comes from Starfleet. All non-Federation personnel are here at their discretion. And Starfleet these days—"

"Means Starfleet Intelligence." Pulaski fell back in her chair. "What have we created?"

There was a pause. "I'm not happy about this either," Tanj said. "If you want, we can speak to Captain Ro. She might be able to assist. Put some behind-the-scenes pressure on whoever can alter this decision."

Pulaski gave her friend a straight look. "This is a deal breaker for me, Maurita."

Tanj looked back unhappily. "Don't issue ultimatums that you can't live with, Kitty. I don't want you forced off this ship at this stage. And I certainly don't want to see you have to eat humble pie. I don't want Alden on board either—"

"So don't *let* him on board!"

"But my hands are tied. We'll take this to the captain and see what she can do."

In the temple, a service was under way. Cory slipped quietly into a seat at the back, closed her eyes, and listened. Prayers were being said, a soft chant in a language that Cory did not know but that seemed ancient and full of power. She ran through what she had learned about Bajor and the Occupation. It seemed remarkable to her that this language and this religion survived. Cory admired survivors, particularly those who venerated their own cultures.

She knew little of religion. For Tzenkethi of her status, the Autarch was the sole focus of their worship. He looked down on them from his palace on the Royal Moon, and they ached to serve him to their best of their abilities in the function that he had ordained for them. They sang songs about him. They knew that he loved them and wanted them to be happy, and that he would take care of them if they became sick and needed to be reconditioned. They trusted him, even if they did not always understand why the world was the way it was.

Religious practice had therefore been one of the things that most interested Cory after leaving Ab-Tzenketh, and, for obvious reasons, she had been particularly interested in those religions whose gods were present. The Bajorans—their gods lived in the Celestial Temple. They had intervened directly in Bajoran history—this was documented fact. And then there were the Jem'Hadar and . . . Now, what were the others called? Cory searched her memory, full of information learned during her recent wanderings. The Vorta, yes, that was it—the Jem'Hadar and the Vorta worshiped the Founders, who, like the Autarch working through his Yai servants, had created people to love and serve them. Cory wondered whether any Jem'Hadar or Vorta had ever experienced what she had. She still loved the Autarch, who had given her everything most beloved about her life. But she no longer believed he was all-powerful. She no longer believed everything he did was for her benefit.

Cory realized that her hand had crept up to her chest to begin the habitual gesture made by all Tzenkethi when they thought or spoke of their beloved Autarch: pressing one's hand against one's heart and then, head bowed, raising one's hand in respectful gratitude to salute the Royal Moon. She thought of what Alden would say if he could see her, and she put her hand back down in her lap. She listened, dully, to the chanting. Cory loved to sing and loved most to sing with others. But out here, in the wider world, there was nobody to sing with. Nobody here knew Cory's songs. They were useless.

Suddenly, the quiet of the temple was disrupted. A handful of children ran in, laughing and shrieking, chasing another of their number who was sprinting ahead and shouting back at his pursuers, "You can't catch me! You can't catch me!" Cory smiled. Even Tzenkethi children knew this game, although children of her status played it quietly, in the moments when they were not working, and under direction.

The children dashed around the temple. The portly vedek who had been leading the service made the mistake of going after them, huffing and puffing, which only served to make the children laugh more. Some of the congregation joined in their laughter, quietly. Eventually the children, thoroughly unquenched, chased their leader out again. Cory listened to their happiness disappear down the Plaza. Meanwhile the vedek mopped his brow, gathered up his robes and his dignity, and shuffled back to the front of the temple to bring the service to a close.

The congregation filed out. Cory pressed back into her seat, but one or two people looked at her with surprise and interest. She lowered her eyes and dimmed her hue, wishing she could fade away. Once the temple was empty, she looked up. One other person remained, sitting on a bench across the room, and he looked at her curiously. She sighed. Would she never be left in peace?

Her observer was an odd creature. His features were half formed, like the dough of the salt breads that Cory used to eat every day. She had not seen anyone like this before . . . No, she thought, remembering, that was not entirely true. She had seen faces like this in some of the many files she had studied while Peteh was busy. Cory found this man's face quite difficult to read, but she did not sense any threat from him. When at last he spoke, his voice was friendly and kind.

"May I join you?"

Cory pondered this. Usually she shrank from interaction with strangers, but she had been feeling lonely. Perhaps some company would be nice. "Yes," she said. "This one . . . I would like that."

The man came to sit beside her. His smile did much to leaven his strange features. "Forgive me for asking," he said. "But—"

"Yes," said Cory, who only a few short months ago would never have dreamed of interrupting anyone, not even one of her workmates. "I am Tzenkethi."

The man nodded and grunted in satisfaction. Cory waited for the inquisition, but no further questions came. The man merely folded his arms and relaxed back into his seat, looking around the temple and enjoying the peace. "I like this new temple," he said. "I knew the old station very well and thought that perhaps I would judge the new one harshly against it. But so far I'm satisfied by what I've seen. My name is Odo, by the way."

"This one is the Ret Corazame," Cory said. "My name is Cory," she tried, before settling on, "I am Corazame."

"Corazame. And before you ask, yes, I am a Founder. Or a Changeling, if you must."

"I would not have asked," Cory said truthfully, although she was quietly pleased that she had recognized him. "And I'll think of you as a Founder, if that's the name you prefer."

He smiled again. "A pleasure to meet you, Corazame."

"Likewise, Odo."

They sat in companionable silence for a while, enjoying the tranquil space. Eventually Odo said, "I imagine you find yourself attracting all kinds of unwelcome attention. Particularly given that your people have been at odds with the Federation. You have my sympathies. It's not easy being the only one of a kind, and not easy being from a kind that is at odds with everyone else."

"No," said Cory, with feeling. "It is not." They sat quietly together again for a while before she dared to ask the question uppermost in her mind. "Can you really change your shape? Is that true? Or simply an unwarranted belief held by those who fear your species?"

Odo's smile broadened. "Never has such an impertinent question been so courteously phrased—"

"This one hopes she has not given offense—"

"Not in the slightest. Watch."

With a golden shimmer, he was gone. In his place was a bird—she did not know what kind, but a grand bird, a great bird, one that would hunt and dive and fly across unbounded skies. It flapped its huge wings and rose up to the ceiling, then flew around the temple, freely, like the children running about. Coming to rest again beside her, it looked at her with one great yellow eye, and cawed—and then the shimmer came again, and Odo returned.

"Oh," breathed Cory. "Thank you! Thank you! That was marvelous!"

And it was marvelous, one of the most wondrous sights she had seen since leaving Ab-Tzenketh, and all the more so because it was a gesture of comradeship. "You watch now, Odo," she said, and Corazame relaxed and let her skin become as luminescent as it could be. She heard Odo gasp.

"So beautiful!" he said. "I had no idea!"

"No," she said shyly, dimming herself again.

"Nobody does." Not even Peteh had seen a display like that.

"It's hard, isn't it," said Odo, "concealing oneself all the time? Suppressing one's physical abilities so as not to frighten others?"

"Very hard," Cory agreed. "But then . . . I did the same at home." She thought about how much to say to this man and decided that she trusted him. "In my old life back home, it was rarely appropriate for someone of my status to show oneself in such a way. Once or twice a year, perhaps, at Spring Festival and the Autarch's Birthday—and then only ever among others of my status."

"Never when you were alone?"

"Oh, no!" Cory was shocked at the idea. "That would be presumptuous. Our beauty exists to glorify the Autarch, not to please ourselves." She smiled at Odo. "And to show ourselves uninstructed to someone outside our status would be very wrong. I have broken a great taboo showing you that."

"Good for you," said Odo. "But it sounds to me that even if you are now free to do what you like, you miss home."

"Of course I do. Do you miss your home too?"

Odo gave a low rumble at the back of his throat.

"This one hopes she is not being impertinent," Cory said. "This one offers her humble apologies if that is the case."

"No, no need—but home is a difficult question for me," Odo said. "My first memories are of Bajor. The old Deep Space 9 was my first home, but that no longer exists. For a while I lived among my own people, in the Great Link. And now I live on Bajor."

"But you are not at home there?"

"Home is where you make it, Corazame," he said. "I've learned that in a lifetime of exile. Even returning to the Great Link was not a real homecoming. I had never lived there before."

"Ab-Tzenketh is where I was born," Cory said simply. "I grew up in the coral schooling chambers, where we were disciplined to our tasks and taught the songs and how to love the Autarch. Where we learned what was needful for us to know, and to obey an Ap-Rej, since he or she always spoke with the voice of the Autarch. I was happy there, at home. Now I am away from home and I am unhappy."

"I'm sorry to hear that," Odo said gently. "Can you go back?"

"I have thought about that a great deal," Cory said. "There are complications."

There was a pause. "You're here with someone from Starfleet Intelligence, aren't you?" Odo must have seen her jump, because he carried on quickly. "Word passes around a place like this. Everyone knows there's a Tzenkethi on board. And I was once a security officer. I can't help myself. I was interested, so I found out more about you."

"Did you know that you would find me here

today?" Cory said. Suddenly she felt wretched. Had this meeting—which had felt so natural, the most natural she had felt since leaving home—been contrived?

"No," said Odo. "I had no intention of coming to find you at any point. I was simply interested in learning more about a fellow exile. It's only by chance that I found you here today. I would not have met you otherwise." He looked around. "There is something about a place like this. It draws the lonely, I think, and those who need peace to reflect upon their lives and choices."

Cory relaxed, a little.

"I've had a busy day, you see, and I needed some time to think," Odo said conversationally. "I'm here on the station to help a friend of mine. Her son has been held captive by the Romulans for ten years. She wants him to come home."

Cory's heart filled with pity. "Do you think you will be successful?"

"We'll see. An old friend of mine is involved now. If he can't do something, nobody can."

"I hope you are successful, for your friend. It is not right to be kept away from what you love best."

"No," Odo agreed, "it's not. Does that mean you intend to go home, Corazame?"

"I don't know. My friend Peteh"—she glanced at Odo—"Commander Alden"—Odo nodded to show he had understood her meaning—"he seems to be in two minds. He thinks that I can remain in the

Federation, but I know that some part of him wants me to go home."

"Hmm." Odo didn't look pleased about that. "I think that if you do return home, it should be on your own terms and not at the request of Starfleet Intelligence."

"I cannot return without their help," Cory said simply.

Odo's eyes narrowed. "I see."

"I owe Peteh a great deal. He has been kind to me. He could have abandoned me—but he didn't. "

"No true friendship takes account of credit and debt. It gives freely, without thought of compensation or reward."

"But a friend wishes to show gratitude and make gestures of love and thankfulness."

"Perhaps. But not at the cost of self-extinction . . . Oho!" Odo said suddenly. "Who do we have here?"

Cory looked around. A child, small and somewhat ragtag, was peeking at them both from behind one of the bulkheads.

"Out you come," Odo said, gruffly but not unkindly. "Let's take a look at you."

The child crept forward. He stood in front of them for a moment or two, wide eyes staring and unblinking. Then he said, "Will you do your tricks again? I liked to see you changing."

Odo looked back gravely. "Very well. What would you like to see? The bird?"

The child nodded and, once again, the great bird

took a turn around the temple, coming to rest by the little boy, who gazed upon the sight, transfixed. Then Cory released her true colors, and the whole temple glowed with her full and unconstrained beauty.

"Are you a demon?" asked the child, looking at her in awe.

"I don't know what one of those is," Cory replied. "I am Corazame. Who are you?"

"Ioemi," the child said. "We were playing hide-and-seek, but no one came to find me. I don't know how to get back home." He said it quite straightforwardly, as if abandonment was a matter of course, but Cory could see his small arms shaking. "I think I am forgotten."

"Are you here with the ships?" asked Odo.

"Yes," said the boy. Suddenly he looked proud. "We're the People of the Open Sky! We're travelers and adventurers!"

And, sometimes, lost children. "I know where you are billeted," said Cory kindly. "I can take you back to your overseers."

"*Overseers*?" Odo muttered. "His parents, perhaps?"

"We're the People of the Open Sky," Ioemi said. "None of us have parents!"

"Your carers, then," said Odo.

"Yes, yes, yes, that's who they are." He looked sad, a small child far from home. "I'd like to go back to them."

"I'll take you." Cory offered the boy her hand. She let it glow a little, and he seized it in delight.

"Overseers," Odo muttered again, looking at her thoughtfully and shaking his head. He sighed. "But what do I know? I grew up in a laboratory."

Four

Captain's Log, Personal.

It is certainly regrettable that much data about other civilizations has, in recent years, been collected by spies and undercover agents. There is surely a debate to be had as to whether knowledge acquired through unethical or dubious means is tainted or disfigured in some way by such modes of acquisition. Certainly the mistrustful mind-set that this characterizes is not ideal for scientific research: nuances may be missed; prejudices may be confirmed. The spy comes to his or her operation with his or her mind already made up: this is the opposite of the approach taken by the scientist, who must remain open-minded and ready to disprove a cherished hypothesis when the evidence stacks up against it.*

Yet many of our recent encounters with alien species have been carried out under the jurisdiction of Starfleet Intelligence—under the auspices of this bureau or that desk—and I fear that exactly such contamination of data (and mind-set) has taken place. What might a xenolinguist, for example, make of the Tzenkethi, coming to them without any preconceptions about their complex and fascinating society?

*I differentiate here between undercover operations and the necessary protocols for first contact with civilizations that are not yet spacefaring or for whom this is their first encounter with alien species. Suspicion is one thing, caution is another—and it is not hard to imagine how the sudden appearance above a world of a space vessel vastly more powerful even than anything that has appeared in that world's fantastical imaginings might have disastrous effects.

Beverly Crusher told herself that the reason she was interested in the People of the Open Sky was that Ro had made them sound so fascinating, but she knew it was also because she missed René. The sight of these children reminded her of him, both sweetly and painfully.

And she *was* interested in the People for their own sake. Crusher had met many species over the years, and part of her work as a doctor, she believed, involved understanding and responding to the specific cultural needs of patients as much as their physical or psychological needs. She would not, she thought, be much of a Starfleet doctor if she ran roughshod over other people's customs or beliefs. Observing the People in order to learn came naturally to her, and when Ro sent Oioli's request that the People might make use of the medical facilities, she jumped at the chance to see more of them at close hand.

So now the medical unit was full of children—many, many children, whom a couple of adults gently corralled past Crusher's tricorder and keen eye. Later she scribbled a few observations in her notes:

Much high tech, but bits and bobs? No unifying design or aesthetic—different sources? Mostly run-down.
Children—many children! No discernible family structure. Care shared among adults and children present when "work" occurs.
Question: what constitutes "work" among the People? What do they trade when in contact with others?
Adults directive but not "hands on." No physical discipline. Children plainly very happy; however—

Here Crusher paused and sighed. She was facing a problem now, and she had to decide what was best to do next. Her hand hesitated over her notes. Then she opened a comm channel.

"Laren," she said, "can I have a quick word when you're next free?"

"The problem is," Crusher explained, when Ro came by her office after her shift, "that while all the children I observed were very happy, and the caretaking I saw was first-class, there were a number of minor medical conditions among them that troubled me."

Ro was immediately on alert. "What do you mean? Not signs of any kind of abuse?"

"No, nothing like that. One or two of them were nearsighted, for example, but didn't even have glasses or corrective surgery to compensate, never mind drugs to correct vision. The People do plainly have some high technology—"

"But not much," said Ro. "And Oioli did ask

specifically if they could have access to our medical facilities. They're obviously underresourced."

"And they appear to have no visible means of support. But some of the other children show the aftereffects of . . ." Crusher leaned back in her chair. "What you need to understand, Laren, is that I had to look up these symptoms. I don't see them very often. But it's plain to me that some of these children have suffered in the past from malnutrition." Seeing Ro's startled response, she added quickly, "Not now. They're not underfed now. As I said, these children are very well cared for and obviously much loved. But for several of them, this has plainly not been the case for the whole of their lives. This leaves me with a lot of questions."

"I'm sure." Ro pondered what Crusher had said. "You know, I bet if you ran the same tests on me you'd find something similar. People can have complicated pasts."

"I agree entirely. Anyway, I'm not sure how best to proceed."

Ro frowned. "What do you mean?"

"Well, this *is* a first-contact situation."

"So?"

"So I can't go barging in accusing them of neglecting their children."

"I don't think you were going to do that, were you?"

Crusher smiled. "I'd like to think I've learned a couple of tricks from Jean-Luc over the years. But it's a sticky situation. How do you phrase it in a way that doesn't give offense? 'Why have some of your children suffered from hunger? Why are their minor ailments not being treated?' We might find ourselves in some kind of diplomatic dilemma."

"They don't seem the type to care about the niceties of diplomacy," Ro pointed out.

"No, but do they, for example, have prohibitions against certain types of care?"

"What do you mean by that?" asked Ro.

"Some cultural or religious groups have taboos against the transfer of, say, blood between people. But let's take an example from what we see here. Perhaps the People see drugs or corrective surgery—for instance, getting rid of nearsightedness—as going against nature."

"Would anyone think that?" Ro said. "Isn't that a disability you'd want fixed?"

"Sometimes what we perceive as disability is in fact an advantage on someone's own world. Someone from a low-gravity world would have difficulty moving under Earth gravity, but wouldn't at home. And then it's possible to see a physical difference as conferring cultural membership. Deafness, for example, allows access to a particular cultural space through sign language."

"Why would anyone not use therapies and cures that were to hand?"

"The Federation has its own cultural taboos on certain genetic therapies," Crusher said. "Ask Julian Bashir."

"I have to admit I don't understand that," said Ro frankly. "If a therapy is available, I think you're morally bound to use it to ameliorate suffering."

"I'd tend to agree," said Crusher, "and I know many other parents across the Federation would too. But concerns about eugenics run deep for some very good historical reasons. Ask another member of my staff, and they might tell you that they would give up practicing medicine rather than turn to eugenics. However, the point is," Crusher went on, "that I don't want to find myself in the position of having to treat any of these children against the wishes of their carers. But my chief impulse is to heal. So I will treat the children. Whatever the Prime Directive says."

"You know," said Ro, "I was never a big fan of the Prime Directive. Bajor might have gotten help sooner, and of a more substantial kind, if it hadn't been for the Prime Directive."

The two women studied each other thoughtfully.

"Still," said Crusher, "we have to show willingness at least."

"Hmm," said Ro. "I suppose there's a simple answer to this."

"What's that?"

"Don't assume that because we're Starfleet we know best. Instead, assume that the People know their own business."

"I think I said that I can't leave these children in these conditions," Crusher said.

"No, but how about starting by asking Oioli if

they'd like our help, and what kind of help that might be." Ro sighed. "Could *you* do it, Beverly? There's a situation brewing on the *Athene Donald* and I've been asked to help."

Crusher smiled. "Oho, is Katherine Pulaski stirring up trouble, by any chance?"

"As far as I can make out, Pulaski isn't the problem," Ro said. "Starfleet Intelligence is."

"The proverbial rock and the hard place," said Crusher, turning back to her work. "Good luck with that."

"I don't understand," said Alden, in a reasonable tone of voice that Ro knew from just ten minutes' acquaintance would only infuriate Pulaski further and that she rather suspected was the purpose, "why this request is unreasonable. This is a Federation vessel—"

"A *civilian* vessel," barked Pulaski.

"A civilian vessel carrying numerous foreign nationals—"

"So?" snapped Pulaski.

"So that means that certain aspects of its operation fall under our jurisdiction." Alden turned to Ro and held out his hands: *Look*, he seemed to be saying, *I am a reasonable man being hectored by the unreasonable.* "All I want to do is travel on board for a few weeks."

Pulaski looked ready to explode. Tanj placed a restraining hand on her arm. Ro felt sorry the Trill.

If anyone was caught between—what was Crusher's expression?—a rock and a hard place, it was surely Maurita Tanj.

"Captain," said Tanj, in a genuinely reasonable if rather strained tone, "you can see that Katherine is unhappy about Commander Alden's request, and I have to say that I'm not thrilled either. It's contrary to the spirit of our mission, and I think it's a bad way for us to start. Is there anything that you can do?"

Ro ran a fingertip along the ridges on her nose. She agreed with Tanj and Pulaski that this was probably a bad idea for their mission. But what could she do?

"I don't have the authority to interfere with Commander Alden's mission," she said. "The decision is yours, Doctor Tanj, although I suspect that your sponsors may have given you directions about what that response might be."

Alden leaned back comfortably in his chair. Pulaski, however, turned to her friend. "Maurita, tell him to get lost."

Tanj sighed. "I can't, Kitty."

"What?"

"The board of the institute naturally wants a smooth relationship with Starfleet. I've been told to make Commander Alden welcome and give him whatever assistance he needs."

Tanj was looking down at her hands. Ro felt a stab of sympathy for her. Rock—hard place. *Welcome to command, Doctor Tanj.*

"Maurita," said Pulaski, "he's here to spy on us."

Alden roused himself. "This is nonsense. A spy almost by definition needs to be concealed. I'm hardly concealed, am I? Certainly not given all the fuss that's being made. And I'm not in the habit of spying on Federation citizens."

"But you will happily spy on others?" Pulaski shot back. "Metiger, for example?"

"I have no evidence to suspect Metiger Ter Yai-A of anything," Alden said smoothly.

Liar, thought Ro. *If you don't suspect her for some reason, you suspect her simply because she's Tzenkethi.*

"Anyway," Alden went on, "traveling openly on the same ship as her is hardly the best way to go about spying on her."

"A check of public records reveals that you're with Tzenkethi Affairs at Starfleet Intelligence," Pulaski said. "I imagine that Metiger Ter Yai-A, who is a brilliant researcher, will be able to find that out. What is she supposed to make of that?"

"Perhaps that I'm interested in her?" Alden said. "That I share some of the same hopes for this mission that you do? That this might be a starting point for genuine dialogue between us?"

There was a brief pause. It was just possible, Ro thought, that this was true.

"What about your friend?" Pulaski said. "The Tzenkethi you're traveling with? Is she your spy?"

Alden laughed. "She's hardly a very inconspicuous one, is she? Everyone looks at a Tzenkethi, even one as quiet as Cory. No," he said, and addressed Tanj, "Cory is my friend. If anything, I'd like to put her into dialogue with Metiger. Cory's lived with us for a while now. She can give assurances for Metiger to take back home that we are not their enemies."

Tanj looked thoughtful at this.

"Maurita," Pulaski said urgently. "Don't be fooled. He's playing you, saying what you want to hear. You are a highly respected scientist—a leader in your field—and the director of this mission. I know that the institute will support whatever decision you make. This is a high-profile project and they can't be seen not to have faith in the director they appointed. It'll make them look like idiots."

"But that's not what they want," said Tanj. "And alienating our sponsors is not a good start for our mission either. I think," she said slowly, "that I'm prepared to give Commander Alden the benefit of the doubt. He's hardly undercover, is he? And if this really is the start of a more general thaw between our intelligence services—well, that falls within our remit, doesn't it?"

Pulaski sighed. "It's your decision. But I think it's a damned stupid one you're making."

Tanj smiled. "Thank you as ever, Kitty, for your support." She rose from her chair. "I appreciate your time, Captain Ro."

"I'm sorry I wasn't able to help more," Ro said as the two women departed.

"Thank *you* for your support," Alden said after they'd gone.

Ro turned her attention to her padd. "Don't mistake my obeying instructions for giving support."

"There's a Tzenkethi on that ship," Alden said.

So he *had* been playing Tanj. "You're *traveling* with a Tzenkethi," Ro said.

"What?" said Alden. "What do you mean by that?"

Ro looked up at him. He was looking back at her with great intensity and self-assurance. She'd met his kind many times before. Good intentions but bad experiences that ran the risk of perverting intentions. "Well," she said, "maybe Metiger is to Tanj and Pulaski what Cory is to you."

"Which is?"

"Friendly."

Alden gave a short laugh. "I doubt it."

Ro turned back to her paperwork. "Things change. Trust me. I never thought I'd be helping Cardassians."

Days like this, Crusher thought, were the reason she practiced medicine. By the middle of the morning, she and her team had corrected the eyesight of nine children and two adults, started several children on treatments that would ameliorate the effects of malnutrition on their bones and muscles, and also given some of the elderly members of the People drugs that would begin to reverse the early signs of dementia she had observed.

The matter of the health of the children of the People had proved entirely nonproblematic. Oioli and the other adults, when Crusher approached them, had jumped at the chance of treating the various ailments afflicting their number. "We are not fools or ideologues," Oioli said, when Crusher explained her hesitancy to offer. "We simply lack resources." As a result, Crusher was carrying out full health checks on all of the People, children and adults.

"It's a pleasure," said Crusher to Ro, when she went to report on what had happened, "to have a first-contact situation not fraught with difficulty or moral dilemma."

"Yes indeed," said Ro with a sigh. "If only the cultures we know could be so obliging."

Crusher's eyes gleamed. "Problems with Cardassians?"

"I was thinking more of humans."

Crusher laughed. "Do I detect problems arising from the presence of a certain doctor of my acquaintance?"

Ro smiled. "In fact, I have complete sympathy with Pulaski. Putting someone from Starfleet Intelligence on the *Athene Donald* makes a mockery of the idea that the ship's goal is to bring cultures together in harmony."

"But it was inevitable that they would send someone," Crusher pointed out. "If Metiger *is* reporting back to her superiors, they need to know. And surely she is? I imagine Tanj's reports and all the medical logs will be pored over by the intelligence services of *everyone* on board, not only ours." Crusher shook her head. "Perhaps one day we can all stop being so damn cloak-and-dagger and simply get on with talking sensibly to each other."

"A pleasant fantasy," said Ro.

"Live in hope," said Crusher.

"I might," said Ro, "if I didn't have to go now and talk to a Romulan about a possible war crime."

The castellan had been back in touch, asking that Odo contact the relevant officials on Romulus and inform them that the matter of the prisoners of war had come to their attention. When Odo asked whether it would be more appropriate coming from someone in Garak's office, Garak shook his head.

"*Too confrontational,*" he said. "*But with luck, the suggestion from a third party that the castellan is now very interested in this affair will be enough to create some movement.*"

Ro had been instructed by Starfleet Command to participate in the conversation: partly to show solidarity with their Cardassian allies and partly to show the Romulans that Starfleet officers were keen to have an open dialogue with them. On Pa'Dan's advice, they approached a Major Varis, head of the repatriation office.

"We're grateful for your time, Major Varis," Ro said to the Romulan political officer on the view screen. "We're eager to find out what has happened to these people and whether their repatriation can be brought forward."

Major Varis, another chilly functionary of the kind that the Romulan Empire seemed to produce as a matter of course, looked back coldly, giving away nothing. "*These people have been in our care for a decade. May I ask what has brought them to your attention now?*"

Odo spoke. "One of the soldiers is the son of a friend of mine. She approached me for help, and I approached Starfleet."

"*An interesting choice of intercessor,*" Varis said. "*Nevertheless, I suggest you approach the relevant offices within the Cardassian government that can proceed in the proper fashion—*"

"They have been unable to help," said Odo. "I have spoken directly to the castellan. He asks—informally, of course—that you do him the courtesy of giving this matter your attention and sending him a short summary of the situation from your perspective."

"As I understand it," said Ro, "this is not to be construed as a demand . . . but he would like a few answers."

There was a pause. Varis was staring at them, barely moving. After a moment, she said, very quietly, "*You chose to approach the Cardassian castellan before coming to us?*"

"We're in an alliance with the Cardassians," Ro said. "It was polite, to say the least, to let the castellan know that I intended to speak to you on behalf of some of his citizens."

"To let the relevant government officials know, perhaps. But to go immediately as high as the castellan? How should I"—she threw the word back—*"construe that?"*

Ro and Odo exchanged alarmed looks.

"This wasn't intended as an offense," Odo said.

"No?"

"Of course not," said Ro impatiently. "Major, I'm sorry this has landed on your desk. But the fact is that the castellan *is* now aware of the situation and he'd like some answers."

"Why now? After ten years?"

"Because it's only now that people are listening. People with the *power*," Ro said pointedly, "to do something about it."

"If the Cardassians wanted these people back, they shouldn't have waited ten years to ask for them."

"Their families *have* been asking," Odo said, "but nobody has been listening."

"Successive Cardassian governments have had a great deal to do," Ro added.

"That's their problem and entirely their own fault. This could have been resolved at a much lower level. I'm insulted, Captain, that you should come to me and threaten me with the castellan."

"I haven't threatened you at all," said Ro. "If anything, I've given you advance warning that people higher than both of us are getting interested—"

But the comm had been cut and Varis was gone.

"Well," said Ro, pushing out a breath, "that didn't exactly go as planned." She glanced at Odo. "What do you think was going on there?"

"I don't know," Odo said thoughtfully. "Something we don't understand."

"You realize what the obvious answer is?" Ro said.

Odo growled.

"That they're all dead," Ro said, "and they have been for some time. Varis is faking being offended in order to cover up a mass murder."

Odo brooded for a moment and then roused himself from his chair. "I won't believe that until I see bodies," he said. "Or DNA evidence. For Mhevita's sake, we have to keep asking. And if there has been an atrocity . . ." He looked grim. "That is an even better reason to keep pressing for the truth." He sighed. "I'll go and tell Mhevita how this went."

Ro nodded. "And I'll inform the castellan's office that we have some unhappy Romulans."

"Under other circumstances he'd be pleased about that," said Odo dryly.

But under these circumstances he wasn't, and neither was Command. *Keep pressing*, came the message back from both. *Keep asking.*

"But ask who?" muttered Ro. Varis was ignoring her requests for a second conversation, and other officers she approached directed her back to one place—the repatriation office, under the care of one Major Varis. They seemed to have reached a dead end, and that surely didn't bode well for Mhevita Pa'Dan's son.

"Well, I guess this is good-bye."

Katherine Pulaski stuck out her hand. Crusher shook it. "You know," Crusher said, "I wasn't really looking forward to seeing you."

Pulaski gave a snort of laughter. "People don't, generally speaking. What did I do this time?"

"You want the truth?"

"Always," said Pulaski.

"I found it hard to forgive your attitude toward Data."

"Quite right," said Pulaski briskly. "I was an idiot. Sometimes I can be thickheaded. Ask Maurita."

It was Crusher's turn to laugh. This was the thing about Pulaski. The frankness encompassed herself. In fact, Crusher reflected, that was probably where it started. Katherine Pulaski cut herself no slack, and she extended the same courtesy to others.

"Have you thought more about what you're going to do?" asked Pulaski. "Whether you need more . . . what was it you said? 'Time to think'?"

"I've thought," Crusher said. "I'm thinking."

"Well, don't think too long. Picard strikes me as a patient man, but not one to jerk around."

Crusher had to agree that that was a fair summary of his personality. "And are you resigned to having an intelligence officer on board?"

Pulaski's brows furrowed. "No! Of course not!

I'm pissed as hell. But I'm going to have to make the best of it if I don't want the mission to start off on the wrong foot. Damn it, Beverly, why don't these spies and spooks get the hell out of the way and let us get on with the real business of life!"

"You've got my wholehearted agreement there," Beverly said fervently. "But why not take the chance to do some observations of your own?"

"Huh?"

"Alden's bringing his own Tzenkethi on board, isn't he?"

"Yes. Cory, I think he said she was called."

"I gather she's had an interesting past."

"Haven't we all," Pulaski muttered. "But yes, I'll be watching this Cory—the same way Alden is watching Metiger."

"When I said make observations, I meant something more benign," Crusher said. "How often do we get the chance to meet a Tzenkethi like her? Someone who lived like most of them must do? We get to see only the ones permitted to leave, the ones trained to interact with us."

"You're assuming that everything Alden has told her about us is true," Pulaski said.

"If I didn't work on the assumption that people were mostly telling me the truth, I think I'd go mad," Crusher said. "And I'd rather be mistaken about others than mistrustful of them."

"It's a good philosophy, Beverly. I wish I had your open-mindedness."

"Keep me informed about the journey, won't you?" Crusher said. "Send me your logs."

Pulaski smiled broadly. There was, Crusher thought, probably no better way to please her than to take an interest in her work. "I will. And thank you for opening up to me. I know," Pulaski said with a laugh, "that I'm not the kind of person to attract confidences. So I appreciate your trust. I've always felt that because of that brief time I spent on the *Enterprise* that people . . . I don't know . . . put us into competition somehow. Compare and contrast us. But I was always more than chief medical officer on the *Enterprise*."

"I know exactly how you feel," said Crusher.

They had reached the docking bay by this point. Pulaski left with a cheery salute and Crusher went to watch the *Athene Donald* depart. She found on reflection that she was glad to have met Pulaski again. She had enjoyed the other woman's prickly, honest, and stimulating company. *Who would have thought?* Crusher said to herself as the *Athene Donald*, bright and brimming with promise, set sail on its voyage. *Katherine Pulaski, marriage guidance counselor. Sometimes you don't need to go traveling to discover something new. Always keep an open mind. People can surprise you.*

She strolled back the long way to the medical unit, enjoying the pleasant walk along the Plaza. Would she like to live here permanently? A charming fantasy unfolded in her mind, of the three of them here, a family, René running in and out of everywhere like the children she had seen earlier . . . It was so safe, so friendly, like a real home . . . Crusher shook herself. Nothing would prise Jean-Luc Picard from the *Enterprise*. If there was going to be a home for their family, that's where it would be.

So what did that mean for their marriage?

Crusher put these thoughts, troubling as they were, aside. She had enough to occupy her for the rest of the day, completing the medical checks on the People and arranging for any necessary treatments. She turned into the unit and greeted her staff, getting an update on how the various cases were progressing. She entered her private office.

It was in disarray. She tapped her combadge. "Crusher to Blackmer. Could you come to the medical unit immediately? Someone has broken into my office."

"Doctor Crusher hadn't been to her office that morning," Blackmer reported to Ro. "So the break-in could have happened anytime during the night."

"But how?" said Ro. "It's not as if the medical unit is left unattended."

"But it's quieter then, and the lights are dimmed. You could get past reception and into her office if you knew your business. And whoever did this knew their business."

"Anything missing?"

"That's the strange thing," said Blackmer. "Nothing. Some samples on her desk seem to have attracted the most attention, but they were left behind. There was an attempt to access her logs, however—and hers are not the only ones. Someone's been trying to gain unauthorized access to station security logs."

Ro whistled under her breath. "Any thoughts yet as to who might be involved?"

Blackmer shifted uneasily in his seat. "I have a few ideas."

"So what's the problem?"

"I know who I *think* it is. But everything I've turned up points in a different direction."

"Evidence can be unhelpful that way," Ro said dryly. "Go on. Who do you think is involved?"

Blackmer lowered his voice. "Well, who do *you* think? Their children are into everything. They're—"

"For your information, Lieutenant Commander," Ro said, "if you mean to imply that homelessness goes hand in hand with a tendency to thieve, you'd better not say that outright to any Bajoran of my generation. Do you have any hard evidence to link any of the People to the break-in or the attempts to access either of the logs?"

"Not as such—"

"But something has come up."

"Well, yes—"

"Which is?"

Blackmer sighed. "There's a Tzenkethi on board DS9."

"A Tzenkethi?" Ro frowned. "But hasn't the *Athene Donald* left?"

"Yes. Doctor Crusher saw it off."

"So who can it be?" Ro turned to the comm and opened a channel to the *Athene Donald*. Tanj was on the line within a few minutes. "*Whoever your Tzenkethi is, Captain, it's not Metiger. I can see her from where I'm sitting.*"

"Wasn't there another Tzenkethi supposed to travel with them?" Blackmer said quietly from across the desk. "Alden was traveling with one."

Alden came on the line. "*Yes, Cory's traveling with me.*"

"Did you go on board with her?"

"*What do you mean?*"

"Did you board the *Athene Donald* together?"

"*No, but she knew the departure time—*"

"Could I prevail upon you to check," said Ro patiently, "whether she is in fact on board?"

The search took no more than a couple of minutes. Alden came back on the line white-faced.

"I'm guessing she's not where you thought she was," Ro said.

"*No,*" said Alden. "*No, she's not. She must have misunderstood when we were leaving—*"

"Or decided not to come along?" suggested Ro.

"*No, no, she wouldn't do something like that . . . Captain, Cory is very vulnerable and not very experienced. I'm concerned she may have got into trouble. She could be hurt, lost—I don't know! But she wouldn't simply miss departure without telling me."*

"Then we'll proceed under the assumption that she's still on board DS9, and we'll look for her."

"Please, and hurry. And let me speak to her as soon as you find her."

"I will," said Ro, and cut the channel. "So," she said, turning to Blackmer, "it seems we now know whom we're looking for. Any thoughts as to why she might have stayed?"

"She could have simply misunderstood when the ship was leaving," Blackmer said doubtfully. "But if you want my guess, she's obeying orders."

Ro almost did a double take. "Excuse me?"

"Alden's bluffing. She was never intended to go on the *Athene Donald*."

"For what reason?"

Blackmer shrugged. "I don't know, I'm not a spy."

"You've got a suspicious enough mind," Ro said. "Couldn't she simply have decided to part company with Alden? DS9 is as good a place as any to set out on your own."

"We'll see. But I'd like to ask her about the break-in."

"And the People?"

"For the moment," said Blackmer, "they're off the hook."

They remained off the hook, but it seemed that Corazame too was not likely to be responsible. A routine check of records showed that she had left on a private freighter for Bajor some hours prior to Crusher leaving her office the previous night. Alden, when pressed, claimed to know nothing about this trip.

"But Odo had some interesting things to say about her," Ro said to Crusher and Blackmer, who had joined her in her office for updates on the situation.

Blackmer frowned. "What does he know about this?"

"Turns out he met her in the temple. They had a long chat. Odo's impression was that she was eager to go home, but not under any condition Alden would attach to her return." Ro gave her colleagues a meaningful glance. "Which, practically speaking, means a return to Ab-Tzenketh is an impossibility for her. She may simply have decided to strike out on her own—and, in fact, there's nothing we can do about it."

Blackmer looked thoughtful. "She's not a Federation citizen, is she?"

Ro shook her head. "No, her status is still asylum seeker, as far as I can make out. But there are no constraints on what she can do and where she can go, provided she keeps her sponsor, Alden, informed. So if Cory *has* decided to go off and spend a month on retreat in the Kasella Mountains, she's free to do so. She's free to do whatever she chooses in Federation space."

"Except Alden doesn't know where she is," Blackmer said.

"That's what he says," Ro said.

"And all the while," Crusher said, pointing to Blackmer's tricorder, "we have Tzenkethi life signs on the station."

Even as she spoke, the pulse on the tricorder flickered and went out. Blackmer shook it, but nothing happened. "Now, that is confusing. And more than a little worrying."

"At least all our facts now tally," Ro said dryly. "We didn't think we had a Tzenkethi on board. And now the machines have caught up with us."

Blackmer tapped the device. "It could be a glitch," he said. "New systems and everything . . . But I was so sure that she was still here . . ."

"It could be another Tzenkethi entirely," Crusher said puckishly, with a wink at Ro.

Don't torment him, mouthed Ro.

"But I didn't . . . I haven't . . ." Blackmer shook the tricorder hard. Nothing changed. "Huh. Well, I guess that's that."

"So, no Tzenkethi, no suspect," said Ro briskly. "Who else do we have in mind? Have you been able to pin anything on the People, Jeff?"

She meant it tongue-in-cheek, but Blackmer shook his head seriously. "To be honest, I'm finding the whole business baffling. The forensic team is struggling."

"Is that surprising? Surely it means that whoever

broke into Crusher's office knew what they were about?" said Ro.

"The problem is being able to tell what's their DNA and what isn't," Blackmer said.

Ro glanced at Crusher. "Is it possible to conceal DNA in that way?"

"We don't know much about their capabilities," Crusher said. "But everything I've seen suggests that what technology they have is decrepit."

"And a burglary isn't consistent with what I've seen," said Ro. "They seem completely honest to me."

"I'd agree," said Crusher.

"But they're into everything," Blackmer said. "The children . . ."

Crusher smiled. "That's one of the things I like best about them."

Ro smiled too. "Sorry, Jeff, but if you want to arrest Oioli and the others on suspicion of burglary, you're going to have to bring me real evidence. In the meantime . . ."

"I know, I know," said Blackmer gloomily. "Round up the usual suspects."

Peter Alden was sitting in the *Athene Donald*'s rec room, staring out into space, when Pulaski found him. He looked preoccupied—worried, even, as well he might. Pulaski glanced around the room, checked who was within hearing range, and eased herself into the seat opposite Alden. After a moment, he noticed her. His face hardened. Pulaski smiled without pity.

"The best-laid plans of spies and informers, eh, Commander?" she said.

Alden made himself visibly relax. "I've no idea what you're talking about."

"Oh, come on! This business with your pet Tzenkethi. Corny."

"Her name is Cory." A little steel had crept into Alden's voice. "And she is nobody's pet. What about her?"

"Well, where is she?"

Alden folded his arms. "I've no idea."

"No idea?" Pulaski tutted. "Careless of you. *Very* careless. Or perhaps it's nothing to do with you."

"I'm afraid you're not making any sense."

"All I mean is that perhaps your asset decided she had her own ideas about how to use her talents?"

"I really don't know what you're talking about—"

"No?" Pulaski leaned toward him conspiratorially but didn't bother to lower her voice. "Come on, Commander. I love a spy caper as much as the next person." The word "caper" hit, she noted with satisfaction. "So what's going on? Did she decide she wasn't interested in being used as a tool by Starfleet Intelligence after all?"

Alden glanced around at their audience, who were pretending not to listen. "This isn't appropriate, Doctor—"

"No! Wait!" Pulaski snapped her fingers. "I've got it! She was never meant to come on board at all, was she? All that fuss about getting you on board was cover for her to slip away. I bet she's halfway back to Ab-Tzenketh right now, to embed herself there—isn't that the word you use for it? 'Embed'?"

"Actually, no," said Alden. "I don't know where you're getting these ideas, but they're fantasy. What do you think I am? I wouldn't send Cory back to Ab-Tzenketh against her will. That would be a death sentence for her—"

"Did I say it was unwilling? I bet she was dying to get back. It's beautiful there, isn't it?" She turned slightly in her chair, calling over to Metiger, who was sitting a few seats away, and had, Pulaski devoutly hoped, been listening to this entire exchange. "Hey, Metiger, I bet it's beautiful on Ab-Tzenketh at this time of year, isn't it?"

Slowly, and with the grace and dignity of a near-supernatural being, Metiger unfurled herself from her seat. Her skin shone so brightly it might almost have been on fire. "Ab-Tzenketh is always beautiful," she said. As ever, people stopped what they were doing when she spoke. Some even closed their eyes. "The Autarch's grace blesses us in all ways, at all times."

"Well, no wonder Corny jumped ship," said Pulaski. "I bet she couldn't wait to get back to the old homestead. But you must be pissed if she's really gone AWOL, Commander. No handy reports coming back your way. I wonder what the folks back at Starfleet Intelligence have to say about that."

Metiger turned and left, leaving the room a little dimmer, as if enchantment had disappeared from the world. There were one or two audible sighs of regret.

"Was it something I said?" Pulaski said. "Or perhaps it was you, Commander. To lose one Tzenkethi is a misfortune. To lose two—"

Abruptly, Alden stood up. "You've made your point. For what it's worth, I have no idea why Cory didn't board the *Athene Donald*, and I'm worried sick about her. But I'll say this—if Cory was our agent, heading back home undercover, this little performance of yours would probably have killed her—"

Pulaski dismissed this idea with a wave of the hand. "Assuming everything we discuss makes it back from Metiger to some imagined superiors—"

Alden leaned forward to speak more confidentially. "I doubt you know much about the Tzenkethi. But I know a great deal. Firsthand. Of course Metiger will be reporting back to her superiors. She has that duty as a loyal servant of the Autarch. He cannot be everywhere at once, so she must act as his eyes and ears in places where he cannot be. She would no more imagine not reporting back to her superiors as you or I would imagine not breathing."

Pulaski held her breath ostentatiously for a few seconds, puffing up her cheeks and then pushing the air out noisily. "Yeah," she said. "We'll see."

Alden left. There was much murmuring around the rec room. Pulaski thought she heard one colleague, a Ferengi first-contact specialist named Delka, mutter, "Harsh . . ." But Pulaski was satisfied with how the encounter had gone. Until—

"Katherine."

It was Tanj.

"A quiet word in my office, please."

"Oh, come on, Maurita, he was asking for it!"

"Maybe, but that doesn't mean you have to dish it out. What were you hoping to achieve by that performance?"

Pulaski shrugged. "I wanted Metiger to know to keep an eye on him."

"And?"

"All right, I also wanted to embarrass him."

"And you have. But you've embarrassed Metiger too."

"Embarrassed Metiger? How on earth—"

"By pointing out to a roomful of people that our intelligence service doesn't trust her. No, don't speak yet. Shut up and listen. It's worse than that. If I was in Metiger's position, I would feel used."

"Used?"

"Used by you to score a few points off a colleague."

Pulaski bit her lip. "I didn't think."

Tanj sighed. "You rarely do, Kitty."

"Sorry."

"Apology accepted. But will you please let this drop? Alden is here for a few weeks only. Let us ignore him as best we can. For Metiger's sake, at least."

"All right," Pulaski said, "I'll behave. It'll be a

long trip otherwise. But damn it, Maurita, I'm furious about this!"

"I never would have guessed. But he'll be gone before you know it. In the meantime, I think we can show Metiger in more positive ways that she is our colleague and that she has our support."

"All right. I'll be good." Pulaski laughed. "This is why I wanted you on this journey. You're more of a diplomat than I'll ever be."

"Kitty, you are no kind of diplomat at all. Stick to the science, my dear. I've got the egos in hand."

Pulaski smiled. "You're the expert—"

Their conversation was suddenly cut short. An alert was sounding about them. Tanj rose to her feet. "There must be a ship—" she began, but she was interrupted by a voice booming through the whole ship.

"Proceed no farther. You are being observed. Stand down all weapons. This is not a request."

Their ship was huge and black, as if the King of the Underworld had sent it as his messenger. It loomed vast and faceless before the *Athene Donald*, which seemed like a child's trinket beside it—tiny, fragile, and crushable. There were no markings, no transponder signal to say who they were, only the instructions booming through the ship that the crew scrambled to obey. They had come as if from nowhere, and with them came death.

Part Two

Cease from Exploration

Five

Captain's Log, Personal.

What form might the first encounter with a new species take?

We most easily imagine the discovery of a new world, perhaps, with numerous civilizations and histories to be learned and understood. Or perhaps a new species suddenly arrives from nowhere, announcing itself to ship and crew? Both of these fire the imagination, and many such cases—and their pitfalls and difficulties—are documented not only in my own logs but also in those of the other Starfleet *captains who have traveled in hopeful search of new life.*

Less common for the starship captain in command of an exploration vessel is the chance, even informal, meeting—the voyager passing through at a deep space station, perhaps, or some other outpost. Here the challenges arising from initial encounters can be more complex, but the rewards are arguably greater, since these travelers are less likely to be typical of their civilizations (being, as they are, away from home for reasons of their own) and more likely to be outliers of some sort. They may not, in that case, represent what is typical of their civilizations, although that does not, of course, prevent them from being equally revealing.

Something, after all, drives us away from our homes to voyage among the stars. Something, after all, has made us . . . I would not say disaffected, but certainly restless in some way, eager for new experiences and adventures.

Are we explorers typical of the Federation? And what might our restlessness say about the civilization that we have left behind?

The black ship sat motionless in space before the *Athene Donald* for hours, uncommunicative and unmoving. The message that had so forcefully penetrated all decks of the ship had, mercifully, gone on for only five minutes before cutting out. After that the ship had fallen completely silent—but terribly, frighteningly present: a vast and steely imposition upon space.

"What are they *doing* over there?" muttered Pulaski, staring at the view screen at the amazing vessel. "Why go to the trouble of making contact with us if you don't then go on to . . . well, make contact?"

The first-contact specialist, Delka, looked up from the notes she had been working through with Tanj. "Their message said we were being observed. I assume they're observing us."

"For this long?" Pulaski said. "We're not that interesting."

Delka smiled, all teeth. She was a bright, no-nonsense Ferengi, one of the new breed of professional women starting to fill up the junior branches of the Ferengi civil service. Pulaski liked her, admiring the guts necessary to make her way in her chauvinist society. Delka, in turn, had shown all the signs of finding Pulaski amusing, which was, as Tanj had found over the years, one of the best ways to handle Pulaski. "Perhaps we have a homespun charm that they find quaint," Delka said.

Alden came over to join them, having requested he be present in the briefings and for formal first contacts. Pulaski hadn't liked the idea, of course, but Tanj had acquiesced. "He's on board now, Kitty," she had said, "so we might as well make use of his expertise. He'll only cause trouble if we don't."

"Any idea how long this might go on?" Alden asked Delka.

"Not a clue," the Ferengi replied. "Their idea of the passage of time might be completely at odds with ours. I suggest that if it gets to a couple of months, we might want to try initiating contact ourselves."

"*Months?*" said Alden, as Pulaski said, "You are joking, aren't you?"

Delka shrugged. "Let me tell you a secret about first-contact specialists. We're mostly making it up as we go along. How else could it be? I've never met these people in my life and neither has anyone else that I've read about."

"So what exactly is the use of you?" Pulaski said impatiently. Again her prejudice against the social sciences was being confirmed: conjecture and intuition dressed up as fact.

"Rather offensive, Kitty," murmured Tanj.

"Oh, I'm not offended," said Delka cheerfully. "It's a fair enough question. I can't speak for my other colleagues, but I at least"—and here she tapped her bulbous brow—"have an encyclopedic knowledge of over four and a half thousand first-contact situations, good and bad. No first contact is the same, but some of this information might come in useful when we try to judge how best to interact with these people. Think of it . . . like case law in the legal profession."

"That's a good analogy," said Pulaski, content to acknowledge expertise when she saw it.

"Thank you," said Delka with a laugh.

"But it's so . . ."

"Uncertain?" Delka smiled. "Imprecise? Isn't that what all science is like? A voyage of exploration, mapping out uncharted territory?"

Suddenly, the view screen shimmered into life.

"Step up, Maurita," Delka said. "Your moment's here."

Tanj positioned herself in front of the screen, settling her shoulders back and folding her hands before her so that she looked authoritative but nonconfrontational. A face appeared on the screen, humanoid but obviously alien, all lines and angles, with grayish skin and dark markings around the throat. Pulaski glanced over at Alden, who was staring at the view screen. His hand, Pulaski noticed, had strayed to his side, where a weapon might be, if weapons were permitted on board the *Athene Donald*. She looked back t the alien. Something about its demeanor reminded her of Alden: taut, severe, and impassive.

The alien spoke. Through the translators, its voice conveyed little in the way of emotion, sounding formal and stiff.

"My name is Tey Aoi of the Chain. I wish to meet your leaders. We will send a team of personnel onto your ship."

" 'Please' goes a long way, you know," muttered Pulaski.

Gently, Delka patted Pulaski's arm.

Tanj cleared her throat. "My name is Doctor Maurita Tanj. I am director of research on the civilian vessel *Athene Donald*. We are a scientific research and exploration ship crewed by representatives from many species. Part of our mission is to seek out new life in order to learn and, perhaps, in some small way, to teach."

A brief flicker passed across Tey Aoi's face. Was it offended? Amused? Intrigued?

"With your permission," Tanj went on, "we would like to send a small team of scientists across to your ship to meet you."

There was a pause. Then Tey Aoi said, "*We know about your ship. We know your purpose. You may not come on board. But we will send our own team over. Wait for our instructions.*"

The comm cut out. "Brisk," said Pulaski, "not to mention bossy. And how do they know about us already?"

Alden looked up from a tricorder. "I'd like t
know that too," he said. "In the meantime, I'd do
what Tey Aoi says. That ship is armed to the teeth."

Pulaski sighed. "Always about the weapons with you lot, isn't it?"

"Somebody has to care about potential threats," Alden said.

"They haven't issued any threats," Pulaski pointed out.

"I said 'potential.' " Alden turned to Tanj. "I'd like to be part of the team meeting the Chain when they come aboard."

Pulaski narrowed her eyes and, glancing at Tanj, shook her head. *No damn way.*

"I'll consider your request, Commander," Tanj said. "There are some obvious candidates for inclusion—myself and Delka. I don't want to overwhelm our visitors with too many new faces."

Alden nodded. "That seems fair." He turned to the view screen, where Tey Aoi's image had been. "Is it me," he said, "or is the universal translator putting their speech into blank verse?"

"So we've got Delka, obviously," said Tanj. "And I'd suggest Metiger, for reasons of internal politics—"

They were sitting in Tanj's office, deciding on the best team to meet the representatives of the Chain.

Pulaski frowned. "What do you mean by that? I'm not sure I like the idea of doing things because of politics."

"What I mean," said Tanj, "is that I want to make sure that the Tzenkethi are given no reason to complain that Metiger was treated in any way differently from the rest of us. This isn't simply a Federation first-contact mission. Delka is a representative of the Ferengi Alliance, and Metiger represents the Tzenkethi Coalition."

"Shouldn't everyone be in on the act in that case?" Pulaski said dryly. "We've some Cardassians you can press into service, not to mention a couple of Romulans lurking around—"

"Fortunately they are too junior to be able to pull rank and insist on their involvement. Besides, Metiger is pretty impressive—"

"Ain't that the truth!"

"And I'd rather like to do something to impress. Despite which, I'm going to let you loose on them, Kitty."

"Oh, thanks!"

"Leaving me with one more person to find—"

"Not Alden," Pulaski said quickly.

When Tanj didn't immediately agree, Pulaski looked at her in alarm. "You're not seriously thinking of including him, are *you*? He's only here on sufferance in the first place! He forced himself on board! We don't have to let Starfleet Intelligence get their finger into every damn pie—"

"That's not why I'm thinking of including him," Tanj said. "Do you know his background?"

"No idea," Pulaski said. "Do they send them to

special spy school, or do they pluck them out of the ether already paranoid and obstructive?"

Tanj smiled. "He trained in xenosociolinguistics. How alien languages work. I gather this is why he originally became interested in the Tzenkethi. Their language has a vast number of dialects that are not all mutually intelligible, and even within these, there are very precise modes of address. These all reinforce social structure, of course. He began a doctoral thesis on the subject but didn't quite complete it before Starfleet Intelligence got their hands on him." She sighed. "So many good minds get sidetracked that way."

"Where are you getting all this information about Tzenkethi language from?" Pulaski said. "Not from Metiger, surely?" Metiger had never shown any sign of being willing to speak about Tzenkethi society before, deftly fielding questions.

"No, from Alden's field reports."

"You have access to them?" Pulaski's eyebrows went up. "I would have thought they'd be classified—"

Tanj gave a noncommittal smile. "Oh, a friend of a friend of a friend was able to help . . ."

Pulaski laughed. "We all need friends like that from time to time. So you're not averse to a little spying yourself?"

Tanj's eyes narrowed. "You don't think I'd let him loose on my ship without being informed, do you?"

Pulaski smiled. "I knew there was a reason I liked

you. You're all warmth and 'let's be friends,' but in fact you're as manipulative as hell."

"Don't you forget it. And right now I'm attempting to manipulate you into letting Peter Alden take part in this first-contact scenario. And it's not because I want to placate Starfleet Intelligence. I think he might have some genuinely interesting insights, but also—"

"Because he will have to work with Metiger," Pulaski said. "You really are a manipulator, aren't you?"

Tanj sighed. "I want this voyage to work. I don't want our first mission soured by distractions."

Pulaski thought carefully about what to say next. "You know, when I realized we were stuck with Alden, I did a little poking around myself. I took a look at his medical records."

Tanj was startled. "Are you supposed to do that?"

"I'm CMO of this ship. If I think there's a reason that something about his medical status might affect the rest of the crew adversely, I can do whatever the hell I like."

"I think you're pushing your luck there," Tanj said. "And are you supposed to tell me what you read?"

"If I think you need to know anything."

"And do I? Need to know anything?"

"Maybe." Pulaski sighed and leaned back in her chair. "The last mission Alden went on where he met a Tzenkethi, the contact nearly drove him to a breakdown."

"What?"

"He had some kind of phobic reaction, apparently. I'm telling you this because if you want to put him into a potentially stressful situation with a Tzenkethi around, you ought to know that there are risks."

Tanj sat deep in thought for a while. "I think we should include him nonetheless," she said. "I've seen no similar reactions to Metiger the whole time he's been on board, and he's been traveling with a Tzenkethi for months now, by all accounts. Perhaps exposure is better than avoidance."

"He and what's her name were traveling as companions, though," Pulaski pointed out. "Not working alongside each other."

"Was he working alongside a Tzenkethi when he had this almost breakdown?" Tanj asked.

"No," admitted Pulaski. "From what I can make out, it was a high-stress situation with a lot of mistrust flying about."

"There you are," said Tanj, satisfied. "Completely different. Working with Metiger might be exactly what he needs to make him understand that he doesn't have to greet every Tzenkethi with fear and alarm."

Pulaski smiled at her friend. "Always the optimist, eh?"

"Always," Tanj said firmly.

"Then Alden it is," Pulaski said. "Will you tell him, or shall I?"

They told him together. Seeing his genuinely pleased expression, Pulaski thought that maybe she was catching a glimpse of why this young man had chosen to go into Starfleet in the first place. It was also, perhaps, an insight into some of the damage done to him on Ab-Tzenketh.

He's an entirely different generation, she thought. *Not like ours. We assume that we'll enjoy whatever the universe has to offer. But his is a generation shaped by war. They came of age in a time not of freedom and exploration but of threat and defense. We didn't have that. It came to us much later. That must make a difference.*

After they left Tanj's office, Alden caught up with Pulaski in the corridor. "I gather I have you to thank for my inclusion in this," he said, falling into step beside her.

"I'll be frank. I didn't want you to go, but Maurita persuaded me not to block your inclusion in the away team."

"Either way, I'm grateful, although I'm interested to know why."

"Why I'm letting you run amok in a first-contact situation? Yes, I'm wondering that myself." Pulaski stopped walking to look at him directly. Yes, he was still a young man, despite the gravity and the world-weariness. Perhaps there was still time for him to remember that this whole business was supposed to be *fun*. Gruffly, she said, "I'm sure you've got enough on your plate given that your Tzenkethi is still on the loose, but it struck me that genuine first-contact opportunities must come your way rarely these days. So who am I to deny you the chance?"

Alden gave a half smile. "Thank you."

He offered his hand. Pulaski shook it, very briskly. "And who knows," she said, "perhaps the experience will convince you to give up your current life of crime and turn your attention back to science. We all win that way."

Behind them, Tanj laughed. "Don't be offended, Commander. This is Katherine Pulaski when she's trying to be nice."

Gravely and gracefully, Alden said, "I think I'd be a fool to ignore career advice from you, Doctor Pulaski. I'll think about what you say."

"Mind you do," said Pulaski, and swept on her way.

"So," said Quark, sidling up the bar toward Ro, "have you found your burglar yet?"

"Prophets, Quark!" Ro gave him an astonished look. "How do you know about that?"

Quark was offended. "How long have we known each other?"

"Far too long."

"Well, there's your answer. Besides . . ." He snorted. "Blackmer's no Odo, is he?"

Ro was amused. "Missing your archenemy?"

"I don't like change," Quark complained. "Things should stay the same."

"You're getting old."

"We're all getting old, Laren. Even you. But enough about me—you're not having any luck with this burglary case, are you? Do you need me to put out some feelers?"

Ro drained her glass. What, she wondered, would Blackmer say if she told him that she'd asked Quark to help with one of his cases? He'd be furious. But the way out of that problem was obvious. She wouldn't mention it to Blackmer. "Quark, the day I come to you to help with security on this station is the day I pack up and go into retirement." She smiled. "The day I *formally* come to you to help with security, that is. What do you know?"

Quark leaned in. "About your burglar—nothing."

"Quark!"

"Wait, wait, wait! But about your missing Tzenkethi . . ."

Ro fell back in her seat. "How do you *find out* about this stuff?"

Quark tapped one earlobe. "I listen to the rhythms of the station. Nobody knows this place like me."

"It's a brand-new station!"

"The spirit remains," he said portentously. "This is the same tributary of the Great River that it ever was."

"Rubbish."

He bared his teeth at her. "Do you want to know what I know or don't you?"

"Get on with it."

"So you—or perhaps I should say Blackmer—have been trying to pin this burglary on the Tzenkethi, haven't you?"

"Blackmer would like to know how she got past him, and I share his concerns there."

"But you found she was off the hook because she'd left for Bajor before the break-in occurred."

"Quark, you are impossible—"

"Let me speak. What if I told you I'd seen her on the Plaza *after* that freighter left? The *Prophet's Tear*, wasn't it?"

"You saw her?" Ro glared at him. "Are you sure?"

Quark was palpably irked. "She is fairly distinctive. How many Tzenkethi do you see wandering around Deep Space 9?"

"Fair enough. Where did you see her? Where was she heading?"

"She was walking along large as life right there." He pointed outside the bar. "Everyone passes by Quark's at some point, even if they don't come inside, more's the pity . . . I've no idea where she was heading, but it certainly wasn't to Bajor on the *Prophet's Tear*." He picked up a cloth and started wiping ineffectually at the surface of the bar. "Anyway, that's all I know. But if you want to frame her for the break-in, she's available. Whether she's still on the station is another matter. And who she's working for now"—he showed all his teeth—"I wouldn't dare to guess. But I know what I'd do in her position."

Ro sighed. "Go on, what would you do?"

He gave her his most ravenous grin. "What else? I'd sell, sell, sell, of course." He stopped suddenly and looked over her shoulder. His expression was one of pure, joyful malice. "Well, look who's come to visit."

Ro turned. There, standing in the doorway, arms folded and face blank, was Odo.

"Quark . . ."

Quark's face was a picture. "The gang's all here," he said blissfully. "Or at least everyone who counts. Laren, think—what would a refugee Tzenkethi who's desperate to get home do with Federation secrets? Excuse me, I have ancient business to attend to."

Ro left them to their reunion. She went back to her office pondering Quark's words. An unhappy scenario was forming in her mind: that Corazame had somehow accessed the meta-genome data via Crusher's files and was now on her way back to Ab-Tzenketh with it. She wasted no time in opening a channel to Alden on the *Athene Donald*. He looked preoccupied, explaining that a first-contact scenario was under way and he was forming part of the team meeting the visitors. Ro quickly brought him up to date on the latest sighting of Corazame and asked bluntly whether he thought she might try to buy her way home.

Alden shook his head. *"No. Cory wouldn't do that."*

"You're very sure of that."

"She wouldn't betray me, but more than that she's

under no illusions as to what would happen to her if she returned. You have to understand that she was one of the lowliest grades on Ab-Tzenketh, practically a slave. They wouldn't reward her for bringing home information about the Federation. They'd take what they wanted, then punish her to the fullest measure. Declassify her—in their terminology, make her null."

"That doesn't sound good. What does it mean, exactly?"

"Public disgrace, for one thing—her genetic material would be permanently removed from the screening programs. But more than that, she'd be the lowest grade of server for the rest of her life—and that really is slavery, Captain, by any definition. Tzenkethi of that level have no future and no voice. I mean that literally. They're forbidden to speak to anyone outside their grade—they have to use a form of sign language in most everyday interactions. In Cory's case, they'd silence her for good and curtail her future severely. They'd cut her vocal cords and work her to an early grave. But they'd make sure she was visible so that people were in no doubt as to what happens to someone who offends the Autarch."

Memories of the atrocities of the Occupation came too readily to mind. "That's obscene!"

Alden sighed. "*I keep trying to make people understand the Tzenkethi, but nobody listens. I guess it takes a Bajoran to understand cruelty and exploitation and to value freedom and self-determination. I know how beautiful the Tzenkethi can look, but it's superficial.*

y knows what's in store if she goes back. She wouldn't Not alone."

Not alone, Ro thought—*but might she go with assistance? And if not Alden's, then who else might help?*

"How do you know that wasn't the plan from the outset?" Ro said. "How do you know she hasn't been playing the part of a refugee to gain your trust and sympathy, to get close to you—and your work—and then leave and go home?"

Alden frowned. *"What do you mean?"*

Patiently, Ro explained. "You only have Cory's word that she is who she says she is. Couldn't she have been undercover when you met her? Posing as a refugee? She could be a much higher grade than she's ever let on to you. This could simply be the point at which she was due to return home, with whatever she's learned from being with you."

Alden didn't reply. He put his hand up to his forehead and rubbed at the worry lines forming across his brow. Ro could see that this hadn't crossed his mind—but surely it should have? That was his job, wasn't it, to imagine scenarios like this? But he'd missed it.

"You've suggested many times," Ro said, "that she [illegible]s capabilities beyond her grading."

[illegible] that's because their grading system is immoral! It [illegible]ntial of hundreds of thousands of Tzenkethi! [illegible]y is a higher grade masquerading as

"But is there anything about this idea
couldn't be true?"

"I can't believe it of Cory . . ."

Or of himself, perhaps, that he'd been fooled, and by one of his enemies. Gently, Ro said, "Betrayal is part of your business. You must have lied to a few people for your own ends over the years."

"Not Cory. No."

No, thought Ro, it wasn't good to think that you'd been played so masterfully, particularly by people you thought of as . . . well, as your archenemies. "I'm sorry to put this to you when you've got plenty else on your mind," she said. "But I needed to ask."

"You're wrong, Captain. I know Cory."

"You didn't know her well enough to guess that she'd jump ship on DS9, though, did you?"

Ro watched doubt settle on Alden's face and decided she'd gone far enough. "It's good to get your perspective. I guess we won't know for sure till we find her. Blackmer's on the case. Good luck with the first contact. I'll get back to you. DS9 out."

She cut the comm and sat for a while pondering the conversation. *Who was she, this Corazame?* Ro had not even seen her while she was on the station and had only the accounts of others to go on. Why, she wondered now, had they been so careless about her being here? Why had they let a Tzenkethi, of all people, wander around the station unaccompanied? Blackmer hadn't trusted her at all. Ro sighed. The likeliest scenario was that Corazame was responsib or the break-in and the attempts to access the security and medical files, and had left for Ab-Tzenketh as soon as she could, concealing her departure from the station. Whether she was returning to throw herself on the mercy of her government, or whether this had been the plan all along, Ro couldn't say. But if she were Commander Peter Alden right now, she'd be reviewing every conversation she'd had with Corazame, every place they'd been to, and everything that Corazame had seen while in Federation space. And if she was in Alden's shoes, she'd be thinking up some pretty good explanations to offer her superiors.

There was another scenario, of course, and one that Ro didn't much like either: that Corazame was still on DS9, and that whatever personal cloaking device she was using to conceal herself was something they hadn't come up against before. That opened up a whole new series of security problems on a station already worried about security breaches. She reached for the comm to bring Blackmer up to date.

"Jeff, I've got some information on the Tzenkethi Corazame. We should talk about it."

"It'll have to wait. Can you get down to the Romulan consulate? Our Cardassian guests are causing a scene, and it's about to turn nasty."

"On my way," Ro said. "Cardassians," she muttered, pulling on her jacket and heading out the door. "You take your eye off them for one minute . . ."

* * *

The Romulan consulate was not generally a site of drama, its denizens preferring to leave the political posturing to superiors at the far end of a comm channel. Ro wasn't even sure that she'd spoken to the envoy, a rather low-ranking political officer who seemed mainly to fulfill the function of messenger service. Today, however, a substantial crowd was assembled outside the consulate and the noise levels were rising by the minute. A small group of Cardassians, Mhevita Pa'Dan among them, was standing outside the consulate chanting: *Where are our children? Send our children home.*

It was not a popular cause on Deep Space 9. A gaggle of Bajorans, none of whom could be old enough to remember the Occupation, had started up a response: *Cardies go home! Cardies go home!* Others were more violent in their disapproval: *I hope they're all dead! Hope the Romulans finish off the lot of you!* In the middle of all this, Blackmer and his team were forming a thin but sturdy barrier between the demonstrators and their critics.

Ro inched her way around to her security chief, clipping a mouthy Bajoran boy around the ear on her way past. "Jeff! What in the name of the Prophets is going on?"

"The Cardassians turned up about half an hour ago," Blackmer explained. "They made a few speeches—"

"Sounds about right for Cardassians."

"And nobody was paying much attention. Then Kala Morio and his cronies came out of Quark's, saw what was happening, and decided to voice their opinions."

"Ah," said Ro, grabbing the shoulder of the Bajoran boy and holding him still. He wriggled against her. Kala Morio was one of Quark's regulars, far too regular. Making his opinion known generally involved throwing a couple of wild punches and then falling over himself, before he was dragged to a holding cell to sleep it off. Today he was having considerably more impact than usual. But then nobody liked a Cardassian, missing children or no missing children.

The boy squirmed noisily in Ro's grasp. "Shut up, you little wretch," Ro said matter-of-factly, "or I'll wallop you all the way back to Ashalla." The boy subsided slightly, although he kept up a few grumbles. The jeering from the crowd, meanwhile, was getting louder, and the jibes were getting increasingly nasty: *Hope they tortured them. Hope you get them back in pieces.* From the corner of her eye, Ro saw one of the Cardassians, a young male, getting angrier. "Commander," she said, "I think we have a problem—"

Too late. The Cardassian male broke through the line made by the security team and pushed his way through to the gang of Bajorans throwing the worst of the insults. The crowd began to bay for blood. Fists were clenched. Arms were raised. "Here we go again," muttered Blackmer, ordering in his team as the brawl broke out in earnest.

It was hardly the worst scuffle in which Ro had

ever participated, although it did have an unpleasantly partisan feel to it. And when she saw the glitter of a knife heading her way, she wasn't surprised, although she was naturally alarmed. With one hand she shoved the Bajoran boy behind her; with the other she made to defend herself.

Someone was there already. A hand, at the end of an impossibly long arm, reached out and grabbed her attacker by the wrist, turning it until there was a howl of pain from its owner and the knife fell to the ground. Ro made the arrest and then glanced across the Plaza.

There was Odo, tucking himself back into his usual shape. He gave Ro one short, brisk nod, and she mouthed back, *Thanks*. Beside her, Blackmer muttered, "Where the *blazes* did he come from?"

After the dust had settled, and everyone who deserved it (and perhaps a few who didn't) was languishing gloomily in the holding cells, Ro and Blackmer convened in the security chief's office.

"I spoke to Quark earlier," Ro said. "He claims he saw Corazame on the station after the *Prophet's Tear* had left."

Blackmer, who had been leaning back in his chair, nursing a cup of tea and beginning to relax, was immediately back on alert. "Do we need to organize another search?"

"I think we should. At the very least, if she is still here, I want to know where and how she's hiding herself. If there's a problem with our systems, I want it fixed, and if she's using some technology we don't know about, I want us covered in future."

Blackmer grunted his agreement, and set about instructing his deputies to start another search.

"There's a great deal we don't know about Tzenkethi biology," Ro said. "Could she have some kind of biological capability to conceal herself?"

Blackmer was unconvinced. "I don't think the Tzenkethi have special powers. If she's still here, she's cloaking herself. Or somebody is cloaking her."

"But you've checked for cloaking devices based on what we know about Tzenkethi capabilities?"

"As best I can," Blackmer said. "There's a great deal we don't know about Tzenkethi technology either."

"She might well have magic powers for all we know."

"If that turns out to be the explanation," Blackmer said, "I'll settle your bar bill."

"If that turns out to be the explanation," said Ro, "I'll be drinking the bar dry. What's our next move?"

"Search," Blackmer said. "Search again. Ask O'Brien if he can come up with something to track her."

"Another fine plan," Ro muttered. "Well, there's nothing much more we can do until we get news of her. Meanwhile, what do you want to do with the people we're holding?"

"The usual. Keep them in overnight, release them

to the magistrate in the morning for a rap on the knuckles. Kala Morio wouldn't expect anything less." He frowned. "This will go on my list of reasons why we should limit the hours during which alcohol can be consumed publicly on the station."

"Send me a memo," said Ro, recognizing a hobby-horse when she saw one and keen to move on. "What about the Cardassians?"

Blackmer gave a grim smile. "I've already had the more sober of their number in here demanding to see their friends."

"Demanding?" Ro frowned. That seemed bold, given the circumstances.

"That's unfair," Blackmer conceded. "The nestor, Pa'Dan, asked politely. The others were demanding stridently."

"That's certainly the Cardassian style," Ro said. "Any reason not to let them go? Some of those taunts were pretty vicious."

Blackmer eyed her curiously. "Giving the benefit of the doubt to the Cardassians?"

"I'm trying to be fair," Ro said. "And you've got to have some sympathy for their plight."

"I'm not saying sympathy isn't appropriate," said Blackmer. "But I'm curious as to what's provoked it in this case."

Because lost children tugged at anyone's heart—if you still had a heart. "Then in the interests of being fair," Ro said, in irritation, "by all means let us keep the Cardassians overnight too."

"The wheels of justice do grind slow," agreed Blackmer.

"And in the meantime, I'll ask Odo to have a word with them to calm them all down."

Blackmer put down his tea and sighed.

"What?" Ro said.

"Nothing."

"Doesn't sound like nothing. Go on, fire ahead."

"Well . . . Odo."

"What about him?"

"He's proving indispensable around here," Blackmer said.

Ro smiled. "That's not jealousy I'm hearing, is it?"

"I'm jealous," said Blackmer, with dignity, "only of his ability to reach across the Plaza and knock a knife out of someone's hand. But since I'll never have that ability I may as well forget about it."

"Good philosophy," said Ro. "I'll never get to drink the bar dry either."

They came aboard the *Athene Donald* using their own means, having no interest in the offer of transporters. There were five of them, all dressed in black with silver markings that—one conjectured—signified rank and status. They were close enough to human that one would think you would be put at ease, but they were different in ways that daunted. They were very tall, and austere, and their eyes were somber and unblinking. Each one, it seemed, was tasked to perform some function: one observed the room into which they had transported; another appeared to be making notes upon the team that had been assembled to meet them—Tanj, Delka, Pulaski, Alden, Metiger: four species under the single banner of friendship and curiosity, a message they hoped would prove universal. Another perhaps took readings: atmosphere, gravity, life signs. When these brief tasks—performed with speed and efficiency—were complete, each turned to report briefly to one of their number, in low voices, and in a soft clicking and whistling language that could not be understood. Only when this was done did one of them speak. This one had remained still throughout, waiting for the others to report.

"My name is Tey Aoi of the Chain. I greet each species gathered here today. Let me assure you all—we come in peace."

Pulaski couldn't help herself. It popped out before either Delka or Tanj had the chance to say something more appropriate. "That's good," she said. "So do we." She thought about that. "Mostly."

Six

Captain's Log, Personal.

Formal study of any civilization usually begins with an overview of its forms of government, a description of its levels of technological development, a general statement of the primary definitive forms of social organization by which the main species arrange themselves, and so on and so on. Naturally such data is of great interest and can be of considerable assistance, particularly in situations where diplomatic relations are being opened and formalized.

But it is very rare that the first face a civilization presents is the definitive face, if indeed such a thing can exist. Whom do we generally meet first? The legislators, the governors, the elite. And their perception of their civilization will surely differ from that of the exile, the runaway, the dispossessed. A careful student of other worlds and cultures quickly learns to look beyond the formal face presented to discover what he or she can about the ordinary people—or, even more wisely, the marginal. One learns the true nature of a civilization from the way it treats its sick, weak, and poor. The extent to which elites wish to deflect you from such a goal can also be illuminating.

But what if such people cannot be found? Perhaps on. indeed encountering that rarity: a world without the dispo sessed, in which all members of a society are truly valued for their individual worth and are not merely vessels for the will of others or means by which the powerful attempt to achieve their ends. Or perhaps, as seems more likely, a harmonious surface conceals something more disquieting underneath . . .

When this mission had been at the planning stages, Maurita Tanj had, in her discussions with the board of the institute, pushed for the best ship available. It was a matter of Federation pride, she said. They should show the other powers the courtesy of the best—and of course it wouldn't do any harm to show them the extent of their capabilities. The board had liked these arguments, which appealed to both their utopian and pragmatic sides. Tanj's reward had been the *Athene Donald*: a brand-new *Olympic*-class vessel, with state-of-the art research facilities that would make any team of scientists drool with envy. The *Enterprise* had been a more impressive ship to serve on as CMO, Pulaski thought, but the *Athene Donald* was the ship upon which she would do her best work.

Tanj therefore took their guests from the Chain around her ship with a great deal of pride. The idea for this mission might have been Pulaski's, but it had taken Tanj to persuade the institute to give them the ship and to assemble this remarkable team from across the political divides. There were not many people in clout to have achieved this, ... pride was well earned, and Pulaski was delighted ... her friend's account that this early on, the mission was offering her the chance to show off.

But as the day wore on, Pulaski became more and more uneasy. The team from the Chain was not hostile or aggressive, but neither was it effusive. They followed Tanj wherever she took them—through extensive laboratories, past the brilliant statistical-modeling teams, in front of beautiful new equipment to study stars and space and the wonders of the universe—but Aoi and the rest seemed largely unmoved. In fact, Pulaski thought, they seemed weary, as if everything they saw was old news, stale and uninteresting. Even the transcendent luminosity of Metiger (who, Pulaski noticed, was putting on an amazing show) seemed not to move them.

Occasionally, a few clicks and whistles passed between them, as if something was found worthy of comment. Pulaski would have given a Nobel Prize to understand what these odd noises meant, but the ship's translators were being somehow bypassed by their visitors and their conversations remained tantalizingly impenetrable. Perhaps they were wondering when they would be offered a cup of tea and a sit-down. Perhaps they were wondering where the toilets were. As the day wore on, and the Chain seemed unmoved by whatever Tanj threw at them, Pulaski became steadily more and more

"Have you met people from our civilization before?" Pulaski said suddenly, cutting Tanj off partway through an explanation of the work being done in Lab 16. "I ask because you look like you've seen all this."

It was as if a bucket of cold water had been thrown over the proceedings. The whole charade was shown up to be exactly that—a charade. Despite all Tanj's effort, there was no meaningful contact happening here: only a series of protocols being enacted.

Aoi turned a pale impassive eye upon her, taking a moment to consider her. Pulaski got the impression the alien was recognizing her independent existence for the first time. Anyone would have bristled at such a realization and Katherine Pulaski more than most. She all but snarled back at him.

"We have not met your species," Aoi said. "You are new."

"But you've met people like us?"

One of Aoi's colleagues whistled something, but Aoi cut through with a sharp click. Turning back to Tanj, Aoi said, "We have met many people in our time."

Tanj said gently, "We would like to hear more about that, if you were willing."

"Perhaps we might arrange a later meeting. For now we shall continue with this tour. You still have much to show us, I believe."

"Certainly," Tanj said. "If you'd like."

Aoi nodded, not particularly enthusiastically, in Pulaski's opinion, and they carried on their way. Pulaski caught Delka's eye and saw at once that the Ferengi woman was sharing her own sense of . . . not unease . . . anticlimax. Perhaps it was vanity, but you'd like to think that an alien species meeting you for the first time would find something of interest to write home about. Alden, brushing past her, muttered under his breath, "Mostly harmless."

The tour continued. Pulaski found the situation increasingly excruciating, but Tanj's enthusiasm remained high throughout, or at least she was putting on a good show. When the last lab had been observed by their visitors' tired, bored eyes, the group convened in one of the ship's reception rooms. A very nice spread had been provided. Pulaski fell on the first bottle of wine to hand, although a sharp glance from Tanj reminded her there was a small protocol to follow first. Glasses were duly filled and handed around.

"It's customary in the Federation to mark special occasions with hospitality, and with a toast—" began Tanj.

"We have seen this ceremony elsewhere," said Aoi.

There was a pause before Tanj regrouped. "Well, then, if you're familiar with it, we can go straight ahead. Allow me to lift my glass and offer a toast to friendship between all our species." She turned to speak to her colleagues as much as to their visitors, and Metiger, at least, appeared touched by the statement and the gesture. Her skin rippled in response and she lifted her glass, smiling at Tanj, and following her example and taking a sip of the wine. From her expression, she seemed to find the taste pleasant, and she immediately sipped again. *Perhaps they might have her in the bar by the end of the mission*, Pulaski thought. She glanced at Aoi and the other visitors. They lifted their glasses in rather peremptory fashion and did not drink beyond the first, necessary sip.

Some rather awkward attempts at conversation ensued. After a few minutes, Pulaski hid herself behind the bottles. She found Delka there already. "Get me out of here," Pulaski whispered.

"If you know a way out," Delka whispered back, "I'll be glad to follow."

Eventually, after what seemed like the minimum amount of time they could politely remain, the visitors exchanged a few quick clicks, and they all put down their glasses. "Thank you for the meeting here today," Aoi said. "We will return and then discuss in detail the nature of your mission and research."

Pulaski stepped forward. "You mean here on our ship?"

Aoi nodded.

Alden said, "When can we come to your ship?"

A few clicks and whistles.

"In due course." Aoi's head bent briefly, and then the Chain's transporters picked up the team, transferring them back to their ship without fuss. The room seemed suddenly very empty.

"For the love of God, somebody hand me a bottle," said Pulaski into the silence. She poured out wine liberally for them all, Metiger included. "Get that down you," Pulaski advised. "It'll make everything seem better. Maurita, that was *awful*."

"You think?" Tanj received her glass gratefully and sank into the nearest chair.

"In many ways," said Delka, "it was a textbook first encounter. Although I don't know the textbook we were working from." She sighed. "It's not as if anything went *wrong*. And we do have these further meetings."

"All to take place here, I note," said Alden.

"I noticed that too," said Pulaski.

"And I'm dying to get a look around their ship," Alden said.

"Me too," said Pulaski.

Alden eyed her. "We'll make a spy of you yet."

"Over my dead body," said Pulaski firmly. "But the fact is we seem to have allowed them direct access to our ship without any reciprocal arrangement." She frowned. "I don't much like that."

"Nor do I," said Alden.

There was a slight cough. The two humans, the Ferengi, and the Trill all turned to look at the Tzenkethi. "Might I suggest," Metiger said, "that we open ourselves to these people fully and without hesitation?" She turned to Tanj. "We must build trust.

If allowing them to see more of the *Athene Donald* is the way to do this, then let us embrace it. I, at least"—and she turned her amber eyes slowly toward Alden—"have nothing to hide."

Tanj smiled warmly at Metiger. "You're quite right. None of us has anything to hide. We can approach these meetings with complete openness and a desire to share knowledge and earn friendship. That's what this ship is all about. Thank you for reminding us of the purpose of our mission."

The Tzenkethi woman pressed her hand against her chest in a gesture of respect.

"Kitty," said Tanj, "you're looking thoughtful. I don't like it when you look thoughtful. What's the matter?"

"Oh, it's nothing. But I don't like feeling tolerated. Humored, even."

"They didn't strike me as having much of a sense of humor," said Alden.

"We might be missing the joke," said Delka.

"It's not quite that," Pulaski said. "You know, I hate to say this, but I think we bored them."

There was a pause as they all considered how that might be the case. "Not possible with you on board, surely, Katherine?" said Alden.

Pulaski raised an eyebrow. "Don't get too familiar, Commander."

"That, incredibly, was my attempt to be gallant."

"Stick to spying, it's what you're good at." But Pulaski was pleased that Alden had relaxed enough to banter with her, and pleased to see the comparative ease with which he was now speaking to Metiger. Tanj knew what she was about, putting them together. Perhaps he might yet shake off his unease around the Tzenkethi. As long as it wasn't replaced by mistrust for the Chain.

Mhevita Pa'Dan sat uncomfortably in the chair in Ro's office, ramrod straight and plainly very embarrassed. "I certainly did not anticipate that there would be such disruption, Captain," she said. "You've been nothing but helpful since our arrival and this is a poor reward for the aid you've given us." She glanced over at Odo. "You too, my friend. I don't want to cause trouble for either of you."

"It wasn't a great turn of events, no." Ro sighed. "I understand your frustration, Nestor Pa'Dan. We've reached a roadblock with the Romulan repatriation committee, and the castellan's office is trying to find out why they're no longer willing to speak to us. If you can have a little more patience . . . "

Pa'Dan started in her chair. Odo, seeing the movement, intervened quickly. "I know that ten years is far too long to be patient, Mhevita," he said gently. "But things are moving forward now. Give us a little time. The castellan will help us, I'm sure. But these behind-the-scenes negotiations can be delicate, and the Romulans took umbrage at the fact that the castellan has become involved, even tangentially—"

"But that sounds like we've taken a step backward!" Pa'Dan said wildly. "Is Varis even speaking to you?"

Ro resisted glancing at Odo. "Varis is proving difficult to get hold of right now." Lifting her hand in an attempt to forestall any more anxiety on Pa'Dan's part, and speaking more confidently than she felt, she said, "Varis was put on the spot, that's all. You've got your diplomatic corps working on this now, and don't forget that there's our tacit support—the support of Starfleet and the Federation—behind what your own diplomats are doing."

"The castellan *will* help," Odo said. "I promise."

"Very well," said Pa'Dan. "I'll be patient. Again. And in the meantime"—she glanced at Ro—"I promise that there will be no repeat of what happened yesterday."

"I appreciate that," said Ro.

Pa'Dan left worried but mollified. "You're quite sure the castellan will help?" asked Ro after she had gone.

"I'll skin him alive if he doesn't," Odo growled.

"That'll look good on the wall of my office," said Ro. But she was comforted that it was, at least, unlikely that there would be more trouble on the Plaza. Diplomacy often moved too slowly for her taste, but she had to admit that, very often, it did get results. She felt she had done all she could for Pa'Dan, beyond what might have been expected.

She certainly did not expect the conversation she had later that day with a Representative Brooking from the Federation Council. He came on-screen crossly red faced and infinitely self-important. Ro took an immediate dislike to him.

"*Captain Ro,*" he said, "*I'm not going to waste time.*"

"Oh, good," she muttered.

"*Is it true that you've had private conversations with Castellan Garak? That you've asked him to put pressure on the Romulans on behalf of one of his own citizens?*"

Since the councilor had not seen fit to introduce himself fully (presumably on the grounds that he was so important that Ro would know who he was), the captain surreptitiously looked him up. Head of a committee tasked to improve relations with the Romulans. She sighed and braced herself for the inevitable drubbing. "I guess you could say that I have—"

"*I've got a message here from a Major Varis saying that's exactly what you've been up to. Captain, this is a delicate time between us and the Romulans—*"

"It's always a delicate time between us and the Romulans," Ro muttered.

"*What?*"

"Nothing, sir. What were you saying?"

"*Look, Captain Ro, we're closer to détente than ever before, and the last thing I need is Starfleet clodhopping around our negotiations.*"

It would be nice, Ro thought, if middle-ranking officers such as herself and Varis could rely on some kind of transimperial solidarity not to carry tales back to the other's superiors, but apparently this aspect of Federation-Romulan relations needed some work too. And since there was no point in saying that she had been specifically instructed by Command to support Odo and Pa'Dan, she let the councilor get on with telling her off.

"You need to apologize to Varis."

"Apologize?"

"You heard me. I don't care if you don't think she deserves it. Varis needs to save face. So get busy face-saving. Get it done within the hour and let me know when it's done. Brooking out."

That was an easy request to make, Ro thought (although it could have been made considerably more politely), but how she was supposed to say sorry to a Romulan major who was steadfastly ignoring her attempts to communicate, Ro wasn't sure. Still, she dutifully sent a subdued message that formally apologized for the offense, regretted that they had got off on the wrong foot, and hoped that Varis would be prepared to speak—and perhaps even come to Deep Space 9 to meet Pa'Dan and the rest. Ro would be delighted to offer her services as arbiter. The message was of course met with stony silence, although Brooking, when Ro reported back, seemed satisfied that she had done what was necessary. Perhaps the Cardassian diplomatic corps could now get on with its business and leave Ro out of this bewildering and strangely escalating situation.

Alas, it was not to be. Mhevita Pa'Dan, requesting another meeting, turned up in a state of barely suppressed and nervous excitement. Ro was immediately on alert. Something new was animating Pa'Dan; something must have happened in the hours since they had last met.

"I'm sorry to say that I wasn't satisfied at the end of our last meeting," Pa'Dan said. "I've been contacted by several senior politicians back on Prime. They listened to me with great sympathy and promised to get behind our cause."

Ro sighed and leaned back in her chair. "Let me guess. Are these politicians by any chance opponents of the castellan?"

Pa'Dan frowned. "I suppose they are—"

"They're using you," Ro said bluntly. "They want to get to the castellan. He's got a high-profile speech coming up and they want to embarrass him."

"They're willing to speak out on our behalf when the castellan isn't," Pa'Dan said fiercely.

"The castellan," Ro said, not quite believing that she was defending a former member of the Obsidian Order (another unexpected bend in the Great River), "is doing a great deal, and you know it. I know it's the Cardassian way, but making noise won't solve this matter. Quiet diplomacy will."

"The Cardassian *way*?" Pa'Dan looked at her in astonishment. "I won't pretend to know what you must have suffered during the Occupation, but I thought that I had done enough to make it clear that I was hardly a supporter of that deplorable policy—"

"That didn't come out right," Ro said quickly.

"What I meant was that making a fuss will only entrench the Romulans further. They already don't want to talk because it looks like they're backing down—"

"'Making a fuss'?" said Pa'Dan icily, and Ro wished momentarily for her own personal diplomat to stop her from shoving her foot in her mouth. "Unfortunately, 'making a fuss' is the only way that I can get people to listen. It's more than ten years since I've seen my son, and four years since I've even heard from him. I'm sick and tired of people not listening when I say this to them and brushing aside my grief and heartbreak as an inconvenience. I'm sorry to tell you"—Pa'Dan sounded breathless now as well as angry; she was well outside her comfort zone—"that there will be further demonstrations on DS9 until our cause is both heard and acted on."

There were other voices behind this, Ro knew. Calmly, she said, "I can't stop you, but you have to understand that if there's any criminal activity on the station, we will be obliged to make arrests. I can't make any exceptions to this, no matter how sympathetic I am to the cause. Please," she said urgently, "think again."

Pa'Dan hesitated—the idea of arrest clearly didn't sit well with her. "I shall be glad if arrests happen." Her hands were trembling. "It will only bring us more publicity."

Yes, indeed, Ro thought as the nestor departed; publicity of exactly the wrong kind—embarrassing the castellan and the Romulans alike. She opened up a channel to the castellan's office. The last thing *he* needed was to be blindsided by this.

Beverly Crusher's word was utterly dependable, and so she had, as promised, been faithfully reading all the reports Pulaski had been sending her about the *Athene Donald*'s mission. Pulaski's trials with Alden amused Crusher (and how typical of Pulaski to be frank about this in a log where others might have chosen to be discreet or equivocal). Did Pulaski always need a battle to fight? Poor Jean-Luc, the windmill at which Pulaski had tilted the whole time she was on the *Enterprise*. It must have been a sore trial. Crusher—who, like many reliable and decent people, was not instinctively jealous—found herself imagining, as she frequently did now that Pulaski had put the idea in her head, what the Picard-Pulaski marriage would have been like. Oh, to be a fly on the wall of those living quarters . . .

The hints at a thaw in the relationship with Alden intrigued Crusher, but the situation allowing this rapprochement interested her more. Pulaski's account of the meeting with the new species was fascinating, taking Crusher back to the time on the *Enterprise* when exploration and first contact had been their primary concerns, before war after war had pulled them away. Consequently, she read the reports avidly, poring over the descriptions of the huge black ship, the grave visitors, and the sense of being in the presence of something powerful but remote. She smiled at

Pulaski's irritation at the tepid interest shown by the Chain throughout the meeting, and was touched by the other woman's annoyance on behalf of her friend Tanj. Pulaski was not exactly a great prose stylist, having learned to write in order to communicate scientific findings as efficiently as possible, but there was nevertheless something in her description of the Chain that made Crusher uncomfortable. "Something nasty in the woodshed," she muttered, reading the report of the chilly first meeting with the personnel (that seemed the right word, impersonal and technical) from the Chain ship. In fact, she was so absorbed and persuaded by Pulaski's description that she overlooked the clues for some time. Only on a second reading, and trying to pronounce the name of the captain of the Chain ship, did Crusher see what she had been missing.

"Yes, that's right," said Oioli. "We are the same. We shared a common sunrise."

"But you're so different!" On some level, Crusher had been expecting a denial ("*Chain? Who's that? Never heard of them*"), but everything was there for someone who looked carefully: the height and the tapering fingers, the markings on the skin, the oddly formed names that rolled around the mouth like marbles, the unblinking eyes that seemed to fix you in place and demand something more of you. Even some of the descriptions of the Chain's hardware, as much as Pulaski had been allowed to see, were familiar—black and silver and functional. The leaders of the People of the Open Sky were the same species as the crew of the Chain.

"We're less alike than similar now," said Ioile. "We've taken different pathways."

"But you came here deliberately. Are you on an exploration mission?" Crusher said. "Is that why you're here?"

Ioile laughed. "Missions, captains, uniforms—does that sound like the People?"

Crusher looked around at the chaos of their quarters. It was as if someone had started unpacking, then changed their mind partway through and decided it was easier simply to rummage through the cases and pull things out as and when they were needed. "No, I guess not. I'm simply trying to understand what brought you here . . ."

"Yours were the next lights that we saw," said Oioli softly. "Need there be more reason?"

"What you see is what you get," said Ioile with another laugh. "We do not hide our purpose!"

"You look like adventurers, I suppose," said Crusher. "Travelers."

"Travelers? Or wanderers." Oioli paused for a moment's thought and then nodded. "Those words, I think, come closest. The People of the Open Sky exist to see what's out there."

"So you're not on a formal exploration mission," Crusher said. "You're traveling, wandering. That sounds like exploration to me, but we'll call it whatever you prefer." She sighed. "You have to understand that I'm a doctor. My choices are always guided by what will help someone who is sick or injured. Going from Pulaski's descriptions of the technology the Chain has, there's some pretty impressive hardware at their disposal. May I ask why you haven't been home? You could easily have cured some of the ailments your children had simply by popping home . . ." Crusher trailed off as she saw the look that Oioli and Ioile were exchanging. "If you're exiles," she said quietly, "it's possible that we can help. The Prime Directive limits our ability to involve ourselves in the affairs of others, but no captain would ignore a direct appeal for sanctuary, and I think you'd find that with her history, Captain Ro would be particularly receptive in that respect."

Oioli gave her a sunlit smile. "We are not running, Beverly. We sail because we want to. Not all journeys seek an end. Some are their own purpose."

Crusher nodded. "We understand that in Starfleet. We're explorers too, at heart." She sighed. "Although we seem not to have done any exploring for a long time."

"I see," said Oioli gently. "I understand. That's often what can happen. People set out to explore and find that years have passed them. Standing still, they reach a point and cannot push on farther. The love of traveling dims and fades. They never travel onward."

"Is that what happened with the Chain?" pressed Crusher. There was obviously some reason why the People would not return, and it had to be good enough for them that the health of these much-loved children had become secondary.

"If people cannot move ahead, their homes will end up stagnant," Ioile said.

"But *you* continued to travel?"

"What else would we do?" Oioli gestured outward. "We have no other purpose. But more than that: the traveling brings joy to us, and meaning. The People of the Open Sky could never choose stagnation."

Perhaps not, thought Crusher, but for the first time in her interactions with them she felt something was being concealed. There must have been a reason that Oioli, Ioile, and Ailoi had left home. Could it simply be that they didn't like it there? Was that enough to keep people wandering, year after year, even when the health of their children was at risk? To be fair, there had been nothing life-threatening, and they had jumped at DS9's medical facilities the moment they were offered, but there was still that barrier to returning that Crusher didn't understand. And surely there would be a pull back home, eventually? A pull to whatever family was there?

"Who else," Crusher muttered as she reread the last missive from René, smiling and waving at her from the view screen, "are you going to show the holiday pictures to?" Who was she to question people who had made their lives a permanent journey? She'd moved around as a child after her parents died and had chosen travel as a way of life when she signed up for Starfleet. And her husband and son—her family—were light-years away from where she was now.

"You think they're the same people?" Pulaski was intrigued.

"Only some of them," Crusher replied. *"There are numerous species on board the People's ships. They take on new members from the worlds they visit. But the core three adults are definitely the same species as the ones you've encountered."*

"Fascinating," said Pulaski. "And yet they're clearly culturally a million kilometers apart." She laughed. "Well, I suppose that's true for any world. Just because you're from the same species doesn't mean you're culturally monolithic. Not everyone on Earth is a white male Westerner, no matter how it seems sometimes."

"There's something else too. Some tension between them. I couldn't get Oioli or Ioile to be specific—they have this vague singsong way of talking that makes them difficult to pin down sometimes. But it has to be a good reason. They love those children too much to make them suffer unnecessarily."

"Are they on the run?" Pulaski said.

"They pretty much said no when I suggested that. They said the journey was their way of life and they had no need to return."

Pulaski grunted. "Sound like a bunch of goddamn hippies."

"Of course, they might lie if they didn't feel safe

enough, particularly once I said that we were in touch with others from their species. I'd like to think we'd done enough to show that we were trustworthy."

"They could simply have different value systems. Perhaps we have walked into a dispute between the hippies and the authorities."

"Oioli did say something about 'stagnation.' That the Chain was stagnant in some way. Does that sound right?"

"They're certainly sticklers for protocol and not much fun," Pulaski said. "From what I saw of the People while I was on DS9, I don't think their laid-back approach would sit well with Aoi and the rest."

Crusher laughed. "*That's certainly true! All those kids! I take it you haven't seen any children on the Chain ship?*"

"We haven't been on board yet, but I imagine it's a blissfully child-free zone. Send across your notes on the People. I'll see if anything strikes me as relevant."

"And then?"

Pulaski shrugged. "If I've got any questions—well, how about I ask them?"

Pulaski spent a happy few hours reading through Crusher's reports on the People: the medical data, the notes and conjectures about their social structure. She admired Crusher's clear style, the care with which she made her observations, and the restraint she showed making assumptions based on them. One or two of the species traveling with them seemed vaguely familiar to her, so she went hunting back through her own files to see whether there was anything there. She wasn't pleased with what she discovered.

"I'm sorry to summon you both in this rather dramatic way," Pulaski said to Tanj and Delka, "but somebody has been rifling through my files."

It was very late at night. Both women had nonetheless come straight to Pulaski's quarters when she'd called and asked them to come on "a matter of some delicacy."

"Your files?" Tanj frowned. "Which ones?"

"Files related to my current research. Someone has been trying to get into them."

There was a silence as both of her guests tried to consider the likeliest candidates.

"I suppose," Delka said slowly, "that the Chain might not be as friendly as they seem—"

"They don't seem particularly friendly at all," Tanj said. "As much as it pains me to say it, we're not really getting much in return, are we?"

"But that's exactly my point," said Pulaski. "We've welcomed them with open arms. We've not hidden anything, and we've promised them free access to pretty much the whole kit and caboodle. So why bother hacking into my files? If they asked me what I was doing, I'd tell them. At length. In detail. If they weren't bored before, they would be after."

"But they haven't shown any reciprocal openness," Delka pointed out. "What we've seen points to a culture of secrecy. Even with the People of the

Open Sky—I gather from Crusher's logs that they have avoided answering specific questions about their reasons for traveling. Not all cultures are as open as the Federation or the Ferengi Alliance."

"And not even the Federation is as open as it once was," said Tanj. "I know that Alden is worried about the access we've given the Chain to the *Athene Donald*. Metiger too."

"Alden," muttered Pulaski darkly. "Now there's a name to conjure with."

Tanj looked at her in surprise. "Are you saying what I think you're saying?"

"That he's my chief suspect? You bet."

"Oh, for pity's sake, Kitty!" Tanj fell impatiently back in her chair. "I thought the two of you were coming to an accommodation."

"He might well be a frustrated xenolinguist dying to fly free," Pulaski said roughly, "but first and foremost he's Starfleet Intelligence—"

"If you think it's unlikely that the Chain would break into your files, how much more unlikely is it that Starfleet Intelligence would?"

"*I* don't know what goes on in the heads of those people!" Pulaski cried. "I don't think they know themselves half the time!"

Delka gave a polite cough. "I do rather feel that I'm intruding on family business. If this is now a discussion about your security services, perhaps I should go?"

"No," said Tanj firmly. "Kitty is being ridiculous."

"You say ridiculous," Pulaski said, "but I bet if we asked Alden who's been at my files, he'd say Metiger. I bet he'd think she was using the convenient presence of the Chain as cover for her own nefarious activities. Here's my guess," Pulaski said, jabbing the air with her finger. "Alden's Tzenkethi came on board exactly as planned on DS9. She's somehow been able to conceal herself. She's been observing us—more specifically, Metiger—the whole time."

"And having gone to these extreme lengths to conceal herself—and I'd like you to tell me how—she's now decided to reveal her presence by having a poke around your medical files?" Tanj shook her head. "There's a simpler explanation, as Delka said. Someone from the Chain is responsible. Perhaps it's even been authorized."

"But this brings me back to my original question: what do they want with my files? They're obviously more advanced than we are. Why bother?"

"Perhaps they aren't advanced as they seem," said Delka. "Or as advanced as they would like us to believe. And while we've seen a lot of hardware, we know nothing about their medical science."

Pulaski hesitated.

"Go on, Kitty."

"Crusher's reports did say that the People had various health problems . . ."

"There are you," said Tanj.

"But I'd assumed that was because they were wandering about, rather than because their civilization isn't advanced," Pulaski said. "It's unlikely they'd have ships like that and be unable to cure conjunctivitis, isn't it? Besides, if it's a question of needing medical assistance, why not simply *ask* for our help?"

"Perhaps," said Delka dryly, "they are a proud people."

Pulaski snorted.

"Who knows," Tanj said. "It's possible there's simply been a misunderstanding—"

"I think I can tell when someone has accessed a secure file!" Pulaski said hotly.

Delka raised a diplomatic finger. "I think that what Maurita meant was that they don't understand the concept of classified information. That they wouldn't have understood that they were doing something offensive, or that could be construed as hostile."

"Thank you, Delka, that's exactly what I meant."

"They don't look like the kind of people who don't understand the concept of classified information," Pulaski said. "Uniforms like that go hand in hand with classified information. A place for everything and everything in its place."

"Here's a thought, Kitty. Maybe they're insomniacs desperate for a good night's sleep and your files seemed the best choice."

"Remind me why I like you?"

"If I can make a suggestion," said Delka "The next time we meet, you should give a presentation on your work. That might send the message that they can ask rather than go looking."

Tanj snapped her fingers. "I like that. Good idea. Kitty? Are you willing?"

Pulaski sat in her chair and sulked.

"Kitty?"

"What? Oh, very well!"

"I knew she wouldn't pass up a chance to talk about her research," Delka said to Tanj, with a smile.

"Shut up, the pair of you," said Pulaski. "And don't be fooled. I'm still keeping my eye on Alden."

"I sincerely hope so," Tanj said briskly. "No doubt he'll be keeping his eye on Metiger. And I'll be keeping my eye on everyone and everything—you included."

Pulaski's shtick when talking about her current research was always to start by claiming she was chasing the secret of eternal life. It usually got a laugh from people and it always got their attention. Sometimes folks would say that if anyone was going to work out how to live forever, it would be Katherine Pulaski. Once she'd warmed her audience up with this opener, she could get down to the science. Sometimes they followed it, often they didn't. But they were always interested.

Except this time. The team from the Chain (she assumed they were the same five, although apart from Aoi, who had a different badge, she struggled to tell these uniform gray-faced, wide-eyed entities apart) sat through the whole hour without even blinking. Literally, not blinking. Just . . . looking. Straight at her. Without as much as a blink. It creeped Pulaski out. At least Metiger was interested. The Tzenkethi had been taking careful and substantial notes from the minute Pulaski opened her mouth.

"Well," said Pulaski, winding up the presentation and deactivating the holographic display, "that, really, is as far as I have gotten." *Which is a damned long way,* she thought bitterly. She looked around the room. "Any questions?"

The team from the Chain continued looking at her politely. One of them blinked, slowly.

"What, nothing?" There was usually some interest in what she had to say. Often there were plaudits. "Zilch, zero, nada?"

"Your work confirms all that we knew already," said Aoi, after a moment.

"Okay, then," said Pulaski. "So that'll be no questions." She leaned one hip against the table and folded her arms. "But that's fine. Less about me and more about you. I've got plenty of questions of my own."

The visitors gave no response.

"So I'll get on and ask them, shall I? We're curious about you, you know. We want to learn."

"All information comes through proper channels," Aoi said.

"Yeah, yeah, I get that. Starfleet's the same. But not everyone's so hung up on the rules, are they? Your friends on DS9, for example—they're a lot more laid-back. That's what a first contact should be. Kicking back and having a cup of tea. Not all this formal nonsense—"

Aoi suddenly leaned forward. "Our 'friends on DS9'? What do you mean?"

"Well, DS9 is a Starfleet space station," Pulaski began, halting when Aoi raised his hand. "Okay, you know that already. There are people from your species there right now. They call themselves the People of the Open Sky—"

After being used to their visitors' lack of interest in everything they had had to say, Pulaski wasn't prepared for the swiftness of Aoi's response. The visitor stood up quickly, unfurling as if a whip had been cracked. "All crew on board at once and then initiate protocol nine-three-sixty. High alert. These are your orders."

"And we will obey," his crew chorused as one. Pulaski had never heard anything so creepy in her life.

"Well," said Blackmer, bringing to a sudden halt his midmorning briefing with Ro. "Look who's turned up."

"Who?" Ro leaned toward the tricorder he was waving under her nose.

"Our missing Tzenkethi. And look where she is. It seems she's been staying with the People of the Open Sky." Blackmer leaned back in his chair. "Can I please arrest somebody now?"

Seven

Captain's Log, Personal.

I should offer some thoughts on the Prime Directive, although I believe that a complete discussion could easily sustain a full-length work in itself. This, the guiding principle behind all exploration conducted under the banner of Starfleet, is of course intended to prevent the hideous forms of exploitation that can come when an advanced civilization makes contact with one that is less so. Even the most cursory reading of Earth history will show the extent to which we should be on guard against these circumstances. Beware of involvement and intervention, the Prime Directive insists, because our history instructs us that that way lies tragedy. In no way do I mean to understate this, and I do not advocate casual meddling in the affairs of others. But I increasingly come to believe that in certain circumstances lofty disinterest can be, in its own way, a form of self-aggrandizement, implying, as it does, that we are in some way superior to the civilizations we meet and must remain aloof. How can one walk away from suffering?

Surely, then, there must be a third way?

I recall an excellent speculative novel in which the explor-

ers from Earth, on discovering a new and technologically less advanced civilization, agonize as to what degree of involvement would be appropriate. They solve this thorny problem by asking the people concerned what they *think would be appropriate; in other words, the humans demonstrate that they have truly learned the lessons of the past by no longer assuming that they have the answers as far as others are concerned . . .*

Sitting in Blackmer's office, looking at the monitor that showed the holding cells, Ro studied Corazame carefully. The Tzenkethi was sitting quietly on her bunk, her hands folded, her head down. Her skin was dulled to a dim brown. She seemed almost absent, faded away, enduring her state until someone came and changed it for her. Such patient resignation made Ro uneasy: she liked movement and purpose, people who made active efforts to change their situation. How could a child of the Occupation be any different? But Corazame, it seemed, was something else entirely: the kind of person who waited for things to be done to her. She pondered again what Alden had told her about Corazame's past: that she had been practically some kind of slave on Ab-Tzenketh, born and bred to wait on others. Was that someone who could act as a double agent? Or was this all performance? It was a good show if it was.

Blackmer entered the room, a frown upon his face. "That was a waste of an hour."

Ro shifted in her chair. "What does she have to say for herself?"

Blackmer flopped into his chair with a sigh. "That's exactly the problem—she's not saying much. She says that she didn't want to travel on the *Athene Donald*, but she won't say why. When I asked her about her association with the People, she says that she met them when she took one of their children back to them." Blackmer frowned. "Those damn children!"

"It's not their fault, Jeff. So what does she say happened next between her and the People?"

"She says that they got into a conversation, she explained that she was of two minds about going on the *Athene Donald*, and they offered her some peace and privacy to do some thinking."

"And the break-ins?" Ro said. "Crusher's files?"

Blackmer shrugged. "She denies all knowledge. She looked shocked when I said she might be responsible—actually the first reaction from her about anything."

"Or certainly the first reaction she wanted you to notice."

"I don't know." Blackmer glared at the monitor. "She's so damn—"

"Passive?" Ro nodded. "I know what you mean. So how have the People been hiding her all this time?"

"Pretty much what we'd guessed. They have some cloaking technology that we didn't know about. I'd like to know what else they have tucked away. I knew we couldn't trust them—"

"To be fair," said Ro, "they're within their rights

to use whatever they have in their possession. And it's not the kind of capability they have to declare. Not a weapon."

"No, but—"

"I don't think there's any 'but' about it, Jeff. What exactly have they done wrong? Any of them? That we can prove?"

"Give me a moment and I'll think of something," Blackmer said.

Ro held out her hands. "Be my guest."

"How about this? Corazame gave false information about her departure from the station. That bears investigation, particularly if the People helped her in any way."

"That's a minor felony, even if she did anything wrong." Ro said. "Perhaps she checked in, and then changed her mind before boarding. And, anyway, it's not evidence to link her to the break-in. Do we have any evidence there, or is everything circumstantial?"

Blackmer shook his head. "There's nothing I can find. Someone got into the room and then left as quietly as he or she arrived. O'Brien and his people still can't find any trace that a transporter was used."

"So we're no farther than we were." Ro sighed, and once again studied the Tzenkethi sitting quietly in the holding cell. Corazame's eyes were now closed. She appeared almost to have powered down. "Have you spoken to any of the People yet?"

"No, but Oioli's here if you wanted a word."

Ro nodded and pushed herself up from her chair.

"Yes, I'll come in on this one. We had a good rapport—or, at least, I thought we had a good rapport. I'd like to hear what Oioli has to say."

They made their way down the corridor to the interview room. "I got a message from Alden," Ro said. "He's eager to speak to Corazame as soon as he can."

"He'll have a long wait," said Blackmer. "She said she didn't want to speak to him."

Ro was surprised by that. What could it mean? If Corazame was working for Alden, then surely she would want instructions now that her cover was in danger of being blown? Ro frowned. Corazame's refusal to speak to him lent weight to her suspicions that she was a double agent: Alden would be the last person she wanted to speak to in that case. Or perhaps she was still working for him, and this was all a feint, to make it seem that they were estranged . . . Ro shook her head. Spy games hurt her brain.

"You know," said Blackmer slowly, "even if the People believed they were simply giving Corazame time to reflect on her next move, that doesn't mean she told them the truth."

"What do you mean?"

"She could have been buying time before her pickup from Ab-Tzenketh." Blackmer sighed. "I hate this spy stuff. Life's complicated enough as it is."

"Tell me about it," Ro muttered.

Oioli stood up when they entered the interview room. Their visitor was plainly upset. Not angry—

that wasn't Oioli's style, Ro imagined—but certainly not happy. Ailoi was there too, also looking displeased. The marks on their skin had gone very bright, almost lime green.

"Well now, Captain Ro!" Oioli said, gesturing around the room, clearly understanding the nature of the place. "This is a disappointment! The People came with open hearts—we thought this was a haven!"

Ro gestured to them both to sit down. "I'm sure there's a simple explanation, and we won't keep you long. This isn't an arrest. I'm grateful for your time and your willingness to speak to us. But the simple fact is that we need to know about your dealings with Corazame. Perhaps you didn't realize there was a stationwide search going on for her?"

"She came to us and sat with us," Oioli said. "She brought one of our children. We listened to her story then. We had no call to doubt her. She asked about our way of life and we were glad to tell her."

"And then she asked you to hide her?" Blackmer said. "Didn't that seem at all suspicious to you?"

"She struggles in her daily life to pass around unnoticed," Ailoi said. "She said she needed time and space, away from eyes that watched her. We had the means to give her all the peace and quiet she needed."

Blackmer, Ro saw, wasn't in the least convinced, and Oioli didn't miss this reaction either. "This is the simple truth of it," Oioli said. "She came, she asked, we helped her."

Ro, after a moment's thought, said simply, "I

believe you." She ignored Blackmer's growl of dismay. She wasn't quite finished with Oioli and Ailoi yet, but she'd ask her remaining questions in her own time.

Or, rather, she would make them ask. Standing up, she said, "Thanks for your time. I'm sorry if we've seemed suspicious. We had a bad breach of security on DS9 recently and now we're hypersensitive." She gestured to the door. "You're free to go."

Oioli hesitated. "And all of our technology? Must this block continue?"

Ro smiled to herself. Her suspicion was correct: Oioli was assuming that Starfleet was responsible for whatever the Chain had done to the People's capabilities. This meant she still had her trump card to play. "I'm afraid there's nothing I can do about that," she said. "That's not us."

She caught Oioli's questioning look and spoke deliberately casually. "One of our science and exploration vessels has made contact with some more of your people. They were very excited to learn you were here and sprang into action straightaway. They're the ones blocking your technologies. Impressive, isn't it?" She looked straight into Oioli's wide and fearful eyes. "You know, I have to wonder what it is about you that's making them so hostile."

Maurita Tanj was able to shed some light on this. *"In effect, Aoi is accusing the People of kidnapping children."*

"Kidnapping children?" Ro glanced over at Crusher, who shook her head and mouthed, I don't *believe that!*

"Aoi says that not all of the children traveling with the People are their own."

"We knew that," said Crusher. "Most of the children aren't even the same species as Oioli and the rest."

"I think Aoi means the children that are from the same species."

Ro and Crusher exchanged a glance. "Are there any?" said Ro.

"I've no idea," said Crusher. "Their family structure is necessarily very loose."

"Aoi also says that the People are irresponsible and not fit to be in charge of children. I understand that the children traveling with them are allowed to run wild, almost feral—"

"Rubbish," said Crusher promptly. "They're lively, yes, but it's only high spirits. Playfulness, that's all. That's because they're children. That's what children do—play. If Aoi thinks that children shouldn't be running around, then that's Aoi's problem."

Tanj gave a small, tight smile. *"I'm only the messenger, Doctor Crusher. This is what Aoi is saying."*

"My apologies," Crusher said. "But I'm having a hard time squaring what this Aoi is saying with what I've seen of the People."

"Does Aoi have anything else to say?" asked Ro.

"I'm afraid so. The claim is that the People's way of life puts the children's health at risk. Apparently they live

according to some back-to-nature principle that means they refuse to use certain technologies?"

"That's simply not true," Crusher said at once. "They *fell* upon the treatments that I offered." She glanced over at her CO. "Laren, I really don't think that any of those children are at risk—"

"But you said yourself that they've continued traveling rather than take any of the children home for medical treatment," Ro said. "So there's clearly some principle at stake. Doctor Tanj, has Aoi made any demands?"

Tanj sighed. *"Aoi requests that the children be handed over to the Chain as quickly as can be arranged."*

"That's not going to happen," Crusher said briskly. "The People haven't broken any laws."

"They did conceal Corazame," Ro pointed out. "And the jury's still out on whether they knew what they were doing there, not to mention whether they're responsible for breaking into your office, or helping Corazame with that—"

"I'm as eager as anyone to find out who was responsible for that," said Crusher, "and if you and Blackmer have evidence to show that they were responsible, I'd be happy to see it. No," she corrected herself, "I'd be disappointed, and I'd be surprised. But I think we should have proof before we start assuming guilt."

"I agree," said Ro. "Doctor Tanj, I'm afraid I don't see what I can do. The People haven't done anything wrong. Everything that has happened can simply be construed as a misunderstanding. I can't force them to give up their children against their will. Never mind the Prime Directive—that would be unjust and immoral."

"*I was afraid you might say that.*" Tanj sighed. "*Aoi did say something else, and I think you'll agree that this bears investigation. Apparently the People take children from the worlds they visit. The advice is that you should put a watch on all the children on DS9, or else they'll take some of them.*"

"That," said Crusher hotly, "is almost certainly a lie." She turned angrily to her commanding officer. "Captain, this is the kind of thing that used to be said historically about Romani people on Earth."

"Romani?"

"One of our ethnic groups. They're travelers too, and historically they suffered dreadfully as a result of this kind of bigotry—up to and including genocide. People accused them of stealing children and it was nothing more than outright racism. People would see blond children among them and say they couldn't be Romani. Sometimes the children were taken away from their parents, all in the name of caring for them. But then DNA tests would prove they were Romani after all."

Ro ran her hand through her hair. "But we know that there are children traveling with Oioli and the others that they're not related to—"

"You know better than to believe this. It's what

oppressors always say about oppressed groups rather than face up to their own guilt. Everything Aoi has said about the People . . . I bet the Cardassians used to say the same kind of things about Bajorans—that they were shiftless, that they couldn't be trusted. I bet Bajorans were accused of harming Cardassian children or even stealing them. Weren't there cases of Cardassian orphans left on Bajor—"

Ro waved a hand to stop the flow. "You're right that casual racism about oppressed groups doesn't play well with me, but then neither does kidnapping. If there's a question mark over the legitimacy of their custody of any of these children, that's something we need to find out."

"And do what?" Crusher said. "What does the Prime Directive allow us to do, exactly? We're not supposed to get involved— "

"The Prime Directive is a nice ideal, but have you noticed it never works in practice? We're already involved."

"*And some of us are more involved than others,*" said Tanj. "*Another point that I need to impress upon you both is that the Chain is significantly more advanced technologically than the Federation. Their ship is vast, and we simply have no idea of the extent of its capabilities.*" *Tanj looked uncomfortable.* "*I can't shake the feeling that there is a veiled threat behind everything Aoi is saying, and I'm terrified that any refusal to assist them might give an excuse for reprisals—*"

"If that's the case, then Aoi is making a mistake," said Ro firmly. "I won't be threatened into any course of action. I certainly won't hand over children at gunpoint. Tey Aoi needs to read up on the Occupation—"

"May I respectfully point out that you are not the ones in Aoi's immediate firing line?" Tanj said. "*The* Athene Donald *is not equipped in any way to respond to Aoi's threats. We are a research and exploration vessel."*

Ro sighed. "I take your point. Let me consider all this, Doctor Tanj. I'll get back to you before the end of the day, station time. DS9 out."

Ro turned to her CMO. "Beverly, you've carried out medicals on most of the People. Can you prove one way or another whether the children are related to the adults?"

There was a moment's hesitation.

"Beverly?"

"Of course I can," said Crusher. "But I'm not sure it's an ethical use of my medical data. And it wouldn't tell us anything about whether they have been legitimately adopted or not—"

"Legality is in the eye of the beholder. I think we can assume that the People will say the children are legitimately adopted, and that Aoi will say that they're not."

Crusher shook her head. "I won't do it, Laren. It's not right—

"Beverly, you heard what Tanj said. Her ship might be in danger if we don't act."

"You said yourself that you wouldn't respond to a threat."

"No, but I won't willfully put the crew of the *Athene Donald* at risk either—"

"Let me speak to the People first," urged Crusher. "Let me get their side of the story. We owe it to them—they've been completely frank with us so far."

"Not completely," said Ro.

"I thought we agreed that concealing Corazame was a misunderstanding."

"That's not what I meant."

"Then what do you mean?"

Ro shrugged. "Do *you* know why they left the Chain? Neither do I. If they're taking children away from their parents, that would explain their reluctance to tell us why they left." Ro held out her hands. "I'm a child of the Occupation, Beverly. That's not going to happen on my watch."

Crusher cross-checked her medical files. What Aoi had said was true: none of the Open Sky children was genetically related to any of the adults. Further checks confirmed what she already knew: some of the children were the only members of their species traveling with the People. They were thus certainly not traveling with any relatives. But there was no proof that any of them had been taken away from their families against their will.

When Crusher reported back to Ro, the captain was ready to move at once to return the children to the Chain. But support for Crusher came from an unlikely quarter: Odo, who was present in Ro's office when the doctor arrived, and listened to Crusher's arguments with interest and sympathy.

"I know that this presses particular buttons, Laren," Crusher said.

"You bet it does," Ro said.

"But families are complicated. They're not all cut to the same size." Crusher took a deep breath. "Look at my own family. René, right now, is living a long way away from his mother. Do you judge me for those choices, Laren?"

"Of course not! It's none of my business! Besides, isn't he with his father?"

"Does a child have to be a blood relative to be with family? What about adopted children? You don't discount those relationships, surely?"

"You know I don't—"

"We don't know enough about the People. We don't even know if family means remotely the same thing to them as it does to us."

"Doctor Crusher's right," said Odo quietly. "Family is considerably more complicated than many of us allow for. The Great Link sent me out to explore the world of solids before I was even aware enough to know what I was. My childhood was spent in a laboratory. Who is my mother, Captain Ro? Who is my father? Doctor Mora was the closest, and he had me performing tricks for his Cardassian paymasters. What sort of family was that?" Odo gave an odd smile. "In truth, when I think of family, I think of the time I spent here on DS9." He frowned. "I would ask you not to repeat that to Quark."

"All right," said Ro, "I take the points you're both making. But Aoi has made some serious accusations. Why do that?"

"There could be thousands of reasons," said Crusher. "The People could be political refugees. They could be like the Romani, victims of racism or some other bigotry. Oh, I don't know, Laren! But let me talk to Oioli before you do anything. There are always two sides to a story."

Ro sighed. "All right. But remember that the clock is ticking on this. Aoi wants an answer—and I have to think of my responsibility to the people traveling on the *Athene Donald*."

When the doctor took her questions to the People, Ioile seemed almost angry: the first sign of anger that she had seen from any of them. Oioli, however, responded calmly.

"Let me tell you, Beverly, how we came to our children. They are the lost from many worlds, the homeless and unwanted. We found some of them on rubbish dumps, eating only garbage. Other sipped from dirty streams. Others we found starving. The litter of the universe—the thrown away, the refuse. But not to us." Oioli smiled. "We are their home. They are safe among us. They eat, they drink, they play and laugh. They are much loved and wanted."

"I have no reason to doubt them," Crusher said to

Ro, when she reported back on this interview. "And no evidence to show that what they've said is untrue." Carefully, she watched Ro as the Bajoran woman considered what she had heard. "You've seen those children, Laren," she said softly. "It's exactly as Oioli says: they eat, they drink, they play and laugh. They are much loved and wanted."

"I have sympathy for the People," Ro said at last, and with a little difficulty. "Any Bajoran of my background would. You spent a lot of time wishing someone would appear from nowhere to take you away . . ." She laughed, rather bitterly. "Where were the People when I needed them, eh?"

"There was Starfleet," said Crusher gently and with great sympathy. Her situation was hardly comparable to Ro's, but she knew how she had found a home there after her parents' death. "They came."

"Eventually," Ro replied dryly. "But that makes me wonder—is this really the best way of life for these children? Wandering about the universe, without access to basic health care or any structure?"

"They are much loved and wanted," Crusher simply said again.

"But what about their education? What about security or stability? These were things I craved as a child. That's what Starfleet gave me. In time."

"Who are we to say that these children are not receiving an education?" Crusher said. "Think of the worlds they must have seen. They're plainly secure—I've don't think I've seen happier children in my life, not even on board the *Enterprise*, with all its riches!" Crusher smiled. "And sometimes, you know, it's that regimentation that people need to escape. That isn't best for them—or their children. They find their own way of life, their own structures—and they pass those on, with love and care."

"I've still got many questions," Ro said. "Are *all* these children unwanted? There might be relatives on their homeworlds, hoping one day to be seeing them again—"

"I doubt it," said Crusher. "I don't think anyone wanted these children until the People arrived."

"And shouldn't they be settled? Is it even fair to drag them around the universe on these ships?"

"Like we do on our starships?" Crusher shook her head. "You can't hand these children over to Aoi, Laren. They're already home. And—most of all—they're not pawns to be used to protect one of our ships."

Ro sighed. "I know, I know. But the simple fact is that ship is still out there—and it's still undefended. So what do I do?"

"What you always do," said Crusher. "Make your decision. And stand firm."

Ro nodded. She had made her decision. Crusher had read her well: no child was going to be removed from his or her home while Ro Laren was in charge. The Chain would have to find a way to get around to liking that. Events, however, were about to overtake them all.

* * *

Later, Pulaski would wonder what their visitor was doing wandering down a quiet corridor of the *Athene Donald* away from the rest of the group over from the Chain ship. Perhaps she (or he, or whatever pronouns these damned people used, and where was a fully trained xenolinguist when you needed one? Sidetracked into spying, that's where) had simply got lost looking for the restroom, or perhaps the reasons for straying were more dubious. But there it was: one of the visitors from the extremely powerful spaceship looming menacingly beside the little vessel had been attacked on board their ship, and nobody knew who was to blame.

Everybody was nevertheless more than ready to make their suspicions known. "My strong advice," said Alden (and he was plainly back in the role of Starfleet Intelligence officer; his body language had shifted to upright and unyielding), "is that you check Metiger's movements at the time the assault occurred."

Pulaski threw her hands up in disbelief. "Here we go again! You think that our guest wouldn't have noticed a *giant glowing alien* attacking them?"

"Tzenkethi can dim their skin tones to whatever hue they like, if the need arises," Alden said. "Metiger's status requires that she put on this show, but she can be as dull as one of their service grades if it suits her. I've no doubt we'll find that she is in some way responsible—"

"Poppycock!"

"You'd be wise to listen to me when I talk about the Tzenkethi, Doctor Pulaski—"

"Back to titles, is it? Well, Commander Alden, you'd be wise to put some of your suspicions behind you—"

"Be quiet, both of you!"

Pulaski had never heard Tanj use so sharp a tone of voice before. Alden too was clearly surprised to see the usually conciliatory Trill so angry.

"I'm sick of all this quarreling," Tanj said. "The pair of you will wreck this mission before it's had a chance! And I'm not having that. Not after all the work I've put into assembling this crew and putting together this mission. You two will speak to each other civilly and work with each other as colleagues or else I'll send you back now. I mean it, Kitty! You can push my patience too far, you know!"

"I'm sorry, Maurita." Pulaski took a deep breath. "I'm on my best behavior now. I promise."

"About time. We'll find out *together*"—she gave both Pulaski and Alden a fierce look—"who is responsible for this assault. Meanwhile, I suggest that we do our utmost to assure Aoi that this is the case—"

"Doctor Tanj," said Alden, "I'd like to assume responsibility for the investigation."

Tanj drew herself up to her full height. "Commander Alden," she said magisterially, "do not try my patience more than you have already. I have gone out of my way to accommodate you. The *Athene Don-*

ald has a security team who are more than capable of conducting any investigation. Leave them to it."

Alden subsided.

"Kitty, don't smirk."

"Sorry."

"And put on your most apologetic face, please. I'd like you there when I speak to Aoi, and I'd like you to be supportive."

"Of course."

But Aoi, when Tanj was put through, was more concerned with other matters. "*The best apology that can be given is that the People of the Open Sky are handed over. Arrange this, please.*"

"I don't understand," said Tanj, after Aoi cut the comm. "You would think that Aoi would care more that one of their number had been attacked. So why so casual?" She frowned. "Almost uncaring."

"Ours is not to reason why," said Pulaski. "Actually, forget I said that. I've remembered the next line."

"Please don't tell me." Tanj sighed. "I'd better contact Captain Ro. But I don't think she's going to like this ultimatum."

At that precise moment, the fate of the People was the least of Ro's problems, since she was, at that precise moment, sitting in front of a view screen getting bawled out by a furious castellan.

"*I believe,*" said Elim Garak (and how did he make his tone so *chilly*?), "*that I indicated that a behind-the-scenes resolution to this matter was what I wanted. And has that happened? No. On the one hand I have half of the assembly demanding to know why I seem to care nothing for the fate of those brave soldiers who faithfully served the Union, and on the other hand I have a very stiff message from a Major Varis asking why Cardassian citizens are besieging the Romulan consulate on DS9—"*

Ro risked an interruption. "Sir, 'besieging' is hardly the right word. There was a minor demonstration—"

"One that ended in arrests, I understand, on both sides. And I'm sure I don't need to say precisely how well that's playing on Prime. The Bajoran commander of Deep Space 9—of Terok Nor!—is arresting Cardassian citizens who are doing nothing more than drawing attention to their plight."

"This isn't Terok Nor," Ro pointed out.

"You know that, and I know that, and everyone saying it knows that, but if it means a point scored off the castellan, then nobody cares."

Odo, sitting beside Ro, looked uncomfortable. "Garak, as much as it pains me to say this, I feel I should apologize. If I hadn't asked you to assist us, you would not be in this position."

The apology seemed to calm the castellan down slightly. "*I appreciate that, Odo. But, to be fair, it sounds as if Mhevita Pa'Dan and her friends would have resorted to these tactics whether I knew about their cause or not. At least this way I haven't been entirely uninformed.*" The castellan sighed. "*Nevertheless, one interpretation of these events—and one that my opponents are very keen to make the accepted one—is that the Romulan diplomatic service is running rings around my office."* He pursed his lips. *"This is hardly the kind of message I want to be sending this close to my speech. It's not the kind of message I want to be sending at all."* He tutted. *"The* Romulans, *of all people! The notion that they could be outmaneuvering me is a personal affront!"*

"I'll speak again to Mhevita," said Odo.

"If you could impress upon her that her castellan is doing everything within his considerable—but thankfully constrained—power that he can to help, I would be grateful."

"It would be helpful if I could tell Mhevita that some progress is being made," Odo said. "Are you getting anywhere, Garak?"

"Not really. No, that's inaccurate. At least Major Varis is now in contact with my people. She was rather a dead end before this. I wondered why she was being so awkward and then I remembered she is a Romulan."

"We had the same experience with her," Ro said. "She made no response to my apology."

"My people will try to keep her talking. Or posturing. Or whatever it takes to keep communications open. In the meantime, Odo, please, get this friend of yours under control! You may not like the idea of me as castellan—"

"Very insightful of you."

"But I can assure you that you'd like some of the alternatives considerably less. I'm doing all I can."

Garak cut the channel and Ro turned to Odo. "Do you think Pa'Dan will be receptive to this?"

Odo frowned. "I honestly don't know. It's not much, is it?"

The lights in Quark's drew Ro toward them like a lost ship glimpsing a safe haven for the first time in months. It was quiet inside, late shift, although the lord of the manor himself was still there, counting his takings and chatting to those stalwarts who propped up the bar until late. Why would he be anywhere else? The bar was Quark's home. You'd have to blow up the station to move him—and even then he'd rebuild. Demonstrably. Whatever shape or form Deep Space 9 took, Quark would be there, selling drinks, making a small but comfortable profit, dreaming of huge riches and never quite achieving them: a quiet small pond to one side of the turbulent Great River.

When Ro sat down, he poured her a drink, handed it over, and leaned on the bar, watching her. "Some days are better than others, eh, Captain?" he said at last.

"Don't start," Ro replied.

"At least you've found your Tzenkethi."

Ro eyed him. "Yes, that's on the profit side, I suppose. Not that we can pin anything on her. Meanwhile I have angry Cardassians, noncommunicative Romulans—"

"Angry Cardassians and noncommunicative Romulans are a fact of life, Laren, particularly for the commanding officer of Deep Space 9. The sooner you learn to roll with that, the better. Besides, Odo's on the case, isn't he?"

"Did he tell you about it?"

"Of course not. But I know the sound of Odo on a case. Anyway, this conversation is about making you feel better. So take it from me: Odo might be a walking, talking bundle of shape-shifting misery, but he's an effective walking, talking bundle of shape-shifting misery. If anyone can calm your Cardassians and get your Romulans talking, it'll be him."

"Blackmer doesn't like him." Ro lifted a finger from her glass. "Correction: Blackmer is *threatened* by him."

"Blackmer's a big boy and can take care of himself."

"It's my responsibility as commanding officer to take care of those serving under me."

"Is Blackmer's self-esteem really what's bothering you?"

"To be honest, no. What's really bothering me is that we seem to have inadvertently walked straight into the middle of a bitter dispute between two factions of an alien species we encountered for the first time only the other day."

"The People of the Open Sky and the Chain, yes?" Quark retrieved her glass. "Don't ask how I know. Assume that I always know and I always will know."

Ro sighed. "We shouldn't even be getting involved, but we are involved. I'm worried it's all going to blow up in our faces—or, more particularly, in the faces of the crew of the *Athene Donald*."

Quark plainly struggled at this point. "I can only say it again. Some days are better than others."

"Some days are downright shocking."

"That's the job you took on." Quark smiled. "Look at it this way—things can only get better."

Perhaps inevitably, that was when Ro's combadge chimed. She had a quick exchange with Blackmer and then turned back to Quark. "Things can only get better, eh?"

"Go on, what's happened?"

"One of the People, Ioile, has been found murdered in their quarters." Her hands, she noticed, were shaking. "Unpleasant, by all accounts."

Quark stopped partway through refilling her glass. "I suppose that really was asking for the Great River to throw in an extra whirlpool."

Eight

Captain's Log, Personal.

One all too easy mistake is assuming that Federation values are default. And indeed why not? Who could balk at values such as freedom of expression, infinite diversity in infinite combinations, et cetera, et cetera?

A thought experiment. How might the Federation appear to outsiders? How might Starfleet appear? Do our rules and regulations appear officious, lengthy, perhaps even preposterous? Does our habit of color-coding ourselves according to some hierarchical ranking system appear ridiculous? And what about the project of exploration itself, which we all hold so dear? Perhaps this indicates some kind of fundamental sociocultural malaise, arising from the stability of our homeworlds, that some of us willingly seek out dangerous situations, putting our lives at risk? What is it that we are trying to escape? Only a few moments' thought and we can appear very different. It is sobering to think that we might require as much explanation as anyone else.

With that in mind, then—what reasons might others have for their cultural norms . . . ?

Ioile's body, in the morgue, was a pitiful sight, with livid bruises across the face that were a grotesque counterpoint to the olive markings. A cover, mercifully, hid the worst of the damage, which, according to the report, was to the back of the alien's head, but what Ro could see was bad enough. She quickly looked away. By the body sat Oioli, holding Ioile's hand. There were no tears that Ro could see (Could Oioli shed tears? The sorrow was plain enough), just those wide unblinking eyes staring down at the body in gentle but all-consuming grief. Ro found herself very moved by the sight. There had been a playfulness about Oioli throughout all of their encounters that had warmed Ro to the visitor from the outset. Grief sat badly on that face.

Blackmer came across to speak to Ro. "A nasty attack," he said quietly. "Really nasty. Someone wanted to make very sure that Ioile was dead."

"Do we have a murder weapon?"

"A sculpture lying on the floor beside the body. We think it's probably that." He sighed. "Laren."

Ro was startled at the use of her personal name. On the whole Blackmer preferred to keep things formal between them. "Something the matter, Jeff?"

He gestured toward the empty pathologist's office. "Could we have a word in private?"

"Of course." Ro followed him in, wondering what this could be about.

Blackmer, when they were alone, didn't waste time. "I want to offer you my resignation."

"Resignation?" Ro was astonished. "What for?"

Blackmer's face, generally so stern and controlled, cracked. Only for a split second, but it was awful to see. Ro came around to him quickly, pressing her hand briefly against his arm. "Prophets, Jeff, what's the matter?"

Blackmer took a deep breath, visibly composing himself. Quietly, he said, "This is the second murder on the station under my watch. I don't need to remind you of the first."

Nan Bacco. The president. Assassinated on the new DS9.

"First her," said Blackmer, "now this. That doesn't say much for station security under my watch, does it? So I think it's only appropriate that I offer to resign."

"I see," said Ro slowly.

"I'll remain here for whatever period of time you need to find a suitable replacement, or, if you prefer, I can be gone within the hour."

"*What*? This is all moving pretty quickly, isn't it? What am I supposed to do in the meantime?"

Rather sourly, Blackmer said, "It's not as if you don't have another candidate ready to take over, is it?"

Ro looked at him in bewilderment. "You've lost me, Jeff."

"Oh, come on! Who do you think I mean? Who is on board the station right now with exactly the right experience and plenty of ability?"

Odo. He meant Odo.

"He's on the spot, isn't he? He even managed to

save you from a nasty injury the other day, when my hands were full."

This, Ro thought, had gone far enough. She said firmly, "I have no intention of replacing my chief security officer. None at all." She thought about what Blackmer had said, and about the tensions there so often were between them. Perhaps this was a signal of a deeper dissatisfaction—with her, maybe, or the way she ran this station. "Jeff, do you *want* to leave DS9?"

"Leave?" Blackmer looked shocked. "Of course not! We're only just back up and running again!"

"Then what are you *talking* about? Look, we've had a run of bad luck, terrible luck. Nobody could have predicted what would happen to the president, and the Prophets know that many of us—and I'm including myself here—have spent more than a few sleepless nights wondering whether there was something else we could have done. Something more. But there *wasn't* anything we could have done. Her murderers were set on committing the crime and that's exactly what they did. If we'd been doing something differently, they would have found a way around that too—"

Blackmer banged his fist angrily against the desk. "But I should have been on to them!"

"That's exactly my point!" Ro said. "*Nobody* was on to them! Not us, not Bacco's own security people, not anyone! It was a tragedy, and it's our horrible misfortune that it happened here. If anyone should be resigning, it is me—and I've no intention of resigning! I've worked hard to get here, and I deserve this post. The same goes for you, Jeff." She shook her head. "I don't want to hear any more of this. You're a first-class security officer and an asset to this station. I know we don't always agree, but that's what makes you right for this job. You keep me from bending too many rules, and you're utterly reliable. I need you here—not Odo, not anyone else. You."

Slowly, Blackmer nodded.

"Is that the last I'm going to hear of this?" said Ro.

"Yes, sir . . . for the moment," he replied. "Let me think some more."

"You don't need to think more about it. Seriously. Put it out of your mind. I mean that."

"All right."

"All right." Ro took a deep breath. She'd been right when she'd told Quark she was worried about Blackmer—but this one had come from nowhere. She could only hope that she had done enough to allay his worries and that she would hear no more of it. "We'll all feel better if we can get to the bottom of this murder. So let's get down to the business at hand. Any thoughts yet on who the killer could be?"

Blackmer sighed. "There's another puzzle. You've visited the People's quarters, haven't you?"

"Only once, but it struck me as a very busy place with lots of people coming in and out. So surely we've got some eyewitnesses."

"We do indeed," Blackmer said. "But you're not going to like what they have to say."

"Why did I have the feeling you were going to say that. Go on."

"Ioile was seen entering one of the bedrooms in their suite to get some sleep at twenty-two nineteen last night. The body was found slightly over two hours later, station time, when Oioli went in to speak to Ioile."

So Oioli had found the body. Ro sighed. No wonder their visitor was in such a state. Nobody should be confronted with that sight of a friend.

"The bedroom has one entry, leading from a shared living room." Blackmer put up a floor plan on his padd. He tapped the largest room. "At least eight of the People were here in that shared space during the relevant time period, and every single one of them swears blind that nobody went in or out of Ioile's room during those two hours." He almost snarled in frustration. "They were all sitting there, the whole time! Unless they're all in it together, I can't see how anyone could have got past them."

Ro studied the floor plan. Blackmer was right. The bedroom where Ioile's body had been found had only one entrance. "I hate to ask this," she said, "not least because I don't think Oioli is capable of an act of violence like this, but—"

Blackmer shook his head. "Oioli cried out on discovering the body. There wasn't enough time between Oioli going into Ioile's room and . . ."

Ro shuddered. "And your idea that they're all in on it?"

"Nonstarter," said Blackmer. "Oioli was one of the eight."

Ro nodded. That chimed with her gut instinct: Ioile's laughing lightness had seemed popular among the People. "So someone must have gone in by transporter," she said.

Blackmer sighed in frustration. "But there are no signs of a transporter being used—or none that Chief O'Brien can find."

"Like the burglary," Ro said.

Blackmer gave a wry smile. "That's something, at least. It suggests that the two crimes are surely connected—if we solve one, we'll have the key to the other."

"That's a start," Ro agreed.

"You'd think so. But of course, if we assume that the crimes are connected, Corazame is out for the burglary." Blackmer touched the padd, and the image of Corazame, now lying on her bunk with her hands folded across her chest, came up. Blackmer said, "Sensors confirm that she was in her holding cell the entire time of the murder."

"Hmm." Ro stared at Corazame. "Although she might still be involved in some way . . ."

"But not directly."

"I suppose the obvious place to look now is among the People themselves," Ro said. "We know they've got some cloaking capability. Would that let someone get past the group that was sitting in the communal room and into Ioile's room without being noticed?"

Blackmer didn't look convinced. "Possibly, if the person was particularly stealthy. There were eight people in the communal room, remember."

"But we know whoever is responsible is probably a burglar. Stealth comes with the territory."

Blackmer smiled. "Fair point."

"I know I'm clutching at straws, Jeff, but we've got to start somewhere." Ro stared again at Corazame. "My hunch is that there's some history among the People that we don't know about. Groups like that, traveling together for a long time—it's easy for hostilities to fester and then suddenly break out into acts of violence."

"Sounds about right. I guess there's a reason golden age detective novels take place in country houses," Blackmer said.

Ro looked at him, puzzled. "What?"

"Forget it. I was agreeing. Small enclosed places, tense relationships, brutal murders. You're right. They go together."

"I've no idea what you're talking about, but I'm glad we're on the same wavelength," Ro said. "So what's Oioli had to say?"

"It seems cruel to question someone who is so devastated, but I've had a quick word. You'll like this: Oioli insists that the Chain is at fault." Blackmer shook his head. "But how could someone from the

Chain ship be responsible? It would take days for any of them to get here."

Ro shook her head. "No, that's not possible. I imagine Oioli's still angry about the jam on their technologies and is lashing out. Grief can make you do that. No, we'll find the murderer—and the burglar—among the People." She sighed. "Whether they'll make investigating easy or not is another matter. Speak to Crusher. She's built some bridges with the People, and they have good reasons to trust her."

"I'll ask," said Blackmer. "She might be able to help the forensic team—they're finding it hard to make sense of the samples they've taken from the body."

"Good." Ro tapped her fingers against the desk. "I suppose there's one positive outcome."

"I'm struggling to think of one," said Blackmer.

"It's cold comfort, but at least I've now got the excuse I wanted not to hand the People over to the Chain—or, at least, to delay any decision for a while." She grinned at Blackmer. "We have to investigate this murder properly, don't we? And the People can't possibly leave the station until that's been done thoroughly."

"As long as Aoi doesn't insist the Chain has superior jurisdiction and insists that they investigate the murder," Blackmer said.

Ro, on her way toward the door, shuddered. "Don't go there." She glanced back at her chief of security. "If it makes you feel any better, Jeff—you called this one correctly. We should have been keeping a much closer eye on the People. So no more talk about resignation, eh?"

He gave her a gray smile. "Not today."

Crusher, approached by Blackmer, agreed to help the forensic team as far as she could.

"But there's a limit to what we can do," she said. "I have the information from the medicals I conducted, but I need to take additional samples from Oiloi and Ailoi, and obviously I won't do that without their permission."

As a result, Crusher found herself sitting in on the more formal interview that Blackmer held with Oioli in his office. "I want to reassure you," Crusher said to Oioli, "that we're not accusing you or any of the People of anything. But if we're going to find Ioile's murderer, we need to know more about you—and about Ioile in particular. We want to understand—"

"Ioile? Ioile? You wish to understand, eh?" Oioli raised long hands upward, as if in supplication to some alien god. For a moment it was as if nobody else was in the room. "Ioile! Ioile!" Oioli cried. "How did I ever fail you?" Tapering fingers covered Oioli's face, the wide eyes closed at last.

Crusher glanced across at Blackmer. The security officer looked uncomfortable and alarmed—but Crusher knew exactly how to respond to such distress. She reached out, placing her own hand upon Oioli's, whose long fingers curled around her own.

The alien's flesh was cool, but not unpleasantly so, and Crusher felt the shuddering of grief beneath her grasp. So many things in the universe were relative, she thought, but the sorrow of bereavement must surely bind together most species—or those that lived linearly, at least. *We all live in time*, she thought. *Time makes all things mortal. Makes them finite. And so we all suffer loss—and can offer comfort and compassion.*

"I am so sorry," Crusher said simply. "I lost a husband." She caught Oioli's questioning look at the word. "A life partner. A lover. A friend."

Oioli's eyes showed comprehension.

"It nearly destroyed me," Crusher went on. "The pain went away, in time, but I was never the same."

Oioli gave her a sad smile. "You say you wish to understand. You understand already. We had been friends for many years. We shared the same horizons." A huge sigh rose up from the depths of Oioli's thin body. "I found Ioile as a child, cold and lost and hungry. Seeing Ioile there that day was when I reached my limit. I could not stay upon a world that starved some of its children. Where some were rich—so very rich!—but some were left to perish. The weakest too, the sick and old, the children and the babies! I took Ioile in my arms, and we became the People. We left our world—our rotten world—which failed so many of us. Ioile was the first of us. Ioile was the reason."

Oioli's eyes closed again. Crusher kept hold of the long hand, gently stroking it. She thought she was beginning to understand now why the People had begun their journey. Their world—the world of the Chain—might have many technological riches, but they were clearly not shared among everyone. " 'The Ones Who Walk Away from Omelas' . . ." she murmured to herself. But why had Oioli been so secretive about this? How had Oioli thought she would not understand a motive like that?

"I promise," Crusher said softly, "that we will do all we can to bring Ioile's murderer to justice. But it might mean facing some hard truths about some of your fellow travelers. Will you trust us, Oioli? Will you help us?"

Oioli looked at her bitterly. "Whatever help you need from me, I am more than willing. But Ioile's murderer is not one of the People. I will help if you can find out why the Chain has done this."

"The *Chain*?" Crusher frowned. "But that's not possible—"

"You want my aid, you'll have my aid. But this is my condition: discover why the Chain did this. You need look no farther."

With a sigh, Crusher said, "I promise. We'll pursue that lead—however we can."

Oioli nodded. Crusher looked over at Blackmer, who was frowning. She bit her lower lip. Grief, surely, was making Oioli say these things, but the truth was that the Chain could not possibly be responsible for the death of the beloved Ioile. They were too far away. Oioli must be mistaken—angry, yes, at what had happened to Ioile, and at the circumstances that had made them leave their home, but mistaken nonetheless. But what was the point of saying so? Crusher simply sat stroking Oioli's hand. Her mind was racing. She needed samples from as many different members of their species as possible if she was going to come up with a test that could reliably differentiate their DNA not only at a species level but also at an individual level. But she had access to only a handful of them: Ioile, Oioli, Ailoi, and a few children. How could she get her hands on more samples? Crusher smiled wryly to herself. If she was going to fulfill this promise to Oioli, she was going to have to enlist the help of Pulaski.

As Crusher's luck would have it, Katherine Pulaski's interests were heading in the same direction—although at first she had a more pressing problem to deal with. A dark and forbidding ship full of aliens armed with unknown weapons was one thing, she was learning, but there were few things in the universe more alarming than a Tzenkethi showing her fury in all its might and color. It was like watching a particularly spectacular and violent fireworks display.

"Doctor Tanj," Metiger said, and Pulaski noted with a wince that first names were off the table again, "I am sorry to say that I must lodge a formal complaint about Commander Alden."

Tanj gestured to Metiger to sit down, but the Tzenkethi woman remained standing. She was much taller than both of the other women, and with the flashing white light crackling from her skin it was rather like a visitation from an archangel. But which one, wondered Pulaski: Michael or Lucifer?

Given the circumstances, Tanj was keeping remarkably cool. "Metiger, please explain what's happened. A formal complaint is very serious—"

"I *am* very serious. You told me that this mission was about building trust."

"It *is* about building trust."

"Why then have I been interrogated by a member of your security services—"

"Interrogated?" Tanj was horrified.

"Am I to understand that you consider me responsible in some way for the assault on our visitor?"

"And this was why I said he shouldn't be let on board," Pulaski muttered to Tanj, who waved an impatient hand to quiet her friend.

"Metiger, I have no idea what you're talking about," said Tanj. "You say that Alden has been questioning you?"

"He came to the lab earlier today and interrogated me for the best part of an hour about my movements during the time of the assault. You know that I was with you and Doctor Pulaski the entire time! It would be a simple matter of checking sensors. He seemed to think I was capable of being in two places at once! Why am I a suspect? What have I done to deserve this?"

"Absolutely nothing, Metiger, let me assure you of

that," Tanj said. "Alden was certainly not acting on my instructions—"

"If I did not know better," Metiger went on, "I would think that your people are setting up this mission to fail."

Tanj shook her head. "You know that's not true."

"Perhaps it's not true of you, Maurita, but is it true of the whole of Starfleet? Is it true of your intelligence service? Not everyone in the Federation is well disposed toward us."

Pulaski glanced at Tanj. Not everyone on the *Athene Donald* was well disposed toward them. Could this be another reason that Alden was on board? It was not beyond the bounds of possibility that there were hardliners at Starfleet Intelligence who would see any movement toward the Tzenkethi as risky and inadvisable. But would they go so far as to try to torpedo this mission before it had the chance to succeed?

"I'll speak to Alden," said Tanj in her firmest tone. "He's gone against my specific instructions speaking to you this way, and it's not acceptable." She offered Metiger her hand. "I want to be completely clear—I have *no* doubts about your commitment to this mission, and no doubts about the desire for friendship that brought you on board. I hope you know that I share that desire."

Slowly, Metiger nodded. The white light was beginning to dissipate.

"I'll speak to Alden," Tanj said again. "He'll be in

no doubt about my opinions. You are not a suspect, Metiger. You are a friend."

"You know," said Pulaski, after Metiger had gone, "I think we'll travel a long way before we see a sight like that again."

"I'd be glad never to see anything like it." Tanj studied her hands, folded before her on her desk. "You know, Alden came to see me earlier this morning."

"Let me guess," said Pulaski. "He thinks Metiger is responsible for the assault on our visitor, for some strange Tzenkethi purpose that you and I cannot divine, but that he, an expert in reading the auspices of Tzenkethi Affairs, can. The man really is obsessed. I bet he didn't mention that he'd been questioning Metiger."

"He didn't. But he did make one good point—"

"A good point? I don't believe he has *any* good points," Pulaski muttered. "Go on, what did he say?"

"He reminded me that this is, ultimately, a Federation vessel. Even if there are other stakeholders in the project, Federation law takes precedence."

"And what did he mean by that? I assume there was a threat behind that. But it can't amount to much, can it?" Pulaski glanced at Tanj. "*Can* it?"

"He implied that if he wasn't satisfied with how our security team progresses with the investigation, he'll apply to his superiors to be given authority to proceed as he sees fit."

"Damn the man!" Pulaski leaned forward angrily

in her chair. "It's obvious that these crimes—the burglaries, the assault, the murder—are all connected in some way. But I don't see how Corazame can be responsible for the murder, and even if she and Metiger are in league, Metiger can't be responsible either—she's too damn far away!"

"Unless the Tzenkethi have transwarp beaming."

The ability to beam an object or person from one star system to another. Pulaski shook her head. "No. We'd know. Our intelligence services would know. Alden would know."

"So you see the point to Alden now?" Tanj said. "But think, Kitty—what if it was true?"

They stared at each other.

"If it was true, Maurita, we'd all have been bowing and scraping before the Autarch years ago. You don't get to transwarp beaming without picking up some fairly powerful capabilities along the way."

"I suppose you're right." Tanj shook herself. "At the very least, I don't want to accept that Metiger has lied to us."

"None of us likes to think we've been hoodwinked."

"No. But if she *does* turn out to be connected to these crimes in some way, we might have to swallow our pride and admit that the Tzenkethi have been playing us." Tanj glanced at the view screen, where the image of the Chain ship loomed. "That ship is big, and it's serious. If the *Athene Donald* and her crew are being put at risk because the Tzenkethi are working to some agenda that we know nothing about, then I have a responsibility to everyone on board this ship to find out what's going on and stop it." She looked past Pulaski, a worried expression on her face. "Perhaps it's time to sit down with Alden and listen to what he has to say. I assume he has information about Metiger and the Tzenkethi intelligence services that could shed light on this whole situation—"

"Sit down with Alden? Over my dead body!"

Tanj winced. "An unfortunate turn of phrase . . ."

"I'd rather sit down with Aoi." Pulaski suddenly brightened. "You know, that's not such a bad idea. We could ask the Chain to act as arbiters in our dispute—"

"I'm not sure Aoi would be receptive to that right now."

"We could *ask*."

Tanj gave a wan smile. "I don't think so, Kitty. Aoi's last message to me was fairly explicit: arrange for the People of the Open Sky to be returned, or else the Chain ship will consider it a hostile act."

"Ro won't do that."

Tanj shook her head. "Not yet. Not while it's possible that the murderer is among their number. And she and Doctor Crusher both doubt that the People are likely to be responsible. They've formed a very positive view of them."

"If Crusher won't accept that the People are behind all this, then I won't accept that the Tzenkethi are responsible either," Pulaski replied. "If only because I want Alden to be proved wrong."

"That's not proof! And you call yourself a scientist."

"Science starts with hunches," Pulaski said. "You know that as well as anyone. Hunches that you either prove or else have the guts to discard when the evidence stacks up against them. And my hunch is that the Tzenkethi are not behind any of this—not Metiger, not this Corazame, friend of Alden or not." She smiled at her old friend. "Will you let me prove it?"

Tanj held up her hands. "I'll take anything, if it can salvage this mission. What do you intend to do?"

"First," said Pulaski, staring out the porthole, "I want to get onto that ship."

Back in her office, Pulaski got a message from Crusher asking for help collecting as many tissue samples from the Chain as possible. Now how, wondered Pulaski, could she go about doing that? "Ship first," she muttered, staring at the big black vessel on her view screen, "samples next." What Katherine Pulaski wanted, she generally got—although not always in a way she liked.

The day had started with a murder, and was ending with a riot. Which was all well and good, thought Ro, but couldn't she have been allowed to get a couple of hours' sleep under her belt first?

She came out of the turbolift onto the Plaza

and sprinted toward the Romulan consulate. As she approached, her heart sank. The scuffle was well under way: Bajorans and Cardassians, and a few of Quark's regulars who had no particular stake in this particular fight but liked to throw a few punches whenever the opportunity arose. Blackmer and his team were already stuck in, trying to pull people apart.

Odo, standing outside Quark's, saw Ro from his vantage point and came over to speak to her.

"I'm guessing you didn't have any success with Pa'Dan," Ro said.

"My apologies, Captain," he said grimly. "Whoever has Mhevita's ear at the moment is obviously more persuasive than I am."

There was one positive outcome to this, thought Ro, ducking sideways as one of the holos of the missing that a Cardassian had been holding came flying her way. Blackmer would feel better if Odo didn't always seem to be on top of things. "Don't worry about it," she said shortly. "I think this was always going to happen."

Odo grunted. Ro, catching sight of her chief of security in the midst of the fray, waved to him, signaling that she was on her way over. She squared her shoulders and began to force her way through the crowd. But before she could get anywhere near Blackmer, she heard an energy blast. Ro ducked—and then realized that the weapon had been fired not into the crowd but above it.

Her immediate reaction was fury. *Blackmer!*

That's not how we do business around here and you know it! And then she registered the sound the weapon had made, and thought, *That's not Starfleet issue! That's Romulan!* Her third thought was, *It's gone quiet . . .*

And it had. Everyone had frozen, midfight. There were a few mumbles and grumbles here and there, but even they were beginning to subside, as people nudged each other and pointed toward the door of the Romulan consulate. Ro looked that way too.

On the threshold stood a Romulan officer—a major, going by her insignia—in full dress uniform. She was incredibly imposing. Some small part of Ro's mind that wasn't busy holding two brawlers apart couldn't help but envy this woman's poise. Ro's dress uniform tended to slump around her, as if knowing how much the body it covered resented being pressed into ceremonial duties. This woman knew how to make a dress uniform work for her. And she'd brought the fight to an immediate halt and was commanding the crowd's attention.

"What is happening here?" she cried.

Whatever noise was still going on disappeared completely in response. Everyone was staring at this woman—or else at their feet. The Romulan stared back imperiously. "Is this how representatives of the Romulan Empire are treated on Deep Space 9?" She looked around. "Who is in charge here?

People looked pointedly at Ro. She put up her hand, like a schoolchild caught in the middle of a playground fight. "That'll be me," she said. "Captain Ro Laren, commanding officer, Deep—"

"Captain Ro," said the woman, saying the name with some distaste. "I am Major Varis."

Varis. Of course. Who else would it be? The person responsible for detaining the Cardassian prisoners of war. Someone Ro needed desperately to impress, and she had failed to recognize her in the melee.

Ro took a deep breath, pushed her shoulders back, and tried to look authoritative. "Major Varis," she said, "welcome to Deep Space 9."

"This is hardly what I would call a welcome, Captain Ro." Varis looked disdainfully around the chaos throughout the Plaza. "Perhaps when your station is once again under your control you might find some time in your schedule for us to talk?"

Part Three

Death Is Her Hobby

Nine

Captain's Log, Personal.

I am often asked the secret of success in assembling away teams. I wish heartily that I could give some clear advice here. Naturally one looks first to specialisms: the security officer in a potentially physically dangerous situation; the xenolinguist when the universal translator fails; the doctor if there is a question of disease or ill health. And of course, all must be willing and able to make swift decisions, and unafraid to live with the consequences of these decisions. (I have seen too many good potential officers freeze when put to the test, to the detriment of all concerned.)

And the captain's role in all of this?

To know the crew. To know who are willing and able, and who are willing but unable; to know who have more to give despite appearances; to know who have reached their limit despite assurances. To give praise where praise is due, but to take on ultimate responsibility at every point . . .

With swabs taken from Oioli, the data from the medicals she had performed, and a not inconsiderable amount of skill on her own part (though she would be too modest to admit it), Crusher inched her way toward a complete DNA map of Oioli's species. It was a slow and slippery process (the proteins seemed to shift and change even as she came close to identifying them), but steadily she found what she believed were their unique features. On a whim, she applied her test to samples taken from her office after the intrusion. The results gave her the first real break since Corazame had been found (and Blackmer would surely be the first to admit that had been a lucky break). But Crusher was now certain that at least one of the three—Oioli, Ailoi, or Ioile—had been in her office.

That opened up a whole new set of questions, Crusher thought as she pondered these results. What if Ioile had been the one to go into her office? Was this connected to the murder in some way? Or was there a simpler explanation? The children, after all, had been running in and out of the medical unit during the time she and her staff had been carrying out the medicals, but Crusher (the mother of a small child) was certain she had taken the precaution of keeping her office door firmly locked throughout. But could this be the innocent explanation that she was hoping for? The one that would clear Oioli?

"All conjecture," she muttered under her breath. "I won't know anything for certain until I get more samples."

She contacted Pulaski, who she knew had been

using her test on tissue samples taken from the assault on board the *Athene Donald*. Pulaski had good news for her: based on Crusher's work, she believed she had pinned down a means of testing for individual members of the species.

"*It's a kind of magnesium signaling test,*" Pulaski had explained. "*We can go into the specifics later, but I'm sure I've got something that will work. Test it against whatever Blackmer and his people managed to get off the murder weapon. And see if you've any match with the samples from your office.*"

Crusher was shocked by the result she got. The sample taken from her office not only matched the sample taken from the murder weapon, but both matched the swabs she had taken from Oioli. If Pulaski's test worked, the burglar—and the murderer—was none other than Oioli.

Beverly Crusher, although a quiet presence, was confident in her abilities as a doctor and a researcher. It was not in her nature to second-guess her own expertise. Nevertheless, this result sent her straight back to her initial work. Had she missed a step when she devised the map of the species' DNA? A careful reexamination said no. So had the samples become contaminated in some way? Again, unsurprisingly, given her careful nature, Crusher found that was not the case. This left another option: there was a problem with Pulaski's work.

That was hard to accept, given what she knew of Pulaski. But could Oioli *really* be the murderer? That did not sit easily with her. Oioli had been plainly devastated over the death of Ioile. Was it possible to fake that degree of distress? Or was Oioli attempting to mask guilt? Crusher recalled something Blackmer had said in passing: that overt displays of grief generally aroused his suspicion, and one should invariably look at those closest to a victim to find the killer. But then Oioli's grief had been in many ways contained—or, at least, it had seemed that way to Crusher. But who knew what was normal for the People?

Which took her back to the possibility that Pulaski had made a mistake. Crusher, reaching toward her companel to open a channel to the *Athene Donald*, sighed at the prospect of that conversation. But a message from Pulaski was already there.

Can't be there yet, it said. *Match between your samples and ours. But not possible for the murderer, the burglar, and the assailant to be the same person. Need more samples! Working on this and will be in touch. KDP*

I wonder what the D *stands for*, Crusher thought, relieved that she didn't have to tell Pulaski that her test didn't work. Picking up her padd, she left her office to go brief Ro and Blackmer on what she had found. Precisely nothing, she thought, and stepped into the turbolift.

Ailoi was there. "Doctor Crusher! I was coming to see you. I understand that you're working on some kind of DNA test for our people . . ."

Holding the turbolift doors open, Crusher frowned.

Surely Blackmer hadn't been talking. "How on earth do you know that?"

"Ioile was my friend," Ailoi said softly. "I wanted to understand what is being done to find the murderer. The barkeep proved very informative."

Quark. Of course, he would know a great deal about the procedures of the security team. "That's standard procedure," Crusher said.

"But you'll be wasting your time." Ailoi touched the olive markings that they had around their throats and necks. They darkened to nearly black beneath long fingers. "It can't be done. Our protein structure changes too much." Ailoi's voice lowered. "I want the murderer found as much as anyone, but this is a dead end. You won't find out who killed Ioile that way."

"That's very helpful, thank you." When the lift reached its destination. Crusher stepped out.

As she walked toward Ro's office, she gave a sigh of relief. It might set the investigation back some way, but at least Oioli was off the hook again. Quickly, she asked the comm officer to send a message to Pulaski summarizing what Ailoi had told her: *Seems what we're trying to do is impossible.* Pulaski's response was prompt and typical: *Nothing is impossible, given time and resources. And more samples.*

"Even you have limits, Kitty Pulaski," Crusher murmured, reading this response. "We exist in a finite universe."

Ro and Blackmer met Crusher's summary of her and Pulaski's work with equanimity. "So based on the results of your tests," Ro said, "we can assume that someone from the People—or their species—broke into your office, but we can't say who, and we still can't explain how somebody managed to get in and out of Ioile's quarters without being seen."

"And even then, all we know is someone from the People—or their species—*went into* Crusher's office," Blackmer said. "It could have been innocent."

"And when it comes to the murder, it could simply be Ioile's DNA that we're finding," Crusher said.

"Of course," said Ro. "Because there isn't a way to differentiate between Ioile's DNA and anyone else's from their species." She sighed. "Do you think Doctor Pulaski will be able to crack this?"

"Katherine Pulaski is many things, but she is not a magician." Crusher smiled. "Having said that, if anyone is going to crack it, it'll be Pulaski. Whether she can do it quickly enough to satisfy Tey Aoi, I'm not sure. And she has to get on board that ship first. She'll need more samples across the set if she wants to study variation among them."

"So for the moment we wait for Pulaski," Ro said.

"Sounds like waiting for the impossible," grumbled Blackmer.

"Where does this leave the Tzenkethi, Corazame?" Crusher asked. "Do we have any reason to continue holding her?"

"Her continued silence does suggest she might be implicated in some way," Blackmer said.

"But perhaps not in the crimes we've been investigating," Ro said.

"What do you mean?" said Blackmer.

"We've been assuming that Corazame is somehow involved in the break-in and then, tangentially, at least, in the murder," Ro said.

"Because she disappeared at exactly the right time," Blackmer said.

"But perhaps for entirely different reasons," Ro said. "I'm going to ask Odo to have a word with her. Try to get her to explain why she jumped ship and hid with the People."

"Odo?" Blackmer looked displeased.

"They struck up a rapport, apparently," Ro said. "She might open up to him where she won't open up to us. After all," she added carefully, conscious of Blackmer's displeasure, "Odo holds no official status on the station."

"I don't forget that," Blackmer said. He sighed. "Very well, let's see what Odo can get out of her."

Cory was used to solitude. She even liked it: a rare commodity in her life. Servers such as she had many workmates and comrades around them all the time (and their Ap-Rejs, of course, always watching to ensure that the Autarch was honored and obeyed through them), and Tzenkethi in general do not like to be far away from their own kind. So Cory did not mind sitting quietly, watching the world go by. She liked to observe, and she liked to think. Her old life had given her little opportunity for this, keeping her hands busy with her tasks and her thoughts busy with the orders of her Ap-Rej and the songs to the order of all things. The holding cells on Deep Space 9, by contrast, gave her all the time in the world. So Cory used it well, lying quietly on her bunk. Since her situation could not be fixed, she reasoned that there was little point in worrying. Something would happen to bring some change. Meanwhile she lay and contemplated all that she had seen since leaving Ab-Tzenketh. All that Peteh had given her.

Despite these gifts of patience and self-sufficiency, she was nonetheless glad to have a friendly visitor in the shape of Odo. The security man, Blackmeh, had been as unyielding as an enforcer, but without the stern charisma and steely beauty that made them a pleasure to obey. She had exchanged a few words with some of the other security staff, but they were mistrustful of their Tzenkethi guest and kept their distance. Odo, however, greeted her with a kindly smile.

"I'm sorry to find you here, Corazame," he said. "I hope you're comfortable at least."

Cory sat up. "I have no complaints."

Odo studied her carefully. "Usually," he said, "prisoners kept in holding cells greet me with grouses about the conditions of their incarceration, or demands to know when they will be released. Often they insist that I hear about their innocence. But not you."

"I am warm and dry, and I have eaten regularly."

There was a pause. "That covers the conditions of your incarceration," Odo said. "What about the rest?"

Corazame considered this. "I would like to be released, of course," she said. "I have told Commander Blackmeh that I am innocent of the crimes that he is investigating. My release must be conditional upon my innocence being demonstrated. Since I know I am innocent, I am content to wait here while that happens, if it puts the station staff at ease."

"Which is tremendously considerate of you," Odo said. "I wish there had been more prisoners like you during my own time as chief of security on this station. So you insist that you have nothing to do with the break-in at the medical facility?"

Cory shook her head. "I have been asked about this already. I know nothing about it."

"You do understand that concealing yourself among the People during this time looks suspicious?"

Cory turned a gentle eye upon him. "I know how it must appear. But I am not responsible. I am not a thief."

"Nor a murderer," Odo said.

Cory shuddered. "I would never kill." In her last moments on Ab-Tzenketh, Cory had seen somebody killed. It had been brutal and shocking. It had also bought her freedom. She had liked the man who had died, an undercover Starfleet Intelligence agent who had been her direct superior for several months, and she knew that Peteh still grieved for him. But only one person had escaped Ab-Tzenketh that day. Cory felt a keen sense of guilt about the price at which her departure had been bought, even though she had not chosen to leave but had been sent.

"Your file," said Odo, "makes for very interesting reading."

"I *am* a very ordinary person."

"Hardly! The only Tzenkethi that we customarily see have been sent by your government to spy on us, or else as diplomats to work against our interests. You are unique. And as for the manner of your escape—"

"But I *am* very ordinary," she insisted. "At home, I mean. I am—I was—part of a maintenance unit. A cleaner. I did not even have Ter status. I received instructions rather than gave them. I knelt to my superiors. I was one of the most ordinary people that you could meet."

"At home," said Odo. "But you're not at home now."

She blinked. "I am aware of that."

"You do not strike me as a stupid person, Corazame," Odo said. "You understand—don't you—the nature of the work that Peter Alden does?"

"Yes, I do."

"And you understand—don't you—that Starfleet Intelligence most likely wants to send you back to Ab-Tzenketh as their person on the ground? After all, who would be better placed to pass as Tzenkethi than a Tzenkethi? Far better than a human or other agent."

"It is true that the undercover agents I met made some very elementary mistakes when it came to our languages and customs."

Odo leaned in. "Was that the plan? Were you ever meant to go on board the *Athene Donald*? Were you always supposed to disappear here on DS9?"

Reluctantly, she said, "I was supposed to travel with Peteh on the *Athene Donald*. My absence was a surprise to him."

"I see. But what about returning to Ab-Tzenketh? Was that the eventual plan?"

Corazame sat back against the wall, curled her legs around herself, and closed her eyes.

"Corazame," said Odo, gently but firmly, "you must talk to me. Do you understand how suspicious your silence looks? Do you understand that it implicates you in a murder? That it makes it seem that you have been a double agent all along?"

Slowly, Cory dimmed her skin tone. If she could have made herself invisible, she would have done so.

"Do you realize that your legal status is very shaky? Do you understand what that means? You are not a citizen of the Federation. Captain Ro would be well within her rights to put you on the next ship back to Ab-Tzenketh. Her superiors may yet decide that this is the best thing to do with you."

A song came to her, one she had loved once upon a time. She remembered singing it at a Spring Festival, with her workmates. So long ago, that seemed.

She had been very happy then. Quietly, she began to sing the tune.

The year turns
The world turns
The springtime is here.
We praise you
Our Autarch
Whom we hold most dear!
We crave your indulgence
We long for your love.
Look down on your servants
From the Royal Moon above.

"Corazame," Odo said urgently, "please, listen to me! You are in real danger of being sent home. And if you are simply what you say you are—an ordinary person who got mixed up in a dangerous game—then I don't hold out much hope for you when you return. Please tell me why you came to DS9. Tell me what plans Starfleet Intelligence had for you. This is the only way that we will be able to protect you."

She sang the tune a little louder, but even that wasn't enough to drown out his sigh.

"Peter Alden isn't worthy of you," Odo said, and then he left her alone again. She lay back on the bunk and closed her eyes and pictured her home in the spring. Would they let her see it again? Would she have one last glimpse, before the end? Patiently, quietly, Corazame surrendered to whatever the future might hold.

Commander Peter Alden was proving to be a difficult man to pin down, but Odo grimly remained on the line until at last Alden appeared on the view screen, a severe and rather preoccupied young man.

"*Constable Odo,*" he said. "*What can I do for you?*"

"Odo will do. I am no longer a constable. I'm surprised that you recognize me."

"The Founder who won the Dominion War for the allies? You're very well known to me and my colleagues."

"Of course. Commander, I hope that you and your colleagues are well disposed toward me as a result, because I would like to speak to you about your friend Corazame."

"*Cory?*" Alden frowned. "*Is she okay?*"

"She thrives upon incarceration. No, that's not correct. She doesn't thrive, but she seems not to suffer any adverse effects."

"Ab-Tzenketh is one giant prison. Much prettier than the average jail, yes, but someone of Cory's class has very little in the way of freedom. I'm not surprised she's coping with being locked up. But surely Ro has no grounds to hold her? She can't still think Cory is responsible for what's been happening on DS9?"

"I believe the captain is still reserving judgment—"

Alden shook his head. "*This is ridiculous. I thought I made it clear to Ro that there was no need to hold Cory. She should let her go—*"

"But there lies the problem," Odo said. "Where, exactly, would she go?"

"I hope she would come and join me on the Athene Donald."

"Cory is very clear that she doesn't want to do that."

Alden sighed. "I know she's saying that, but it really would be for the best."

"So she is still not free to choose?"

Alden gave Odo a cold look. "*That's not the case. But Cory has led a sheltered life and she's much better off with me to look out for her. Look, do you think I could speak to Ro again?*"

"I'm sure you can speak to her whenever you like," said Odo. "But that might be too late for Corazame."

"Too late? What do you mean?"

"Corazame's legal status is unclear—"

Alden shook his head. "*She's an asylum seeker.*"

"Nevertheless, she remains in the Federation under certain conditions. Jumping ship and remaining on DS9—not to mention concealing her whereabouts—are most certainly not part of those conditions."

"I've explained this. She must have misunderstood the departure time—"

Odo shifted impatiently in his seat. "Come now, Commander! Don't treat me like a fool! I've spoken to Corazame. She had no intention of traveling on the *Athene Donald*, and you know that. I'm prepared to believe that this was not your plan for her, but it was certainly her plan for herself. And unfortunately that puts her in violation of the conditions placed upon her remaining in Federation space. This means she's likely to be deported—unless somebody is willing to speak up on her behalf."

Alden had gone very still. "*You can't send her back to Ab-Tzenketh. That's as good as killing her!*"

Odo held up his hands. "There's nothing that I can do. I'm merely the messenger."

"*You are the person who ended the Dominion War,*" Alden said. "*I'm sure that you can influence whoever you choose.*"

"Perhaps I could. But why should I do that?"

"*Because Cory is innocent!*" Alden was starting to sound frantic. *Good*, Odo thought. "*They'll destroy her if she returns to Ab-Tzenketh!*"

"You misunderstand me," Odo said. "What I meant was why should I speak up on Corazame's account when *you* are not prepared to?" He leaned forward in his seat. "Whatever plans you had for her," he said softly, "now is the time to admit to them. Corazame seems to be keeping silent out of a misguided sense of loyalty to you. If *you* won't protect her, then she's lost."

Alden sat for a while in thought. Eventually, he said, "*I suspect you've guessed most of it. Yes, the plan was to send her back to Ab-Tzenketh eventually to work on our behalf. But not for a while. She wasn't anywhere near ready. She's still . . ."*

"Innocent?"

"*Yes, that.*" Alden sighed. "*I thought she was willing. I thought she understood our reasons. Apparently not.*" He shook his head. "*I shouldn't be telling you any of this.*"

"It's way past time someone acted on Corazame's behalf."

"I suppose so. I can't have her deported . . ."

"Not least because she knows a great deal about you," Odo pointed out. "I'm sure the Tzenkethi would like to find out everything Corazame knows about such a key figure in Tzenkethi Affairs."

"That's not the reason why."

"I'll give you the benefit of the doubt."

"I'm not proud of any of this. But Cory was a unique opportunity."

"She's not an opportunity," Odo said. "She's a person."

"Don't twist my words! You know what I mean!"

"I'm rather afraid that I do."

"Isn't it enough to know how she would be treated if she went home for you to fight these people? You should understand, given how the Founders treated the Jem'Hadar."

Odo gave a low warning rumble of anger. "It's a risk you were prepared to have her run if she went back there working for you."

"We're not that callous! She'd have a new identity.

She'd be safe! The last thing we want is for her to get caught—"

"Of course not," Odo said sourly. "She is a unique opportunity."

"*Yes, she was,*" Alden said. "*She was going to do good work for us—help us stop the Tzenkethi attempting to undermine our interests at every turn.*"

"There are better ways to prevent that," Odo said.

"Such as?"

"Get to know each other better. Work together."

"That's a fantasy. A pleasant one, but a fantasy nonetheless."

"That's what happened in the end with the Founders," Odo said. "Perhaps a little time on the *Athene Donald*, working with the Tzenkethi as colleagues rather than adversaries, might work wonders for your perceptions of them."

"*I've spent a lot of time among the Tzenkethi. I know enough about them. That was another reason for wanting Cory here, of course,*" Alden said. "*I wanted her to get as close as possible to Metiger."* He laughed. *"Not that Metiger would have much time for someone like Cory. I doubt she would lower herself to speak to Cory directly. They're such* charming *people!*"

That, Odo thought, took some nerve, coming from this man. "I assume you had some less than legal activity planned on the *Athene Donald*."

Alden stared back and did not reply.

"Corazame would do her best to protect you from

any potentially negative consequences. She believes she is in debt to you."

"*I'm sorry,*" Alden said, and he seemed to be genuine. But who could tell? The man's trade was duplicity. "*Tell her that. Will you tell her that? Tell her I'm sorry. That she should do whatever she wants with the rest of her life. I won't come looking for her, and I'll stop my superiors from coming looking for her too—as best I can.*"

"That might not make her feel particularly safe."

"It's the best I can do. She's . . . she's not to feel she owes me anything. She doesn't owe me anything."

"This is all very noble of you, Commander, but it's all moot while she remains a suspect in this murder."

Alden sat in thought for a while. "*If we found out who did that,*" he said at last, "*would she be able to go?*"

"It might help," Odo said. "But you'd better hurry. Sending her home is an increasingly attractive option for the powers that be."

"*All right,*" Alden said. "*I'll hurry. But please, in the meantime—hold Ro off from making any decision about sending her back.*"

"I'll try," said Odo.

"*Thank you,*" said Alden.

"I'm not doing it for you," said Odo, and cut the comm.

"I gather you're hoping to get on board the Chain ship," Delka said. She had come to see Pulaski in her office. "Any particular reason why?"

"Is curiosity not a good enough reason?"

Delka gave an unnervingly rapacious smile. "It would be—if it was the only reason. But it's not, is it?"

Pulaski snorted with laughter. "Not much gets past you, does it? Should I be telling my intentions to a representative of a foreign power? I suspect not."

"That's a big ship pointing its weapons at us," Delka said. "We're all in this together."

"Fair point. Yes, I do want to get on board that ship. I think I've worked out a way of identifying individual DNA from their species. That will help us find out whoever committed the assault on our visitor, and also whoever committed the murder on DS9."

"So what's the problem?"

"The test doesn't work yet and I need more samples."

"You don't think someone from the *Athene Donald* was responsible for the assault?" Delka said.

"No," said Pulaski.

"Not Metiger?"

"Certainly not!"

Delka's eyes narrowed. "And Peter Alden?"

Pulaski paused before answering. "I don't like spies. I think I've made that clear."

"You've left me in no doubt."

"Maybe Alden and his associate back on DS9 *have* somehow orchestrated this between them. But it can't be coincidence that this all started when members of the Chain met us, while others of the same species arrived on DS9. There'll be a connection somehow. But I need to get onto that ship if I'm going to prove it."

"All right," said Delka. "I'm persuaded. I'll get you on board."

"Don't make promises you can't keep," said Pulaski.

"I never do," said Delka.

"You know from all that we have told you that we are here to learn," said Delka. "That's the mission of our ship—our sole purpose in traveling. We want to understand you better."

Aoi wasn't biting, Pulaski thought. The alien's pale unblinking eyes showed a distinct lack of interest in what Delka was saying.

"More particularly," Delka said, "we want to understand what we can do to help."

Aoi's eyelids narrowed, ever so slightly.

"We are as frustrated as you by the delay in answering your request to return the People to your care. We would like to be able to put your case more fully to the people making the decisions back on DS9. If Doctor Tanj can only explain your position fully . . ." Delka smiled. "And of course the aid of a superior species will no doubt be invaluable in helping us persuade the people back on DS9 to make the right decision."

"A what?" Pulaski muttered. "Come off it, Delka, Aoi's not going to fall for that . . ."

"Our rule is not to meddle in the business of lesser species," Aoi said. *"This includes you."*

" 'Lesser species'? I'll 'lesser species' you," Pulaski growled. Delka laid a restraining hand upon her arm.

The ghost of a smile passed across Aoi's narrow face, the transitory amusement of someone ancient when confronted with the hotheaded impudence of the young. *"I am permitted to make some exceptions. You may come on board,"* Aoi said, and the comm cut. A series of instructions followed shortly afterward: no more than two people from the *Athene Donald*, a specific time, and using the Chain's transporters.

"I'll be honest and say I didn't think you'd manage that," Pulaski said.

"I know you didn't," said Delka.

"And I can't quite believe that tack worked."

"We have nothing to bargain with," Delka explained. "We have nothing that they want—other than the People of the Open Sky. Aoi knows that we have no power to hand them over. But hinting that we are breaking rank with our own people and supporting them? I thought it was worth a try." Delka breathed out suddenly in relief. "I'm glad that worked!"

"And the other stuff? All that business about being a superior power?"

"Everyone likes a little flattery," Delka said. "Speaking of which, I imagine Peter Alden will want to come across. He's not going to pass up the chance to get on board that ship."

Pulaski sighed. "I fear you may be right. But he's going to be a disappointed man."

Delka cocked her head. "Why not simply let him go?"

"Because I'm a stubborn old woman and I don't like him. Isn't that enough?"

Delka was right. Pulaski, answering a request to come to Tanj's office, discovered Alden already there with Tanj.

"Now, don't get angry," Tanj said, "but the commander has asked to go across with you and I think it's a good idea." She lifted her hand in anticipation of the onslaught that was bound to follow this statement, but Alden spoke first.

"I'm asking this as a favor, Doctor Pulaski. I understand that you're working on devising a DNA test that will differentiate among individual members of the Chain's species. I think I can help, but I must have access to that ship. Please—let me come along with you."

Pulaski turned to Tanj and gave her a hard stare. "Did you tell him all this?"

Wearily, Tanj said, "We're all in this together. Aoi isn't going to continue being patient with us. If Peter thinks he can help in some way, perhaps it's worth listening to what he has to say."

"Oh, it's 'Peter' now, is it?" Pulaski turned a sharp eye toward her bête noire. "Go on, then, *Peter*—what do you think you can do for me?"

Alden folded his arms. "If you want a more accurate test, you're going to need more tissue samples. Am I right?"

Pulaski shrugged.

"So how do you propose to do that?" Alden asked. "I assume you're not going to set up a stall over there and ask them to line up one by one while you take swabs?"

Pulaski, hardly an expert in subterfuge, had been struggling to think of a way to achieve exactly this. Bullishly, she said, "I'll think of something."

Alden smiled. "You don't have a clue, do you? That's all right. You don't need to think of anything. I already have."

"I won't be party to anything illegal or unethical—"

"No? Doctor, you disappoint me."

"I'm sure you'll live with the disappointment," Pulaski said. "Why do you want to come with me anyway?"

"Why else?" Alden's smile broadened. "Because my superiors want me to have a good look around that ship."

"Oh, of course!"

"Yes, you'd like that to be the reason, wouldn't you? But things are never that simple." He took a deep breath. "If what you're doing can clear Cory in any way, then I want to help."

"You haven't exactly jumped forward before now to help her," Pulaski pointed out. "What's caused this change of heart?"

Alden's whole demeanor altered. He looked tired

and worried. "They're threatening to send her back to Ab-Tzenketh," he said in a quieter voice. "They're saying that by staying on DS9 when the *Athene Donald* left she violated the terms under which she can remain in the Federation, and that she has to go back. I can't let that happen—"

Pulaski laughed. "No, I don't think your bosses would be pleased if you let an asset like her slip through your fingers—"

Suddenly, Alden lost his temper. Gray eyes flashing like steel, he snapped back, "For god's sake, why is it impossible for you to believe that I might be acting in good faith? She's my *friend*! I have a responsibility toward her. I don't want her to come to any harm. If Cory returns to Ab-Tzenketh, they'll kill her! Not quickly—slowly. They'll pull her apart and they'll take their time over it."

"So speak to your bosses," Pulaski said. "If she's so valuable—to you and to them—then I bet they can prevent Ro from sending her home." She studied him closely. He was staring at his feet. "You haven't told them about any of this, have you? Do they think you told her to stay on DS9?"

Alden bit his lower lip.

Pulaski gave a bark of laughter. "Oh, mister! You'd better have one *hell* of a good plan for getting those samples!"

Alden flashed a rakish smile.

"Go on." Pulaski was intrigued in spite of herself. "What is it?"

Alden lifted up his right hand. "By the pricking of my thumbs, something wicked this way comes."

Pulaski, grasping what he planned, laughed again. "We come in peace," she said. "Mostly."

Beside them, Tanj sighed. "I've no idea what you're planning, and it's probably better that I don't know. But can I take it as settled that Peter will be joining you when you go onto the Chain ship, Kitty?"

Pulaski nodded. "Settled."

"Good," said Tanj. "I'm sure that you'll work together like the professionals you both are."

"Oh, yes," said Alden dryly. "We're a screwball comedy in the making."

Ten

Captain's Log, Personal.

A great deal of what I have written thus far assumes that our mission involves an encounter with species hitherto unknown to the Federation, and this is often the case during deep space voyages. But the captain of a Starfleet vessel—even one equipped for and tasked with exploration—may also find himself or herself involved in diplomacy with species that have long been known to us.

This brings unique challenges in turn. Even to the most open of minds, prior knowledge of such species brings with it certain preconceptions—prejudices, even—that Romulans will be duplicitous, Cardassians bombastic, Klingons warlike. These assumptions can easily distort one's dealings with such species.

It is extremely difficult when dealing with familiar species, but particularly in the case of species with which one has been at war, to approach individual representatives with an open mind and bring to the encounter a freshness that allows one to achieve understanding. But this is what the true explorer must do: be prepared to leave behind one's preconceptions and approach each meeting as an opportunity to learn something new. A closed mind will see nothing other than what it already knows—but there is always something else to discover . . .

"An interesting introduction to your station, Captain Ro," said Varis. "Is it usually so chaotic here?"

Ro gave the other woman a frosty smile. "Commanding a space station is never easy. But I have to say that I'd far rather do that than move paperwork around. I don't know why people accept military commissions when they really want to be bureaucrats."

If Varis realized she was being insulted, she didn't show it. "It was alarming to see such strength of feeling outside our consulate," she said. "What do you intend to do about that?"

"My chief of security will get matters under control," Ro said.

"As I recall, he needed my assistance. Perhaps rather than simply bringing out the security team when a riot occurs, the underlying cause should be addressed?"

Ro leaned back in her chair. "If you know of a way to make Cardassians and Romulans friendlier, Major, I'll be happy to listen. But the solution lies squarely in your hands. The Cardassians outside your consulate were requesting the return home of their prisoners of war from the end of the Dominion War. Which falls under *your* jurisdiction . . ."

Varis waved her hand impatiently. "Security on the station is not my concern."

"But the prisoners of war are."

"We can come to that in a moment. First I want your assurances that the Cardassians will not be allowed to besiege our consulate in this way again."

"*Besiege*? That's not what happened."

"That's how it seemed—"

"It was a protest that got noisy, that's all." Ro shook her head firmly. "I'm sorry, but I can't stop the Cardassians protesting. This is a Federation space station: freedom of expression is a cherished right. The Plaza is a place where anyone is free to say whatever he or she likes. I can get involved only if trouble arises as a result of their protest."

"Which you must admit is likely to happen with so many Bajorans on the station," Varis said.

"Bajorans are free to make their opinion known too."

Varis frowned. "This is hardly the signal of mutual respect that my government was hoping to receive from the Federation."

"No, it's not," said Ro. "Neither is your government's unwillingness to answer questions about the Cardassian prisoners of war." In fact, Ro wasn't entirely convinced that the Romulan government cared one way or the other about the prisoners. It was Varis who seemed to be the sticking point.

"Nevertheless, it was extremely unpleasant to see," Varis said. "I'd hate to have to mention it to my superiors in my report."

A report back to her superiors? So Varis wasn't

here entirely under her own volition. Ro smiled to herself. She wasn't sure if Varis knew what she had let slip, but Ro was going to press her advantage as far as she could.

"I'm sorry that your introduction to my station wasn't as welcoming as it could have been," Ro said smoothly. "We shouldn't let that get in the way of our conversation. Tell me, why exactly are you here?"

Varis looked past her. "This is an unusually difficult case," she said. "I have a passing interest in it."

Rubbish, thought Ro. *You're in as much trouble as I am. My superiors don't want to see a minor issue like this ruin the possibility of détente, and neither do yours. So what's the problem? Why don't you tell me what's going on?* To Varis, she said, "I'm glad that we're talking now and I hope we can carry on in this vein. As a first step, I suggest you speak to the families concerned. Nestor Pa'Dan is anxious to meet you—"

"If they were among the protestors," Varis said quickly, "a meeting would not be appropriate. We can't be seen to be bowing to such pressure."

"Nobody would see," said Ro. "It would be a private meeting. I'd get assurances from the people concerned that it would remain confidential."

Varis sighed.

There's something else here, Ro thought, *something you're keeping quiet, to the extent that I don't think even your superiors know about it. And now you're on the spot, because you've been ordered to sort this issue out.*

"Major," Ro said quietly, "are these people still alive?"

"What do you mean?"

"You know what I mean."

Realization dawned, and Varis shot her a furious look. "These were prisoners of war!"

"On the Cardassian-Romulan front. I've heard the stories. *Everyone* has heard the stories."

"Whatever the Romulans may be, we at least are not monsters!" Varis shot back. "I'm surprised to find a Bajoran prepared to believe such a thing of us—and on account of some Cardassians!"

"You won't believe how sick I get of hearing that as a Bajoran I should be holding the Cardassians in contempt," Ro said. "Don't push that one any farther with me. If a war crime has been committed, it doesn't matter who the victims are—the perpetrators should be punished. That means Cardassians during the Occupation and Romulans during the Dominion War." She paused. "You didn't answer my question. Are these people dead?"

There was a pause. Then, grudgingly, Varis said, "No."

Ro nodded. That, at least, was some good news to take to Mhevita Pa'Dan. "And are they in good health?"

"They were the last time I saw them," said Varis.

"And when was that?"

Another pause. "Last week."

"Last *week*?" Ro fell back in her chair. "You and I

were talking by that point! Did you not think I might be interested to hear that you'd seen Terek Pa'Dan and the rest?"

"It was only a brief conversation—"

"You *spoke* to them? *Kosst*, Major, what is going on here? Where are these people being held? *Why?*"

"They are not being held. They remain quite willingly."

"Willingly?"

"I said that this was an unusually difficult case." Varis sighed. "Captain, if I gave you my word that the people concerned are all well, happy, and living a life they have chosen, would you press this issue no farther?"

Ro considered this. "I can believe that you don't give your word lightly—"

"Thank you."

"But I can't let this lie. It's gone too far now. The castellan requires answers—"

"As you know," said Varis dryly, "I would have preferred it if the castellan had not become involved."

"Yes, I gathered that. But unfortunately that's where we are now. The castellan *is* involved, and more than that, his political opponents are using the case to stir up public opinion against him. Hence the trouble you saw on the Plaza. Castellan Garak is not a happy man. I don't know about you, but that makes me slightly uneasy."

"I see." Varis pressed her hands together before her face.

"My superiors want answers too," Ro went on. "And—if you'll forgive me—I think that's the same for you and *your* superiors."

Varis raised her eyebrows. Then she gave a short, brusque nod. "All right. I'll speak to Pa'Dan and the rest. But I want to be very clear that I'm not bowing to any pressure—whether from the castellan or from Starfleet. I would also like to see a resolution—as discreetly as possible, please, Captain, if that could be arranged."

By which you mean without your superiors finding out whatever secret you're keeping.

"We're talking the same language, Major," Ro said. "I'm sure we can find a way through this. I'm sure that we can be sensitive to the needs of *all* parties concerned."

Despite the conciliatory note on which that conversation ended, Varis was late for the meeting with Pa'Dan and the other Cardassians in the new briefing room: not very late, but sufficiently that the nestor began to get anxious.

"Are you sure she will come, Captain? Did you make clear the time and the place? She would not return to Romulus without seeing us?"

Ro assured Pa'Dan that the major would come, although after twenty minutes she began to feel anxious herself. But Varis did appear—prim, uniformed, and standoffish. Ro wasn't surprised by this show of formality. Yes, she would be keen—for whatever reason—to keep her superiors off her back, but she would also want to make as clear as possible that she was the one calling the shots.

Ro took her seat at the head of the table, with Odo to her left. The Cardassians—four in total, including Pa'Dan—gathered on one side of the table; Varis on the other.

"Nestor Pa'Dan," Ro said gently, after the introductions had been made. "Perhaps you might like to say a little about why you're here."

"Why we're *here*? To get news of our children, of course!" Pa'Dan turned away from Ro to address Varis directly. "You know something about my son, don't you?"

Varis didn't reply.

"You knew he was alive—all this time you knew he was alive! You know where he is right now, don't you?"

Varis still didn't answer. She folded her hands on the table in front of her and examined them rather than look at Pa'Dan.

"My son's name is Terek," said Pa'Dan. "Look. Here. Here he is." She pushed forward a holo of a young male, handsome even by Cardassian standards. "This was taken the year before he was caught in Dukat's Draft. Look, here he is receiving his license from the School of Art in Cemet. He was the best sculptor in his year. Here he is as a boy . . ." Pa'Dan stopped speaking for a moment as she looked at those images. "I could show you more, many more. All of us here could. These are our sons, our daughters. Our *children.* We are desperate for news of them. Why won't you help us?"

Varis looked up from her hands. She glanced briefly at the images of Terek Pa'Dan. "How strange," she said, "that Cardassians require licenses in order to be able to produce and display art."

"That's not the case any longer, in fact," Odo said. "And I fail to see how this is relevant."

"I'm merely reflecting on the differences between us," Varis said. "No Romulans would be so cowed by their government. But you're right—a great deal has changed about Cardassian society. For one thing, there is a greater tendency toward unruliness." She pushed the images back toward Pa'Dan—gently but firmly. "There can be no more public demonstrations, here on DS9 or anywhere. I must have this assurance."

"Is that all?" Pa'Dan said. "Is that all you have to say to us? Do you understand how desperate we are?"

"Nevertheless, I must insist. No more demonstrations."

Ro watched Pa'Dan carefully. She knew that this tactic hardly sat well with the nestor, and while the whole business had caused Ro numerous headaches, she sympathized with Pa'Dan's plight. What else was the woman supposed to do?

"Why?" said Pa'Dan. "Why should we stop?" Her hands and her voice were shaking—she looked frail, Ro thought. Recent events were starting to take their toll. "What have you done to make us feel that we should stop? Why should we believe that we are being heard?"

Varis turned to Ro. "There can be no further discussion if these people insist on using such aggressive tactics as they have done so far."

"Aggressive?" Ro said mildly. "All they've done is stand outside your consulate and ask for some questions to be answered."

"The consulate was attacked!"

"No," said Ro, "that's incorrect. The *Cardassians* were attacked—verbally, at least. Admittedly, they hit back, but the consulate wasn't the target at any point."

"We will not have demands made on us in this way."

Ro held up her hand. "This is a distraction. All these people want is news—real news—about their missing family members." She reached for the holopics and pushed them under Varis's nose. "You can save these people a lot of heartache. Why are you so resistant?"

Varis studiously avoided looking at the pictures. "You've heard my condition. No more attacks on our consulate."

"You've heard my response," Ro said. "There have been no attacks, and I'll not prevent anyone from expressing an opinion on this station. And, if I'm not mistaken, Nestor Pa'Dan is not prepared to back down either."

"Please, Major Varis," Pa'Dan said softly. "Tell us *something*. Then we'll be quiet again. But until then?" Pa'Dan shook her head. "For the sake of our sons and our daughters, we will not be silenced."

"That's a great shame." Varis stood up. "I'll be here on the station for the next two days. If you change your mind, Nestor, and can assure me that there will be no more demonstrations, then perhaps we can talk once again." She nodded to Ro and Odo.

"I don't understand this," Ro said to Odo, after she had gone. "What's the sticking point?"

Odo shrugged. "A puzzle to me too. Perhaps she's been given specific orders. Perhaps there's something she has to conceal . . ." He glanced over at his friend. "I hope it's not bad news."

"She said that she'd spoken to them recently," Ro pointed out. "So why this posturing? What's the mystery here?"

"Nobody likes to lose face," Odo said. He turned to Pa'Dan. "This is still progress," he said. "Varis is talking to us now, at least."

But tears were rolling down Pa'Dan's face. "Am I doing the right thing, Odo?"

Odo glanced at Ro. "You know what we think about these demonstrations," he said frankly. "But it's up to you to decide what's best."

"I feel more hopeless than ever," Pa'Dan said. "Perhaps I should give up. Perhaps I should go home and put out the *perek* flowers for my boy, and chant his name and say good-bye."

"Don't do that," Ro said. "Don't give up." She thought of her own mother, who had given up on life. Given up on *her*. "Don't say that he's dead until you have proof. He wouldn't want that."

"If he's still alive," said Pa'Dan. "Varis could have lied to you."

"She *could*, but I don't think she has." Ro leaned over and gently placed her hand upon the other woman's. "We'll work this out. We'll bring them home."

Would they notice, Pulaski wondered, that Peter Alden was making such a point of shaking hands with everyone who passed him? And would they notice that every so often he apologized for not cutting his nails?

"I'm sorry," said Alden, after shaking hands with yet another alien and drawing blood yet again. "I really must cut my nails."

All this cloak-and-dagger business was such nonsense. A quick glance down at Alden's hands would show that his nails were bitten down to the quick. A tense man, Peter Alden. But perhaps they didn't know what nails were, Pulaski thought. She suppressed the laughter suddenly bubbling up inside her. Perhaps they thought this was a standard part of a human greeting. She pictured representatives from the Chain arriving in the Federation, stopping everyone they met and solemnly proffering their long thin hands: *We are sorry*, they would say gravely to each passing stranger. *We really must cut our nails.*

She looked at Alden. He seemed to be having a whale of a time. Perhaps because he was proving to her how indispensable he was; perhaps because he liked the risk he was taking. With every long thin hand that Alden shook, he was snagging the flesh with a microscopically small needle and thereby collecting the samples that Pulaski wanted. "If you get caught," she'd said, when Alden explained the details of his plan, "I'm denying all knowledge. You'll be on your own, mister."

"Kitty," he'd replied, "'twas ever thus."

And this pantomime was getting in the way of her concentrating on being on the Chain ship at last—although somehow it was turning out to be exactly as Pulaski had imagined it. Steely halls filled with sleek but opaque black equipment, none of which seemed to show any visible controls. Tall and lugubrious aliens, one of whom was now leading them along a metaled corridor, communicated tersely through clicks and whistles that she could not decipher. Others glanced their way, but without much interest in their guests, and what appeared to be salutes were exchanged at every available opportunity. The whole place was horribly claustrophobic.

"Stuffier than even the stuffiest Starfleet vessel," Pulaski muttered to Alden.

"Fewer laughs than the funniest Tzenkethi ship," Alden replied.

Pulaski eyed him. "Perhaps you'll tell me about that one day," she said.

"Perhaps," he said.

They were brought into a spherical room that contained a large round black table and nothing else: no pictures on the stark walls; no decoration—not even a rivet. The room was entirely smooth and featureless. At the far end stood the tallest and most lugubrious alien they had seen so far. Tey Aoi, Pulaski presumed. Aoi came around to greet them, and Alden grasped and pumped the long pale hand.

"*Don't say it*," muttered Pulaski, but Alden was already grinning.

"I'm *so* sorry," he said. "I really *must* cut my nails."

Aoi looked down at Alden's hand. There was a moment's pause, during which Pulaski held her breath, and then Aoi let go of Alden's hand and, turning to the alien who had brought them here, issued a clicked instruction. Their guide took a few steps back and stood quietly waiting by the door.

"So now you find yourselves aboard our ship," said Aoi. "I hope sincerely it is to your liking."

"It's ever so impressive!" Alden was beaming like an idiot. "I mean— wow! Look at it! Amazing! We're incredibly honored to be here. Aren't we, Doctor?"

"What?"

"Honored. Us. To be here. Once-in-a-lifetime opportunity, isn't it?"

"Oh, yes," said Pulaski. "Hard to think of anything better that has ever happened to me."

Aoi eyed them for a moment and then sat down, without extending an offer to either of them to do the same. "I bring you here for one quite simple reason. So that you will understand that my demand to come into possession of the People is that exactly—not a request but a demand. I will not rest until I have them."

Pulaski glanced at Alden. The playfulness that had hitherto been at the fore had vanished. "We're not in the business of handing over people who have come to us in friendship," Alden said softly. "Particularly when there's a threat behind the request—"

"You may be members of a lesser species," said Aoi, "but you are not fools. You understand. The People will be handed over to me, willingly or not. Take back this message to your superior officers." Aoi glanced at the alien waiting behind them and issued a few short whistles. Then, to Pulaski and Alden: "Time runs short."

And so they were dismissed. The alien standing behind them moved forward and gestured to them to follow. They were led back down the corridor toward the small chamber in which they first arrived. When they reached this room again, their guide stopped, looked around, and then whispered: "Listen now! Not all of us want to pursue the People! The Tey, we think, is wrong in this. They deserve their freedom!"

Pulaski opened her mouth to ask a question, but the black ship shimmered around her, and the familiar surroundings of the *Athene Donald* were there once more. Pulaski turned to Alden. "I didn't expect that."

Alden was tugging at one ear. "No, neither did I. It seems they're not as uniform as they'd like to appear."

"Who is?" said Pulaski, and shuddered. "I didn't like it over there. There's something nasty in that particular woodshed."

"I agree," said Alden. "There's something . . . *hard* about them. Worse. There's a rot beneath all that glamour."

"You'd know all about that, would you?"

"I've been on Ab-Tzenketh," he said simply. He reached up his sleeve and handed her the tiny tricorder hidden there. "I think this is what you need. I hope I'll be able to pass on good news to Cory soon."

But even with the samples Alden had collected, Pulaski found that analyzing them was a laborious process.

"It's taken sixteen hours to isolate the cell structures in the first one," she complained to Tanj, who had come to her office to check on the progress being made. "I've never seen anything like their DNA before—shifting all the time! It's hard to tell what's significant and what's not." She sighed. "I think I've got a good basic model, though."

"But you're still not even sure that your test will work?" asked Tanj. "You still have no idea whether or not it's actually possible to identify individual DNA?"

"Of course I'll be able to do that," Pulaski replied testily. "But it might take some time."

"Kitty, I don't think Tey Aoi is going to give us that time. Is there anything you can do to speed things up?"

Miles O'Brien came to the rescue, as he so often did.

"*Sounds like a job for the transporter,*" he said. "*I can use it to target specific extraneous structures in the cells and filter them out. If we do that to all the samples, that should speed up the analysis.*"

Pulaski nodded. "Sounds like a good plan to me."

O'Brien smiled. "*Saved by the transporter again, eh?*"

"All right," Pulaski muttered. "Don't rub it in."

The filtering worked, and by the end of the day, Pulaski believed she had a set of samples from both the Chain ship and DS9 that she could compare with the samples taken from Crusher's office as well as those taken from the murder weapon and after the assault. And there was a match. A single, impossible match. The murderer, the assailant, the burglar—they were one and the same person. "*Who?*" Pulaski muttered. "*And, more to the point—how?*"

"That's Ailoi," said Crusher. "But that's not possible! The murderer, maybe, and the burglar—but how could Ailoi have been on the *Athene Donald* to carry out the attack?"

"*I don't know, Beverly, but that's what the test says. That's what the science says.*"

"Is it at all possible," said Crusher tentatively, "that you could have made a mistake?"

"Of course it's possible, *but I don't think I have! Look, I'm not being awkward old Katherine Pulaski here. I'm not bragging, I'm not being big-headed, and I'm not being any of the other things that everyone thinks I am. But I'm not wrong either."*

Carefully, meticulously, Crusher went through Pulaski's work. "No," she said slowly, "I don't think you're wrong either. But still it's not possible! How can it be the same person on the station and on your ship? Could it be twins?"

"*Oh, give me a break*," said Pulaski. "*Look, do you have an image of this Ailoi? Can you send it over to me?*"

"On its way." Crusher waited while the file reached Pulaski and saw the other woman's eyes widen in recognition and alarm.

"*But that's the security officer who took me and Alden about the Chain ship! Beverly, it's the same person! Beverly?*" Pulaski's voice became anxious. "*Beverly?*"

But Beverly Crusher couldn't answer. Long hands had grabbed her from behind, and thin fingers, snake-like and terribly supple, were covering her mouth and inching their way up toward her nose to smother her. She struggled, desperately, but her assailant was strong, the fingers relentless. Gagging and choking, she again tried to push back—and then, distantly, she heard her office door burst open and Blackmer's voice, yelling out: "Stop! Let her go! I'll shoot!"

Then, suddenly, the hands and the fingers were no longer there. They were gone as quickly as they had come. Crusher caught a whiff of something burning in the air. She fell to the floor, gasping, her own hands coming up protectively to her throat. Dimly, she realized that Ro was beside her, hand upon her back. "It's all right," Ro was saying. "You'll be fine. You'll be fine."

"The bastard's gone," she heard O'Brien say from across the room. "And who knows what the range of that transporter could be?"

"When you've eliminated the impossible . . ." said O'Brien.

"I know," said Crusher wearily. "I've played the same holodeck programs. Whatever remains, no matter how improbable, must be the truth. But how can one person be on DS9, the *Athene Donald*, and the Chain ship all at the same time?"

"Transwarp beaming," said O'Brien promptly.

"Is that even *possible*?" said Crusher.

"We don't know much about what the Chain can do," O'Brien pointed out. "But if they *do* have transwarp beaming, that explains how somebody could commit a theft and a murder on DS9, and an assault on the *Athene Donald* star systems away."

"I suppose it would also explain how somebody could enter Ioile's quarters without being seen," Crusher said slowly. "I guess our usual methods of tracing transporters wouldn't be any use?"

"Not entirely true," O'Brien said, "although you have to know what you're looking for. I had a quick look at those samples Doctor Pulaski sent over. One of them showed some cellular damage that suggested transwarp beaming. I bet if we checked, it would turn out to be Ailoi's. Anyway, I was curious, so I rigged up a detector to alert me if anything like that was used on the station again. That's how we knew Ailoi had been transported into your office."

"And that's how you were all there exactly when I needed you." Crusher touched her throat. "I dread to think what would have happened if you'd been much later. Thank you, Miles."

"All part of the service."

"Do we have any idea where Ailoi might be now?"

O'Brien shook his head. "Not a clue. Back on the Chain ship, probably. But it doesn't have to be that far. No reason why Ailoi couldn't still be here on DS9."

Crusher shuddered. "I hope not."

"Still, Blackmer's looking."

"Hope springs eternal," Crusher said. Gently, she rubbed her throat and neck.

"Doesn't still hurt, does it?" said O'Brien

"No, it's fine." She sighed. "But now I have to go and explain all this to Oioli."

Oioli met the news that Ailoi was a crew member of the Chain ship with dismay. "I knew they had a hand in this but not how far their reach was!"

"Did you have no idea at all?" said Crusher. "When did Ailoi come on board? Not at the start of your journey?"

"No, not then, but later on," Oioli said. "Our fame had gone before us. Ailoi came from our homeworld to travel with the People." The marks around Oioli's throat were very dark. Crusher, who was starting to be able to read these signs, recognized anger. "But not to live with us, it seems," Oioli continued. "To watch, to spy, to listen. I know this kind. They are the rot that will destroy our people."

"Whatever the reason for traveling with you, Blackmer has not been able to find any trace of Ailoi on DS9. And given what we know now about the range of the Chain's transporter, Ailoi could be anywhere—on DS9, on the Chain ship—"

"Ailoi could be farther now—back upon our homeworld."

"That's an even greater range than we guessed." Crusher frowned. "Did you know that the Chain had transwarp beaming at their disposal? I understand if it's a technology you take for granted, but it would have made life a lot easier if you'd mentioned it sooner."

Oioli's head was shaking. "I did not know of such a thing. I did know it was wanted. I left my world because of this—this and other reasons. New gadgetry, new toys, new tools—and yet no end to misery. This is not how I want to live. I do not want such trinkets. I want a life that values life. I did not know they had this."

Oioli sat brooding for a while and, as Crusher watched, the markings, which had turned jet-black, slowly returned to something close to their usual olive green. "I think perhaps that Aoi and I should take the time to speak now," Oioli said slowly. "There are questions that I have that Aoi must answer."

Crusher nodded. "I'll speak to Captain Ro. She'll get it done."

Ro arranged for the conversation with Aoi to happen under the pretext of having come to a decision about returning the People. When Aoi appeared on the view screen, Crusher was struck by the resemblance to Oioli. Yes, members of their species were very similar in general, more so than Crusher felt comfortable admitting, but this likeness was particularly close.

"Well now, Tey Aoi," Oioli said, voice quiet, "do you remember Oioli? I've kept my peace on your account, but this has gone too far now. Did you know spies were on our ship? Is this how far you've fallen?"

Crusher caught one quick glance of Aoi's expression, furious and stormy. Then the comm was cut.

Eleven

Captain's Log, Personal.

What constitutes a successful outcome to a first-contact mission? To diplomacy? To exploration?

Perhaps it is easiest first to say what constitutes failure. It surely goes without saying that the outbreak of war must constitute the greatest and most grievous of failures. But any historian worth his or her salt would say that it is hardly conceivable that a single encounter would cause such a deleterious outcome. We may wish for history to be straightforward—to be able to find single chains of cause and effect—but in truth the universe is complex. War arises as a result of multiple factors over a long period of time. We should not fall into the trap of pride, assuming that our actions have such great significance.

There are moments when a captain must face up to the truth that a mission has been a failure—with the loss of a crew member, or any loss of life. It is some small consolation here to bear in mind that even the most unsuccessful mission may hold within it some promise of future success. One day, the knowledge acquired might be of use, of value—perhaps when least expected . . .

Metiger had been an impressive sight, Pulaski said, but Tey Aoi, appearing suddenly in Tanj's office, certainly gave her a run for her money. Tanj attempted a formal greeting, but Aoi turned at once to Pulaski and Alden. "Explain again to me why you came over. You did not wish to learn—"

"No," said Pulaski, shaking her head. "We would like to learn from you, although I doubt you would have been willing to teach. We came on board because we believed one of your people was responsible for the assault on the *Athene Donald*, and that there was a connection with the murder committed on Deep Space 9. We wanted evidence. And what do you know? We were right to want it!"

"You both came over under false pretenses. You lied to get yourselves on board our ship—"

"*We* lied?" Pulaski gave a hoot of laughter. "You've got some nerve! Accusing *us* of bad faith, when there's been an undercover agent on a Federation space station this whole time?"

"This was unknown to us—unknown to me," Aoi said.

"And yet Ailoi has been on Deep Space 9 throughout," said Alden. He was in full Starfleet Intelligence mode now, and Pulaski found it strangely satisfying. "Whatever you may claim about your ignorance, Ailoi surely wasn't acting independently. *Somebody* must have known that there was an operation under way. The *Athene Donald* is a Federation ship, Aoi, but there are representatives from five different powers on board. I doubt that any of our governments would be happy to discover that your government—or some agency empowered by your government—has been so cavalier about our territorial integrity." Alden raised his right hand and spread out his fingers. "*Five* different powers."

The markings around Aoi's throat were very dark, Pulaski noticed. What did it mean? Strain? Anger? Certainly Alden's meaning was plain enough.

"You cannot make a threat that would alarm us," Aoi said. "You know our capabilities are vast compared to yours. You are no threat."

"Your technological capabilities might well be superior to ours," said Pulaski, "but your ethics certainly aren't. You've made no secret that we bore you, that you've seen everything we can do before. But where has all this experience brought you? One of you has tried to steal from us, has committed an assault on one of our ships—has *murdered* on Federation soil! And now you threaten us with greater firepower!" Pulaski shook her head. "Is this superiority?"

"Was this the introduction to the Alpha Quadrant that you wanted?" Alden said. "Was this the kind of first contact that you wanted to make? You know, the powers on this ship have been struggling to find grounds for peace and friendship between us. Do you want to be the enemy that unites us?"

There was a pause. Aoi had gone very quiet. Pulaski shot Alden a quick look: *Have we gone too far?* He shrugged in response. *I've no idea.*

"You make some valid points that must be answered," Aoi said at last. "I did not know that Ailoi was empowered to act this way. I shall get answers." And with a shimmer, Aoi was gone.

"*It seems,*" Pulaski explained to Ro and Crusher, "*that Ailoi was traveling on board the People's ships without the knowledge of Aoi and those higher up the chain of command. Ailoi seems to be from some kind of covert organization . . .*" She looked at Alden. "*You'll know more about this kind of thing than I do.*"

Alden seemed to choose his words carefully. "*There are intelligence agencies, and then there are . . . Then there are little groups within groups, sections within sections, organizations within organizations. They don't have official status, and they operate on the quiet. Everyone has them, although nobody admits to them. The Chain is no different. This is who Ailoi represents. Aoi would not have been told about Ailoi's dual purpose, even when Ailoi was assigned to the ship.*"

Ro frowned. "You believe that? That Aoi knew nothing?"

Alden nodded. "*Absolutely. These kinds of organizations thrive on secrecy.*"

"*If Alden can believe it, so can I,*" said Pulaski. "*Give the man credit for knowing his job, dirty though it is.*"

"*Thank you for that vote of confidence, Doctor.*"

"You're welcome, Commander."

"I can see why they might place someone within the People," Crusher said. "But what was their interest in DS9?"

"*Easy*," said Alden promptly. "*Aoi all but admitted that the Chain has been observing events in the Alpha Quadrant for some time—since well before the outbreak of the Dominion War. I'd guess there's been some anxiety about preventing the Chain from becoming embroiled in our very messy affairs.*"

"*Who wants to wander into the middle of a cold war between us and the Typhon Pact?*" said Pulaski.

"*More than that*," Alden said. "*They'd want to prevent any of their technological advantage being lost.*"

"Another reason to have someone traveling with the People," said Crusher slowly. "To prevent them from giving away anything that the Chain might prefer to keep under wraps."

"*As the People drew closer to the Alpha Quadrant, this became more of a worry*," Pulaski said. "*That's when Ailoi was assigned to the nearest Chain ship—Aoi's ship—and also placed among the People.*"

"And used the transwarp beaming to switch between ships," Ro said.

"*It's not a way of life that anyone could sustain for long*," Alden said, "*but the first encounters were the key ones.*"

"Poor Ioile must have realized that Ailoi was not really one of them," Crusher said.

"And being able to transport such a great distance would have made access to Ioile's room easy," said Ro. "Presumably Ailoi was able to beam from the Chain ship onto DS9, kill Ioile, and then transport back. And we weren't on the lookout for a transporter as powerful as that." She pondered the situation for a while. "Where does this leave us? Do we have *any* chance of finding Ailoi?"

"*Aoi has promised that the agent will be found and punished,*" Pulaski said. "*But whether that will actually happen . . .*"

"*If you'll take my advice, Captain,*" said Alden, "*you'll say that's not acceptable. Ailoi, once found, should be handed over to you. Ailoi has committed crimes on Federation territory.*" Alden gave a wry smile. "*Aoi won't agree to hand over Ailoi, of course.*"

Ro frowned. "So why would I go to all the trouble of making that demand?"

"*To argue for the release of the* Athene Donald," said Pulaski.

"*You might be able to secure the unconditional release of the People too,*" Alden added.

"I can see how this might save the *Athene Donald*," Ro said. "As for the rest, I have a feeling that this is something that Oioli and Aoi will have to work out for themselves."

Yes, thought Ro, when Oioli at last sat down in her office to speak to Aoi, her hunch had been correct. There was a history here, a personal history that went well beyond this immediate crisis. Oioli sat quietly in a chair, but Aoi looked stiff and formal.

"*You must submit yourself to my authority,*" said Aoi. "*When you left home, you broke your oath to serve—*"

Oioli looked at Aoi in sorrow. "Aoi! Aoi! Can you hear yourself now? The oath I took was one to serve *all of our people*! And yet we broke it every day. We served the rich and chained the poor. We hurt the lost and lonely. Have you forgotten who we were? Can you not remember? The life we led a long time back? Those lost and lonely children?"

With a flash, Ro understood. Aoi was now the captain of a great ship, but that had not always been the case. Aoi and Oioli had been children once—and from what Oioli said, they had not been members of the Chain's highest castes. The story was not hard to imagine: it was, after all, a story much like hers. A poor child, a homeless child, had found a way out of desperate circumstances by joining up. Aoi, it seemed, had been able to continue serving. But not Oioli. Oioli had left to find a different life. A better life? Better for Oioli, certainly.

"How do you serve these masters, Aoi? How can you continue?"

Aoi replied in a rough voice. "*The point remains that you are still a citizen and subject. You had responsibilities—as I have—to those children. How can I leave them traveling without care and schooling?*"

"Without care? Without care? Remember who you speak to! And would you truly care for them? They were like us—uncared for! I found them dying on the streets. I saved their lives. I saved them. Where were our masters then, Aoi? As ever, they were uncaring." Oioli pressed a long hand against the view screen. "We want to journey on in peace. Will you now prevent us?"

Carefully, Ro intervened. "I know that you are genuinely concerned about the well-being of the children traveling with the People, Tey Aoi. But the Federation can replicate medical supplies for them. I'm even prepared to supply a replicator for this purpose. If this is your only reason for preventing the People from continuing on their journey, you no longer need to worry. Unless you have other, more specific reasons to keep Oioli here?" Taking a risk, she continued. "But I think that this would mean your crew learning more about your past than perhaps you would like them to know."

Aoi's head bent. Ro smiled sadly to herself. Her guess had been right. Aoi's insalubrious background would not play well with the crew of the Chain ship.

"There is no shame in what we were or in the world we came from," Oioli said. "There is no shame beyond the shame of those who seek to shame us."

Aoi's head shot up. "*And yet you left, Oioli! You ran away from it, no? If there truly was no shame, you could have just ignored it!*"

"I left because I could not bear to stay and watch

injustice. I went and found a better life. I will not be returning. I will not come to you, Aoi—but you could still come to me?"

Ro held her breath. She was not clear on the relationship between these two—whether they were siblings or merely children who had found each other and saved each other when they were small—but would it persuade Aoi? Was that tie enough, or had other ties replaced it?

"I wish I could. I wish I might. But I have my duties—"

"The time has long since passed since they were duties worth fulfilling!"

"But here I might still make some change. Make a little difference—"

"You cannot save the Chain alone. The Chain is long past saving."

Aoi became formal again but not hostile. *"I thank you for your offer, Oioli. I cannot travel with you. Do not ask."*

Oioli sighed. "Then go your way. But don't forget what we once were and what we hoped we would be."

Aoi's long hand reached up to the screen, and the fingers met Oioli's, rising to meet them. *"Never. Never."*

Then Tey Aoi was gone, and a few moments later a message came through from the *Athene Donald* informing the commander of Deep Space 9 that the great black ship was moving away.

Meanwhile, Oioli sat deep in thought and, stirring at last, said, "Old friends. Old times. Sometimes they wait to meet you on your journey. Past and future are the same. The end is the beginning . . ." Turning to Ro, and speaking unusually sharply, Oioli said, "You will find Ailoi here on the station. Trans-warp beaming is by no means stable. If Ailoi uses it again, the risk is great that damage will occur beyond repair."

A chill went down Ro's spine. *What had Oioli been*, she wondered, *in that previous life? What life had Oioli left behind to know about a technology that had clearly baffled Aoi? Groups within groups*, Alden had said. *Sections within sections.* With a shaky hand, she reached over to her companel. "Blackmer, the jam on the People's technologies should be lifted now." She looked at Oioli, who nodded. "I believe they'll be able to help you find Ailoi."

They ran Ailoi to ground in one of the cargo bays. Ro saw the alien's long hand stretching to touch a button at the wrist. "Don't use it!" she begged. "It's too great a risk!"

But Ailoi was not prepared to be taken—and was prepared to take the risk. The sight of Ailoi's body self-destructing, the screaming and writhing, was too much for any of them to bear—with the exception, perhaps, of Oioli.

They were gone. The huge ship, black and faceless, had disappeared in the blink of an eye, and there were only the stars, beckoning. The crew of the *Athene Donald* breathed a collective sigh of relief. Some went back to the peace and quiet of work. Some went to the bar. And Tanj and Pulaski retired to Tanj's quarters, kicked off their shoes, and chewed over the past few days.

"I don't feel as if we *learned* anything from them," Pulaski said.

"Sometimes there's nothing to learn," said Tanj. "Unless we want to take the Chain as a warning."

"Of what?"

"Oh, I don't know, Kitty. Perhaps of what happens if the push for technological advancement displaces social progress? What's the point of toys if they don't alleviate suffering?"

Pulaski frowned. "I imagine that Alden and his kind would say that technology gives a strategic advantage."

Tanj smiled. "I imagine they would. But let's forget about the spies for tonight, shall we? He'll be leaving us soon enough."

They sat pleasantly for a while, talking about the next stage of the journey and where it might take them. Shortly before Pulaski got up to leave for her own quarters and bed, the door chimed softly.

It was Metiger. She stood uneasily upon the threshold, eyeing both women. Her skin was dimmed to a low-key yellow-white, what Pulaski had come to think of as Metiger's working clothes. So this wasn't a social visit—but then Metiger wasn't exactly someone with whom you sat down and enjoyed a glass of wine once the day was done.

"I am glad to find you both here," she said, and the tone of her voice was lowered too, more like the single line of an oboe than the sweet strings of a harp. "I was hoping to speak to you. I was hoping . . . to confide in you."

Tanj and Pulaski exchanged looks. "Come in, Metiger," said Tanj. "And rest assured that anything you say in here will not go beyond these walls."

The Tzenkethi woman came in, taking the seat that Tanj offered but refusing any refreshment.

"I have a confession to make," she said. "If you decide afterward that I am no longer welcome to remain on board the *Athene Donald*, I will accept that decision, abide by it, and leave the ship without rancor."

Tanj and Pulaski looked at her in alarm. "Hell's bells, Metiger!" said Pulaski. "What have you been up to?"

"Exactly what your colleague Alden has said," Metiger replied. "I was allowed to come on this mission by the Department of the Outside on condition that I reported back to them."

"Reported back to them?" Tanj said. "Reported *what*?"

"On our research, I should imagine," said Pulaski roughly. "Carried out by people from across the Khitomer powers—even by their allies, the Romulans. What intelligence service wouldn't be interested?" She was feeling rather queasy. "I know ours is."

"Not only that," said Metiger, "I was instructed to give full accounts of all cross-species interactions that I saw on board the *Athene Donald*. We know very little about your worlds. Any information is believed valuable."

"At least that's a vote of confidence in your research, Maurita," Pulaski said sourly.

"I am sorry," said Metiger. The Tzenkethi was shaking slightly. "You must understand that the person from the department who spoke to me is my Ap-Rej. I am bound to obey."

"Your 'Ap-Rej'?" Tanj shook her head. "I'm afraid I don't understand. What does that mean?"

"That he or she speaks in the voice of the Autarch," Pulaski said. "Their most beloved and exalted Autarch Korzenten Rej Tov-AA, absolute ruler, top dog, and Lord High Tickety-Boo of the Tzenkethi Coalition."

"Kitty . . ." chided Tanj. Metiger touched her chest gently and raised her hand upward, as if to apologize for hearing such blasphemy.

"He can't be everywhere, you see," said Pulaski. "Being only mortal like the rest of us. So some people speak in his voice, and if you're loyal to them, you're loyal to him through them."

Metiger turned her amber eyes on Pulaski. "You are well informed."

Pulaski shrugged. "Peter Alden is well informed. And I've read his files."

"I see." Metiger blinked. "So I was not taken entirely on trust."

"I was curious," Pulaski shot back. "I'm a scientist. Curiosity is my business."

"Stop this," said Tanj. "I won't have this. I won't have another quarrel between us."

"We already have it, Maurita," said Pulaski. "She's admitted to us that she's here to spy on us—"

"Which she didn't need to do," said Tanj. "So I want to understand what the stakes are. Metiger, what would happen if you went against these orders?"

Again, the hand to the chest that was lifted upward. "I could not disobey!"

"Taboo?" said Tanj. "Or something else?"

There was a pause as Metiger visibly struggled to put into words what compelled her to obey. "I could not disobey," she said at last. "Not an Ap-Rej speaking on behalf of our beloved Autarch. Disobedience is unimaginable."

"Taboo," said Tanj again.

"It might mean reconstruction," Metiger said. "Perhaps even . . . recalibration."

"Something else," said Pulaski. She leaned forward in her chair. "Recalibration. Let me guess. Loss of status?"

Metiger's hand twitched.

"Metiger Ter Yai-A . . ." Pulaski thought it over. "You wouldn't be 'Ter' any longer, would you? Not an order giver. I bet you wouldn't get near any scientific research again either. And as for that A grading . . ."

"That would be gone," Metiger agreed softly. "I

would be null. Contaminating. Unfit to contribute to our stock."

Tanj shuddered. "Horrific."

Metiger looked at her impassively. "That is the nature of things."

"No it's not," said Pulaski briskly. "As well you know. Why else did you come to see us tonight?"

Metiger's skin was rippling now, alternating between the yellow-white and something brighter. "I . . . do not know. I am uncertain."

"It's easy enough," said Pulaski. "You came because you thought something was wrong about what you were being asked to do—"

"I would not think that about the orders of an Ap-Rej! They are the orders of the Autarch!"

"Oh, please," said Pulaski. "You're not talking to the boss now. What's holding you back?"

"You trusted me," said Metiger simply. "You defended me when Commander Alden accused me of crimes that I did not commit."

"That's the universal brotherhood of science," said Pulaski cheerfully. "Or sisterhood, in this case."

"Tell us," said Tanj, "what have you sent back so far?"

"My first report is due shortly."

"So you've sent nothing back yet?" Tanj said.

"Not yet." Metiger flashed a quick amber glance at Pulaski. "Although I have read Commander Alden's files."

Pulaski cawed with laughter. "Quite right too!"

"I believe in the mission of this ship," Metiger said. "I believe in what you want to achieve, Doctor Tanj. I want to be part of it."

"And I see no reason why you can't be," Tanj replied. "I'm glad you felt able to come to us, Metiger. I'll think about what we can do to protect you—"

"That's easy enough," said Pulaski. "Write your reports, Metiger. Send them to us. I'm sure we'll enjoy reading them. We might make a few, um, minor amendments, but then feel free to send them to whoever you like."

"That's certainly one way around the problem," said Tanj dryly.

"But when you send them upstairs, make it look good. 'Many men died to bring this information,' that kind of thing. That should keep your superiors happy. And with luck"—Pulaski leaned back in her chair—"we can all be left in peace to get on with our research."

"To lie to an Ap-Rej . . ."

"Not a lie," said Pulaski firmly. "Window dressing. They love that kind of thing."

Metiger sat for a while. "I will consider what you said, Doctor Pulaski. It might be an acceptable solution." She stood to leave. "I am grateful for your time, and I am grateful for your understanding."

"We all want this mission to work," said Tanj. "And we are all intelligent enough to find a way to make it work."

Metiger nodded. At the door, she stopped for a

moment. "There are some errors in what Commander Alden has written about us," she said with a luminous smile. "Perhaps one day *I* shall note down some amendments."

Ro had summoned Varis to her office. Odo was there too, fully briefed on what Ro intended to say to their visitor.

"There are children, aren't there?" Ro said to Varis. It was the dispute between the Chain and the People that had given her the insight. What did people battle over? Territory, yes, and resources—also children.

The Romulan officer froze. "I have no idea what you mean—"

"I think that you do," Ro said. "Children. Products of liaisons between Cardassian prisoners and their Romulan captors."

Varis smiled. "I don't think that's very likely, is it, Captain Ro?"

"Unlikely, maybe, but not impossible. Love is a strange thing. Why wouldn't Cardassian POWs, drafted into a war that they had no desire to fight, find consolation and peace elsewhere after years in captivity? Why wouldn't a Romulan officer be sympathetic toward their plight?"

"It is a big step from a love affair to children, and a fanciful one. Love between a Cardassian soldier and a Romulan officer? This is the stuff of cheap holo-fantasies."

"I've heard rumors in the past—Klingon POWs

and Romulan captors? Does that sound familiar?" When she got no response from Varis, Ro pressed on. "Unless you want me to believe that the truth is more unpleasant? There are Cardassian females among the prisoners of war. If they've been raped, made pregnant, and either harmed or killed as a result, then that is a war crime. We will find out, and we will support our Cardassian allies in any reasonable course of action they choose to pursue."

Varis shook her head. "Nothing like that happened on my watch! I would not allow it!"

"But you're preventing Cardassian citizens from returning home," Ro said.

"Nobody who has remained has preferred to go back."

"Because they now have children?" Ro said.

"I have not said that that is the case either way," Varis pointed out.

Odo leaned forward. "Major Varis," he said in a soft voice, "you must understand that the castellan is particularly sensitive when it comes to people being denied knowledge of their parentage or access to their heritage."

Ro nodded. She knew about the short life of Tora Ziyal and the place the young woman held in the castellan's heart. "We've discussed our suspicions with him," she said, "and he is waiting for a full answer from you. Either there is some movement at your end or . . ." She shrugged. "The castellan has nothing to lose by going public. But I suspect that you—or friends of yours—do."

Varis was examining her hands. "None of the children are products of rape," she said, after a while and with some difficulty. "They were born of love," she said and, looking up straight at Ro, added, "If you can believe that. We love our children too, you know, hybrids or not. We would not want to part with them."

"Born of love, perhaps," Ro said, "but not of equality. These people were prisoners of war! How could it be equal between them?"

"They are not persecuted," Varis said quickly. "There is a settlement on one of the smaller worlds, a quiet place, where they live quite happily—"

"You'll forgive me if I'm not blown away by that assurance or description of their situation," Ro said. "These people must be free to make their own decisions about where and how they want to live. At the very least they must be granted full recognition and rights within the Empire."

"That might be difficult," said Varis.

"Then if their lives—and the lives of their children—would be better on Cardassia, they will have to go back."

"Mixed-species children on Cardassia Prime?" Varis laughed. "How welcome do you think they will be? How welcome did they make their Bajoran bastards?"

"That situation was different—"

"You think Romulan bastards would be made more welcome?"

"There will be somewhere they can be at home," Ro said doggedly. "The Federation would welcome them: the Federation has no qualms about interspecies relationships. They can live on DS9, if needs be. I am the commander here—I make that offer formally, now, to you."

Varis seemed to be wavering, so Ro pushed her point. "Anyone could come here," Ro said. "There would be a place for all members of these families: children, Cardassian fathers, Cardassian mothers, Romulan fathers . . ." She paused before completing the set. ". . . Romulan mothers."

Varis's eyes narrowed slightly.

"DS9 has always been a home for the homeless," Odo said.

For a moment, Varis looked tempted—wistful, even—but then she shook her head. "A pleasant fantasy, Captain, but nobody's duties are ever so clear cut. Families exist within wider kinship structures, and these exist within polities. Within empires, if you like. We have responsibilities to all of these."

"Yes," Ro said, "but they have a responsibility in turn to you. What kind of state puts people into a kind of exile, simply because of accidents of birth? And that's what is happening to these families right now, isn't it? You're not telling me that a family with Cardassian and Romulan parents is welcome in polite society on Romulus, are you? These people are not integrated, are they?" She pressed on with her suspicions. "I imagine an officer found with such a liaison might find her commission in danger."

Varis did not blink. "That is one possible scenario, yes. But an officer who was discreet and did not parade her family in public—or embroil her family in a diplomatic incident—might live quietly with them away from the center of power."

"But do their partners enjoy full rights as citizens? Do the *children* enjoy full rights as citizens?"

There was a pause before Varis admitted, "That might be a request too far on the part of any officer who found herself in such a situation."

"Then I have to insist that these people are given permission at least to travel to Cardassia Prime, where their citizenship—and that of their children—is assured."

"Assured by whom, exactly?" Varis said quickly.

"By the castellan," Odo said at once. Garak had said so flatly in his last communication, when Ro had explained her hunch to him about the children. "Not to mention a resettlement stipend to help all those who want to return home."

Varis's lips twisted. "I imagine that the castellan sees some political advantage in this."

"I'm sure it will do him no harm," Odo said. "Did you have any particular reason for wanting to see the castellan disadvantaged?"

"No," Varis said. "Cardassian domestic politics are hardly my concern."

"Then what is preventing you from accepting his offer?" Ro said.

Varis thought for a while before replying. "It is possible," she said slowly, "that some of the families concerned may be willing to make the journey to Cardassia. For others, however . . ." She shook her head. "The price of such publicity would be too high. They might be prepared to speak privately to family back on Cardassia, but a journey would be out of the question for some of them. I think," she added, "that you will need to let each individual family make the choice that serves their situation best. There are"—she lowered her voice—"some high-ranking cases involved."

"I understand," Ro said. "I accept that."

"But about Terek Pa'Dan?" Odo said.

"I am . . . friendly with the family," Varis said. "His partner is a colleague of mine. I believe that they might be prepared to return—for a short visit, at least. But I'll need a little time to inform them of this change in circumstances. I believe they may have thought that they were not welcome on Cardassia."

Ro nodded. "A little time is reasonable—but not too much, Varis."

"I'll be speaking to Mhevita Pa'Dan after this meeting," Odo said. "I'll tell her that she will hear from you by the end of the week."

Varis nodded.

"And after that," said Ro, "I expect to hear that a family reunion is in the cards. Deep Space 9 will be honored to welcome them here."

Twelve

Captain's Log, Personal.

I am one of the most experienced captains of a deep space exploration vessel in Starfleet's history. This is not meant as a boast (I hope that I am not generally known as a boastful man, but rather as moderate in most things), but I believe it to be a fair assessment of my career. I have traveled far; I have seen many remarkable and wonderful (and terrifying) things; I have spoken on behalf of the Federation to many different and new species.

It comes as a great surprise to me, therefore, to find myself suddenly learning to look at the world entirely differently. Each day, René surprises me. Each day this child, with the unerring sense of the born explorer that is the gift of every child, makes me look at the world anew. How little I expected this, and most certainly not in that most private of spaces—my home. The domestic, it seems, contains as much adventure and novelty as the whole uncharted universe.

I did not expect this. But then what else is life about if not to continue learning? And to receive the chance to learn afresh, at home, this late in my life—this I can only count as a great gift . . .

She thought she would find him in the temple. And there he was, sitting quietly by himself, hands folded upon his lap, a calm expression upon his half-formed face. There were not many people who knew how to sit and be still, Corazame thought. Too many people dashed here, there, and everywhere, always moving on to the next task, the next project, the next distraction. Corazame suspected that they did not want to be alone with themselves. It took strength to be able to sit with oneself and simply be. Corazame had discovered that she had that kind of strength. There was nothing about herself she wanted to run away from.

Odo, seeing her, lifted his hand in greeting and beckoned to her. He smiled as she sat down beside him.

"I came looking for you this time," she said.

"In fairness to me, I didn't come *looking* for you," he chided her gently. "Although I was hoping to meet you and suspected the temple might be a good place to start. It's where I would go if I wanted some quiet."

"I am glad that we met," said Corazame. "Very glad. I am grateful for the faith that you showed in me."

Odo merely grunted, as if to say, *It was nothing.* Corazame smiled. She would never forget that somebody had been on her side throughout all of this.

"I gather from Captain Ro that you've made a decision about where to go next," Odo said.

"The People have been very kind to me. They

understand my situation. And when I was with them . . . I liked them. They are so comfortable with themselves. I find them very restful."

Odo thought of the many children running around and the chaos in the People's quarters that Ro had reported. To each their own. "And what about home? What about Ab-Tzenketh?"

Corazame shook her head. "That was the fantasy of a lonely person. I can never go back to Ab-Tzenketh. There would be no Corazame left." She smiled at him. "And I like being Corazame."

"So you should."

"And I have a new home now, if I take the time to make it. The People of the Open Sky are giving me that chance."

"I hope you travel forward in happiness and find your place among them."

"I am sure that I will." She stood to go, but before she left, she let her skin shine brightly; filling the temple with white light that seemed very close to bliss. "Good-bye, Odo."

She had one last farewell to make, which she did in the privacy of the quarters she and Alden had shared briefly on DS9. "Hello, Peteh," she said when his handsome, grave face appeared on the view screen."

"Cory. I've been so worried about you—"

She believed him. He could care about her and yet still want to make use of her—and that was something for him to reconcile with himself. Commander

Peter Alden was not a man who could sit for long with himself. There would always have to be a distraction. If he reflected too long, he would see too clearly the gap between the man he was and the man he had hoped to be.

"You don't need to worry about me."

"*I can't help that. I always will.*" He looked down at his hands. "*When I first met you, you were so helpless, so afraid . . .*"

"I was very lost," she admitted. "One of the first people I saw had four arms!"

He smiled in memory. "*It was not the easiest of introductions to the wider universe.*"

"You know that given the choice I would never have left Ab-Tzenketh. I was happy there. No," she said, seeing his expression, "I *was* happy, even if you cannot bring yourself to believe that. Life was peaceful. My surroundings were beautiful. I had plenty of time to think and to be with myself. I loved to sing with my friends. Yes, my work was arduous and repetitive—but not unduly so. No more than that performed by many on so-called free worlds. We were always rested well and never lacked food or comfort—"

"*You were a slave, Cory.*"

"I didn't feel like a slave. And please, Peteh—my name is Corazame. I never liked Cory."

He looked at her in surprise. "*You never told me that.*"

"I never knew until recently. But I am Corazame."

"Nothing else?"

"That is enough."

They stared at each other. He looked awkward, as if he could not grasp how the balance of power had shifted so radically between them, and this shift had left him disoriented. He had never understood her.

"I would like to give you some advice, if I may," she said.

"*You are so different . . . Go ahead,*" he said with a smile. "*Give me some advice.*"

"The life you lead now," she said, "it doesn't make you happy. You work all the time. You obsess about my world and its people, and the damage that was done to you when you were among us. You are stuck in that moment. You are less free than I was on Ab-Tzenketh."

"*This doesn't sound like advice to me.*" He was frowning. "*More like character assassination.*"

"Give it up, Peteh. Now, before it consumes you completely. Do something else. Find something to do with meaning."

He gave her a sad smile. "*If only it was that simple.*"

"It *is* that simple," she said. "I've done it twice now. Once was not my choice, that is true. But this time?" She smiled. "Yes, this is my choice. To travel with the People."

She let all her colors go free. He gasped—he had never seen her like this before and perhaps had never realized the full extent of her capabilities. But here she was, and she was beautiful and unconstrained. She was Corazame.

"Be brave. Be bold. Don't wait for change. Seize your own life and make it."

Beverly Crusher went down to the docking bay to see the little ships leave. The People were departing in their usual chaotic fashion: half-closed packing cases with clothes hanging out; children underfoot; a few of the adults milling around and chatting, showing no particular signs of urgency about their departure time. Oioli was there at the heart of things, counting them all, a mother hen looking over her chicks. But of course, one was missing.

"I'm sorry," Crusher said, offering Oioli her hand. "Your time here on Deep Space 9 was so marred by tragedy. I wish I could send you on your way with better memories of us, and of this place."

Oioli placed long fingers gently upon Crusher's. "Yes, there was grief, but friendship too. For which I remain grateful. You helped us when you had no need. I won't forget your kindness."

"I'll remember Ioile," she said, pressing her hand around Oioli's. "I'll remember that Oioli loved Ioile."

"Yes, Ioile was much loved. And now there is but one of us." Oioli frowned, thinking, no doubt, of Ailoi's treachery. "Two set out so long ago. And now I travel lonely."

"*Lonely?*" Crusher looked at the busy ragtag family that Oioli had assembled over the years. "How can you be lonely with so many around you who love you? The children, Oioli! The children!"

Oioli smiled. "The children, yes. Oh, yes indeed! Without them we'd be nothing!"

They embraced, and she left Oioli to corral the People into some kind of order. She saw Corazame, her skin glowing a beautiful copper, enter the docking bay, but the Tzenkethi woman seemed not to want to be noticed, so the doctor did not approach her, and Corazame slipped unobtrusively on board. Crusher silently wished her well in her new life.

Somehow, under Oioli's gentle direction, the People sorted themselves out. The children were gathered up and herded onto their ships. The packing cases followed. The adults, in lazy and comfortable fashion, ambled on board. They even made their departure time—give or take a minute or two. The docking bay felt empty once they were gone, Crusher thought, as if they had taken something with them—some goodwill, some kindliness of spirit that animated whichever space they currently inhabited.

"Travel safe," she murmured. "Carry on. Gather up more children. Find the lost and sad—and give them homes and hopes and family."

Crusher left the docking bay. *So many good-byes,* she thought. *Where did one start?*

Command could bring with it so much grief, so much worry and heartache, that it was important to savor the good moments. And this, Ro thought, was definitely going to be a good moment.

Mhevita Pa'Dan stood to one side of Ro's office, fussing nervously at the sleeves on her dress. Ro could only guess at the complexities of the emotions the other woman must be feeling: the happiness for the reunion that was about to come; the passing of old sorrow. She leaned over to touch, briefly, Pa'Dan's hand. "You look great," she said. "You look . . . grandmotherly."

A beautiful smile curved across Pa'Dan's face. "Yes. Who would have guessed? Whoever would have guessed? After so long, so many gifts, all at once."

"You deserve them," said Ro. The door to her office opened. "Look," she said, "they're here."

And there they were: a young Cardassian male, tall and handsome by his people's standards, and, very tiny beside him and reaching up to clutch his hand, a little girl. She had a long face, with ears that tapered upward, but there were also little ridges along her neck and the faintest hint of a spoon upon her forehead. Behind them both stood a Romulan colonel. Her relationship to the child was obvious.

"Oh, Terek!" gasped Mhevita. All thought of propriety (and, presumably, dress) was clearly gone from her mind as the mother dashed across to her long-lost son. Ro, from the sidelines, saw the little girl push a fist into her mouth and watch curiously as her father was embraced by this stranger. Then Terek bent down to her, lifted her up, and presented her to her grandmother. The girl eyed the older woman while her father whispered to her—an introduction, presumably. The child chewed her hand for a moment longer and then shoved it forward—small and soggy—to offer it to her grandmother. Two hands, one old and gray, one young and pale, entwined. Ro blinked, rubbed an eye, and turned away.

"A tear, Captain?" Odo murmured in her ear.

Ro cleared her throat. "Perhaps a small one."

"Perhaps I'd shed one myself if I could."

Once Varis had been confronted with their knowledge of the children, it had been only a matter of time before the truth of what had happened to Terek and the other missing soldiers had been revealed. It was quite simple: they had fallen in love. In Terek's case, this had been with a Romulan colonel who also served on the Repatriation Committee. When they learned they were to have a child, Terek sent his mother a message explaining why he would not be returning to Cardassia Prime, and inviting his mother to come and meet his partner and child. But Major Varis, afraid of how the family would be treated and in an attempt to protect her colleague's reputation (and perhaps, Ro speculated, her own), had intercepted the message. Terek, believing that Mhevita had cut him off at the news of her grandchild—half Cardassian, half Romulan—had not tried to communicate again.

But now they were together—all of them, mother

and father and child and grandmother—and it would be hard to think of a happier family reunion. Ro had dreamed of moments like this after her father died and she had left her mother, but of course that had never happened. She would enjoy this vicariously, she thought, and let it bring her joy.

"I understand from the castellan," Odo said quietly, "that he has invited Terek and his family back to Cardassia Prime. The whole family, mind—Colonel Veelak included. And there's an open invitation to all the other former soldiers and their families to come. No expense spared."

Ro smiled. "I imagine the castellan has quite the ceremony planned for their homecoming. Will he be the one to meet them at the spaceport?"

"Oh, I should think so," Odo said. "And I won't begrudge him that." He smiled. "I begrudge him so much else, after all."

"So, Kitty," said Tanj as they relaxed in the director's ready room. The *Athene Donald* was on its way again, speeding on into uncharted space. "I think we can call that first encounter a success."

"As long as I don't have to see Aoi and that ship of fools again," said Pulaski. "A more miserable bunch of paper pushers I've never seen, and I've a long career in Starfleet behind me." She leaned back comfortably in her chair. "But for now I intend to get on with enjoying this part of the trip—"

The door to Tanj's office chimed.

It was Peter Alden. "Maurita, can I have a word?"

Pulaski started to lever herself up out her chair. "I'll leave you to it—"

"No, I'd like you to hear this too, Doctor Pulaski."

There was something odd about him, Pulaski thought. His hair was crumpled, and the collar of his uniform was slightly undone. His face was shining with . . . was that happiness? Pulaski leaned back. Yes, this she had to hear.

"I've resigned my commission," Alden said. "I no longer work for Starfleet Intelligence."

Tanj and Pulaski looked at each other in amazement. "Congratulations?" Tanj said uncertainly. "If that's in order?"

"Yes," Alden said firmly. "Absolutely in order. And, if I may, I'd like to sign up with the mission."

"I beg your pardon?" said Tanj.

"You'd like to which with the what?" said Pulaski.

"The mission." He gestured around him. "This mission. I want to sign up. I want to join the crew of the *Athene Donald*."

Pulaski snorted. "Not a chance."

Tanj waved her hand. "Hush, Kitty, let's hear what he has to say."

"I've had enough," Alden said. "The life I've been leading . . . It's made me do things I'm ashamed of. When I think of Cory—Corazame . . . She's so brave, and all I could think of was how I could use her, how she'd be an asset to me. How is that any different from the way her masters on Ab-Tzenketh treated her?" He shuddered. "I don't ever want to find myself in that situation again. I want to be free. I want . . ." He held out his hands. "I want to explore."

"Do you want my advice, Commander?" said Pulaski. "It's free."

"Of course, Doctor."

"Don't give up your day job."

Tanj covered a snort of laughter.

"Too late," said Alden. "It's done. I've quit. I'm not going back."

"You're assuming a great deal, mister!"

"I'm not assuming anything," Alden said. "If I'm not welcome on the *Athene Donald*, then I'll return home by private freighter. I'll find something else to do with my life. I'll do that doctorate I always wanted to do—"

"Pull the other one," said Pulaski. "Do you think we're idiots? You'll be reporting everything back to Starfleet Intelligence."

"I really won't. I'm done. Finished." He reached up to his collar, pulled off his pips, and threw them down on Tanj's desk. "There," he said. "Done."

Tanj looked at Pulaski. "This seems pretty convincing to me. And it's in the spirit of what we do—"

"It's the maddest thing I've ever heard."

Tanj turned to Alden. "What would you do if you were on board? Go back to your original studies?"

"I . . . guess so," Alden said.

"Do that doctorate?"

"If there was someone here to work with . . ."

Tanj nodded. "I'll speak to Delka. I think that between us we can cook up a supervisory team."

Pulaski leaned forward in her chair. "Now hold on a minute! This sounds like the decision is already made!"

"You're right," said Tanj. She stood up, leaned across her desk, and offered Alden her hand. "Welcome aboard, Mister Alden. We'll make a doctor of you yet."

"Maurita, you're an idiot!"

"Thank you."

"They don't let them walk away, you know," Pulaski said. "They'll make him work for them whether he wants to or not."

"So help me get one past them," Alden said. "Help me get away."

Tanj burst out laughing. "Oh, Kitty, he's got the measure of you!"

"Well, Doctor Pulaski," said Alden, lifting his chin and looking her straight in the eye. "You wanted me to give up my life of crime."

"Humph," said Pulaski.

Tanj laughed. "Be careful what you wish for, Kitty!"

"Are you willing to work together, Katherine?" Alden said. "In the spirit of science and exploration?"

"Oh, all right," Pulaski groused. "If I must. It'd be a damned long voyage otherwise."

After dealing with the castellan at such close quarters, Ro could hardly miss his Shape of the Union address. Quark had expressed an interest too (of course, thought Ro, they had been fellow entrepreneurs on the Promenade once upon a time), so they watched together in the bar.

"Of all the people to become castellan, I would never have bet on Garak," Quark said. "But then, what do I know? Of all the people to become nagus, I never would have bet on Rom."

"Stick to fiddling the dabo wheel," Ro advised.

Brash music signaled the start of the broadcast. Quark smiled. "Garak must *loathe* this," he said.

"What? Journalism?"

"Yes, that. But mostly democracy."

"What?" Ro was baffled. "Then why would he stand for election?"

"Why else?" said Quark. "Because he thinks he deserves punishment, and this is the most ostentatious way he can come up with to do his penance. Garak is all about show. But at least he's showing remorse."

"So he should," said a gruff voice from beside them. "And he's not the only one."

Quark smiled. "Good evening, Odo! Come to watch our favorite tailor in action?"

Odo sniffed. "Garak's doings are of little interest to me."

"Of course not," said Quark. "Pull up a seat. Your lurking always puts the customers off their drinks."

Odo, with a growl that came from whatever

counted as the back of his throat, sat down, folding his arms and turning his back to the barkeep. Quark winked at Ro.

On the view screen, Garak was in full flight. And it was a good speech: well written, funny at appropriate moments, and full of the kinds of progressive and democratic policies that would make the Federation Council and Starfleet Command sleep peacefully in their beds. This was certainly, Ro thought, a new Cardassia—even with the last of the Obsidian Order at its head.

Ro's ears pricked up when she realized that Garak was talking about Mhevita Pa'Dan and her family.

"Those of you who follow the news will have seen that certain members of the assembly have been complaining that I have been slow to act on behalf of several of our citizens who had been held prisoner by the Romulans since the end of the Dominion War. They suggested that I—a former operative of the Obsidian Order—was falling into my old ways, using citizens as political pawns, without care or concern for the lives that were being affected by this tragedy."

Garak took a breath before continuing.

"I am proud to say that through the efforts of our diplomatic corps and with the help of our friends in the Federation—"

Quark nudged Ro. "That'll be you!"

"Ssh!"

"—these families have now been reunited. As to the

accusation that I am careless with the lives of our citizens—let me address this here and now."

Suddenly Garak grasped the lectern with both hands. His eyes became wide and unblinking.

"Hang on a minute," said Ro. "Has he gone off script?"

"Probably," said Odo.

"Garak always did like to improvise," Quark said.

"He's *improvising* the most important political speech he'll do this year?" said Ro.

Quark shrugged. "He's Cardassian. Speeches come naturally, like breathing—and murder."

"*Let me be clear,*" Garak said. "*The days of the Obsidian Order and the Central Command running roughshod over our citizens are over. All citizens are now protected under the law. It is your right to speak your mind, and you can do so safely. Those who violate this principle will be prosecuted to the fullest extent of the law. People of Cardassia, you no longer have any need to be afraid of your representatives. We do not rule you. We serve you. But that brings a responsibility on your part—to ensure that we perform our tasks adequately, to hold us to account, and—most of all—to participate.*"

"He's . . . quite good at this," said Ro.

"Of course he's good at it," Odo said. "He's always been a smooth talker. But how anyone could let a man like that anywhere near so much power, I simply don't understand. A murderer, a torturer, an assassin—"

"I hired him to assassinate me once," Quark said in a tone of fond reminiscence.

"A rare and unfortunate failure on Garak's part," Odo said. "If there were any justice in this universe, Garak would be locked up for the rest of his natural life. But, to the best of my knowledge, he's been incarcerated in total for no more than six months." He preened, slightly. "That was under my jurisdiction, of course."

Quark winked at Ro, who covered a smile. "Of course."

"Cut him some slack, Odo," said Quark. "He's trying to make amends."

"As well he might."

The speech had moved on from the question of the repatriated soldiers. Garak was now talking about ensuring voter rights in some of the Union's more far-flung colonies.

"The Federation must *love* all this," Quark muttered.

"The Cardassians are our allies now," Ro pointed out. "For better or worse."

"I suppose at least that means Starfleet has its eyes on them," Quark said.

"And I have my eyes on Garak," said Odo.

"Even from your hermitage?" Quark said.

"My hermitage?"

"You'll be going back to Bajor now, won't you?" Quark said. "Burying yourself in some miserable old monastery in the middle of nowhere and sulking about . . . whatever it is that you're sulking about now."

"Who says I'm returning to Bajor?" Odo said. "No," he went on, looking around the bar like a man surveying a new kingdom and not entirely liking what he saw, "I've found my time here on the new station . . . exhilarating. I think I'll stay awhile yet."

Ro didn't think she'd ever seen Quark look so rapturous. "Take up your old job!" he pleaded. "It'll be like old times!"

Ro lifted a finger. "Er, I do in fact have a chief of security—"

"Oh, *him*," Quark scoffed. "He's not worthy of the title. Come on, Odo. Let's do it all over again."

"I don't have space for a chief security officer," Ro said. "But I do have an opening for a chief medical officer. Beverly Crusher is going back to the *Enterprise*." She saw Quark's expression. "What? You hadn't heard about that? You must be slipping, Quark. I said you were getting old."

Her office was empty. Her quarters too: the packing cases already loaded onto the ship. She had said her farewells. But something was still holding her back.

Crusher walked slowly around the bare room. There was nothing to show that she had been here, nothing to show that she had been chief medical officer on Deep Space 9. She felt she had barely arrived—and now she was leaving.

The companel gave a soft chime: a message had

arrived. Crusher went around to sit down at her desk—her former desk—to listen.

It was from Pulaski. *How strange*, Crusher thought, but she was grateful as she started the playback that this correspondence had begun. Who would ever have thought that she and Pulaski would become friends? But there it was. Life changed you, and the people you thought you could not stand suddenly made sense to you.

"So we're on our way again, and you won't believe who's signed up for the mission—only that damned Starfleet Intelligence flunky Peter Alden! He says he's quit his day job. We'll see. I have my eye on him." Pulaski sniffed. *"I will say, though, I'm getting some great reports from Delka on the work they're doing together. So if he is faking it, he's doing a good job. Anyway,"* she said, *"enough about me. I heard on the grapevine that you're done with DS9 and you're heading back . . . well, home. I guess that's the right thing to say about you and the* Enterprise*? Not that it's any of my damn business, but I think you've made the right choice. But don't let family get in the way of work, Beverly. Find a way to have both, a way that satisfies you. God knows I never did, but if anyone can, I'm sure it's you."* She smiled, rather evilly. *"And give my love to Jean-Luc. Tell him I miss him. Tell him I'll come and visit when the* Athene Donald *comes back your way. Pulaski out."*

Crusher laughed at the thought of Pulaski coming to stay. She imagined Jean-Luc would arrange a short vacation. And of course she was going to enjoy passing on Pulaski's regards to him once she was—

Home.

Yes, she thought, switching off the companel, she was going home, or as close to home as she had ever been, out among the stars. She would see her husband, and her little boy, and that would be enough. Leaving the office for someone else, she headed toward the docking bays where her ship was waiting to take her on her way. Soon she was in flight again.

Acknowledgments

Grateful thanks to Professor Dame Athene Donald, who greeted my request to name a starship in her honor with kind enthusiasm.

Thank you to Daniel Tostevin, who thought that Pulaski should have her own book. Thank you to Margaret Clark, editor extraordinaire, who was very patient with my rapidly declining outlining skills as I entered the third trimester, and equally patient with my need for extensions as I learned to juggle writing and motherhood.

Thank you to my smashing daughter, Verity, who let Mummy work in the mornings and evenings. And thank you as ever to Matthew, without whom nothing is possible and with whom everything is possible.

About the Author

Una McCormack is the author of five previous *Star Trek* novels: *The Lotus Flower* (part of *The Worlds of Deep Space Nine*), *Hollow Men*, *The Never-Ending Sacrifice*, *Brinkmanship*, and the *New York Times* bestseller *The Fall: The Crimson Shadow*. She is also the author of two *Doctor Who* novels, *The King's Dragon* and *The Way Through the Woods*, and numerous short stories and audio dramas.

She lives in Cambridge, England, with her partner of many years, Matthew, and their daughter of one year, Verity.